In 1793, at the tender age of just seventeen, Horatio Hornblower was forced to find his sea legs as a midshipman. After suffering his first bout of seasickness, the hapless doctor's son quickly rose through the ranks to become Admiral of the Fleet Lord Hornblower. In between, Hornblower must sail back and forth along the coasts of Europe and the Americas, repeatedly engaging or eluding the mighty ships of Napoleon and Spain. His heroic exploits in the French revolutionary war and his many other adventures in service of his country have made the name Horatio Hornblower into legend.

C. S. Forester was born in Cairo in 1899, where his father was stationed as a government official. He studied medicine at Guy's Hospital, and after leaving Guy's without a degree he turned to writing as a career. His first success was *Payment Deferred*, a novel written at the age of twenty-four and later dramatized and filmed with Charles Laughton in the leading role. In 1932 Forester was offered a Hollywood contract, and from then until 1939 he spent thirteen weeks of every year in America. On the outbreak of war he entered the Ministry of Information and later he sailed with the Royal Navy to collect material for *The Ship*. He then made a voyage to the Bering Sea to gather material for a similar book on the United States Navy, and it was during this trip that he was stricken with arteriosclerosis, a disease which left him crippled. However, he continued to write and in the Hornblower novels created the most renowned sailor in twentieth-century fiction. He died in 1966.

Bernard Cornwell is the bestselling author of the Sharpe series of novels.

Flying Colours

C. S. FORESTER

Introduction by Bernard Cornwell

PENGUIN BOOKS

PENGUIN BOOKS

Published by the Penguin Group
Penguin Books Ltd, 80 Strand, London WC2R 0RL, England
Penguin Group (USA) Inc., 375 Hudson Street, New York, New York 10014, USA
Penguin Group (Canada), 90 Eglinton Avenue East, Suite 700,
Toronto, Ontario, Canada M4P 2Y3
(a division of Pearson Penguin Canada Inc.)
Penguin Ireland, 25 St Stephen's Green, Dublin 2, Ireland
(a division of Penguin Books Ltd)
Penguin Group (Australia), 250 Camberwell Road, Camberwell, Victoria 3124, Australia
(a division of Pearson Australia Group Pty Ltd)
Penguin Books India Pvt Ltd, 11 Community Centre,
Panchsheel Park, New Delhi – 110 017, India
Penguin Group (NZ), 67 Apollo Drive, Mairangi Bay, Auckland 1310, New Zealand
(a division of Pearson New Zealand Ltd)
Penguin Books (South Africa) (Pty) Ltd, 24 Sturdee Avenue,
Rosebank, Johannesburg 2196, South Africa

Penguin Books Ltd, Registered Offices: 80 Strand, London WC2R 0RL, England

www.penguin.com

First published by Michael Joseph 1938
Published in Penguin Books 1956
This edition published 2006
001

Typeset in 11/13pt Monotype Dante
Set by Palimpsest Book Production Limited, Grangemouth, Stirlingshire
Printed in England by Clays Ltd, St Ives plc

ISBN-13: 978-1-405-92447-4

www.greenpenguin.co.uk

Introduction

Flying Colours was the third Hornblower story to be written, but the seventh in chronological order, and it was written hard on the heels of *Ship of the Line*. That book ends in disaster. Hornblower has been taken prisoner by the French, after losing his ship in a battle against overwhelming forces. *Flying Colours* was published in 1938, the same year as *Ship of the Line*, so at least the growing number of Hornblower fans did not have long to wait to discover the fate of their hero.

They discover that Hornblower is now a prisoner in Rosas, a Spanish fort in French hands. His companions are Lieutenant Bush, who was grievously wounded at the end of *Ship of the Line*, and Coxswain Brown. The three men face a grim future. Forester, in his wide reading, had been struck by Napoleon's vengefulness, 'perhaps traceable to his Corsican childhood?' Suppose Napoleon wanted to make an example of Hornblower? A captured British naval captain would make a fine trophy for the vengeful Emperor so why not rig a trial and condemn him to death? So the story begins and you must discover the rest, right up to the splendid final scenes with the *Witch of Endor*.

The speed with which the first three Hornblower books were written shows that Forester knew he had struck a vein of purest gold. He was already a successful author, but the Hornblower tales were to make him famous. Cecil Scott Forester was born in Egypt to British parents in 1899. His real name was Cecil Lewis Troughton Smith and he was raised in Britain where, as a child, he was an avid reader, usually the first step in the making of a writer. In 1917, before his eighteenth birthday, he volunteered for the British army, fully expecting to fight on the Western Front, but he was rejected as medically unfit. He was a skinny, short-sighted six-footer who enjoyed sports, but the army's physical examination revealed a dangerously weak heart. So instead of serving as a soldier, Forester entered Guy's Hospital as a medical student – an experience as unhappy as it was unsuccessful – but Forester's ambitions were already fixed on writing. His first efforts failed, but in 1924, with *Payment Deferred*, he enjoyed his first success. During the Second World War he moved to the United States at the request of the British government, who wanted him to produce articles and stories that would encourage American support for the British war effort. It was sophisticated propaganda, and Forester was good at it. He also liked living in the States and most of the Hornblower books were written in California where, with his second wife, he remained until his death in 1966. By then he had become one of the world's most popular authors with almost sixty novels to his name and, even if he had never dreamed up Hornblower, he would be famous as the author of *The African Queen*, *The Gun*, *Brown on Resolution* or *Hunting the Bismarck*.

Flying Colours is an escape story, a tale of illicit passion, and a superb study of the three main characters. The relationship between Hornblower and the sturdy

Coxswain Brown is done especially well. Brown, aged twenty-eight, had served in the navy since he was eleven. 'He could knot and splice, hand, reef and steer, cast the lead or pull an oar, all of them far better than his captain. He could go aloft on a black night in a howling storm without thinking twice about it, but the sight of a knife and fork made his hands tremble.' When Brown is forced to eat off china in front of the officers, Hornblower immediately senses his embarrassment and makes it easy, but he also invites Brown to help himself to wine. This is not generosity, but 'a good moment for ascertaining if Brown could be trusted with liquor.' Brown could. Later Hornblower feels pangs of jealousy because of the pleasure Bush and Brown take in building a simple rowing boat. Hornblower could contribute nothing except 'unskilled labour' and it galls him. But then Hornblower is a complicated man, while Bush and Brown are simpler souls. Hornblower is complicated enough to envy 'Bush his complete inability to speak any other tongue than English'; an extraordinarily acute observation.

The writing of *Flying Colours* was interrupted by that most aggravating of duties, the need to read the proofs of the previous book. Forester was checking the proofs of *Ship of the Line* when his elder son, then a small boy, asked him to hurry with them. 'I want to read it,' he said, 'I liked the first book so much.' It was, Forester said, a reward for the trials of writing. He always claimed that writing was a difficult task, but reckoned *Flying Colours* was especially exhausting. He was filled with 'horrible doubts'; he was 'faced with disaster'. Yet he admitted that there were 'one or two mornings when I actually observed, with considerable astonishment – perhaps even dismay – that I was going eagerly to my worktable, that I was looking forward to a morning with Hornblower'. Dismay? It is a typical Forester touch in case we should believe he might actually have enjoyed himself too much, but those happy mornings show in this most intimate of Hornblower adventures and, if it does not give too much away, this story with the happiest of endings. And it was a good thing that *Flying Colours* ended so satisfactorily, for the world was about to be engulfed with horror and it was not until the Second World War was over that Hornblower, Bush, Brown and Lady Barbara would return.

I

Captain Hornblower was walking up and down along the sector of the ramparts of Rosas, delimited by two sentries with loaded muskets, which the commandant had granted him for exercise. Overhead shone the bright autumn sun of the Mediterranean, hanging in a blue Mediterranean sky and shining on the Mediterranean blue of Rosas Bay – the blue water fringed with white where the little waves broke against the shore of golden sand and grey-green cliff. Black against the sun above his head there flapped the tricolour flag of France, proclaiming to the world that Rosas was in the hands of the French, that Captain Hornblower was a prisoner. Not half a mile from where he walked lay the dismasted wreck of his ship the *Sutherland*, beached to prevent her from sinking, and in line beyond her there swung at their anchors the four ships of the line which had fought her. Hornblower, narrowing his eyes and with a twinge of regret for his lost telescope could see even at that distance that they were not ready for sea again, nor were likely to be. Even the two-decker which had emerged from the fight with all her masts intact still had her pumps at work every two hours to keep her afloat, and the other three had not yet succeeded in setting up masts to replace the ones lost in the battle. The French were a lubberly lot of no-seamen, as might be expected after seventeen years of defeat at sea and six of continuous blockade.

They had been all honey to him, in their French fashion praising him for his 'glorious defence' after his 'bold initiative' in dashing in with his ship to interpose between their four and their refuge at Rosas. They had expressed the liveliest pleasure at discovering that he had miraculously emerged unhurt from a battle which had left two-thirds of his men killed and wounded. But they had plundered in the fashion which had made the armed forces of the Empire hated throughout Europe. They had searched the pockets even of the wounded who had cumbered the *Sutherland*'s decks in moaning heaps. Their admiral, on his first encounter with Hornblower, had expressed surprise that the latter was not wearing the sword which the admiral had sent back to him in recognition of his gallantry, and on Hornblower's denial that he had ever seen the weapon again after giving it up had instituted a search which discovered the sword cast aside somewhere in his flagship, the glorious inscription still engraved upon the blade, but with the gold stripped from hilt and guard and scabbard. And the admiral had merely laughed at that and had not dreamed of instituting a search for the thief; the Patriotic Fund's gift still hung at Hornblower's side, the tang of the blade protruding nakedly from the scabbard without the gold and ivory and seed pearls which had adorned it.

The French soldiers and sailors which had swarmed over the captured ship had torn away even the brass-work in the same fashion; they had gorged upon the unappetizing provisions in a way which proved how miserable were the rations provided for the men who fought for the Empire – but it was only a few who had swilled themselves into insensibility from the rum casks.

In face of similar temptation (to which no British officer would have exposed his men) British seamen would have drunk until nine-tenths of them were incapable or fighting mad. The French officers had made the usual appeal to their prisoners to join the French ranks, making the usual tempting offers of good treatment and regular pay to anyone who cared to enlist either in the army or the navy. Hornblower was proud that no single man had succumbed to the temptation.

As a consequence the few sound men now languished in strict confinement in one of the empty storerooms of the fortress, deprived of the tobacco and rum and fresh air which for most of them represented the difference between heaven and hell. The wounded – the hundred and forty-five wounded – were rotting in a dank casemate where gangrene and fever would soon make an end of them. To the logical French mind the poverty-stricken Army of Catalonia, which could do little even for its own wounded, would be mad to expend any of its resources on attention to wounded who would be intolerable nuisances should they survive.

A little moan escaped Hornblower's lips as he paced the ramparts. He had a room of his own, a servant to wait on him, fresh air and sunshine, while the poor devils he had commanded were suffering all the miseries of confinement – even the three or four other unwounded officers were lodged in the town gaol. True, he suspected that he was being reserved for another fate. During those glorious days when, in command of the *Sutherland*, he had won for himself, unknowing, the nickname of 'the Terror of the Mediterranean', he had managed to storm the battery at Llanza by bringing his ship up close to it flying the tricolour flag. That had been a legitimate *ruse de guerre* for which historical precedents without number could be quoted, but the French government had apparently deemed it a violation of the laws of war. The next convoy to France or Barcelona would bear him with it as a prisoner to be tried by a military commission. Bonaparte was quite capable of shooting him, both from personal rancour and as a proof of the most convincing sort to Europe of British duplicity and wickedness, and during the last day or two Hornblower thought he had read as much in the eyes of his gaolers.

Just enough time had elapsed for the news of the *Sutherland*'s capture to have reached Paris and for Bonaparte's subsequent orders to have been transmitted to Rosas. The *Moniteur Universel* would have blazed out in a paean of triumph, declaring to the Continent that this loss of a ship of the line was clear proof that England was tottering to her fall like ancient Carthage; in a month or two's time presumably there would be another announcement to the effect that a traitorous servant of perfidious Albion had met his just deserts against a wall in Vincennes or Montjuich.

Hornblower cleared his throat nervously as he walked; he expected to feel afraid and was surprised that he did not. The thought of an abrupt and inevitable end of that sort did not alarm him as much as did his shapeless imaginings when he was going into action on his quarterdeck. In fact he could almost view it with relief, as putting an end to his worries about his wife Maria whom he had left pregnant, and to his jealous torments of longing for Lady Barbara who had married his admiral; in the eyes of England he would be regarded as a martyr whose widow deserved a pension. It would be an honourable end, then, which a man ought to welcome – especially a man like Hornblower whose persistent and unfounded disbelief in his own capacity left him continually frightened of professional disgrace and ruin.

And it would be an end of captivity, too. Hornblower had been a prisoner once before, for two heartbreaking years in Ferrol, but with the passing of time he had forgotten the misery of it until his new experience. In those days, too, he had never known the freedom of his own quarterdeck, and had never tasted the unbounded liberty – the widest freedom on earth – of being a captain of a ship. It was torture now to be a prisoner, even with the liberty to look upon the sky and the sea. A caged lion must fret behind his bars in the same way as Hornblower fretted against his confinement. He felt suddenly sick and ill through restraint. He clenched his fists and only by an effort prevented himself from raising them above his head in a gesture of despair.

Then he took hold of himself again, with an inward sneer at his childish weakness. To distract himself he looked out again to the blue sea which he loved, the row of black cormorants silhouetted against the grey cliff, the gulls wheeling against the blue sky. Five miles out he could see the topsails of His Majesty's frigate *Cassandra* keeping sleepless watch over the four French ships huddled for shelter under the guns of Rosas, and beyond them he could see the royals of the *Pluto* and the *Caligula* – Admiral Leighton, the unworthy husband of his beloved Lady Barbara, was flying his flag in the *Pluto*, but he refused to let that thought worry him – where they awaited an accession of strength from the Mediterranean fleet before coming in to destroy the ships which had captured him. He could rely upon the British to avenge his defeat. Martin, the vice admiral with the Toulon blockading squadron, would see to it that Leighton did not make a hash of this attack, powerful as might be the guns of Rosas.

He looked along the ramparts at the massive twenty-four-pounders mounted there. The bastions at the angles carried forty-two-pounders – colossal pieces. He leaned over the parapet and looked down; it was a sheer drop from there of twenty-five feet to the bottom of the ditch, and along the bottom of the ditch itself ran a line of stout palisades, which no besieging army could damage until they had sapped right up to the lip of the ditch. No hurried, extemporized attack could carry the citadel of Rosas. A score of sentries paced the ramparts, even as did he; in the opposite face he could see the massive gates with the portcullis down, where a hundred men of the grand guard were always ready to beat back any surprise attack which might elude the vigilance of the twenty sentinels.

Down there, in the body of the place, a company of infantry was being put through its drill – the shrill words of command were clearly audible to him up here. It was Italian which was being spoken; Bonaparte had attempted his conquest of Catalonia mainly with the foreign auxiliaries of his Empire, Italians, Neapolitans, Germans, Swiss, Poles. The uniforms of the infantry down there were as ragged as the lines they were forming; the men were in tatters, and even the tatters were not homogeneous – the men wore white or blue or grey or brown according to the resources of the depots which had originally sent them out. They were half starved, poor devils, as well. Of the five or six thousand men based on Rosas the ones he could see were all that could be spared for military duty; the others were all out scouring the countryside for food – Bonaparte never dreamed of trying to feed the men whom he compelled to serve him, just as he only paid them, as an afterthought, a year or two in arrears. It was amazing that his ramshackle Empire had endured so long – that was the clearest proof of the incompetence of the various kingdoms who had pitted their strength against it. Over on the other side of the Peninsula the French Empire was at this very minute putting out all its strength against a man of real ability and an army which knew what discipline was. On the issue of that struggle depended the fate of Europe. Hornblower was convinced that the redcoats with Wellington to lead them would be successful; he would have been just as certain even if Wellington were not his beloved Lady Barbara's brother.

Then he shrugged his shoulders. Not even Wellington would destroy the French Empire quickly enough to save him from trial and execution. Moreover, the time allowed him for his day's exercise was over now. The next items in his monotonous programme would be to visit the sick in the casemate, and then the prisoners in the storeroom – by the courtesy of the commandant he was allowed ten minutes for each, before being shut up again in his room, drearily to attempt to re-read the half-dozen books which were all that the garrison of Rosas possessed, or to pace up and down, three steps each way, or to lie huddled on his bed wondering about Maria and the child that was to be born in the New Year, and torturing himself with thoughts of Lady Barbara.

2

Hornblower awoke that night with a start, wondering what it was that had awakened him. A moment later he knew, when the sound was repeated. It was the dull thud of a gun fired on the ramparts above his head. He leaped from his bed with his heart pounding, and before his feet touched the floor the whole fortress was in a turmoil. Overhead there were guns firing. Somewhere else, outside the body of the fortress, there were hundreds of guns firing; through the barred windows of his room came a faint flickering as the flashes were reflected down from the sky. Immediately outside his door drums were beating and bugles were pealing as the garrison was called to arms – the courtyard was full of the sounds of nailed boots clashing on the cobbles.

That tremendous pulsation of artillery which he could hear could mean only one thing. The fleet must have come gliding into the bay in the darkness, and now he could hear the rolling of its broadsides as it battered the anchored ships. There was a great naval battle in progress within half a mile of him, and he could see nothing of it. It was utterly maddening. He tried to light his candle, but his trembling fingers could do nothing with his flint and steel. He dashed the tinder-box to the floor, and, fumbling in the darkness, he dragged on his coat and trousers and shoes and then beat upon the door madly with his fists. The sentry outside was Italian, he knew, and he spoke no Italian – only fluent Spanish and bad French.

'Officier! Officier!' he shouted, and then he heard the sentry call for the sergeant of the guard, and the measured step of the sergeant as he came up. The clatter of the garrison's falling in under arms had already died away.

'What do you want?' asked the sergeant's voice – at least so Hornblower fancied, for he could not understand what was said.

'Officier! Officier!' roared Hornblower, beating still on the heavy door. The artillery was still rolling terrifically outside. Hornblower went on pounding on the door even until he heard the key in the lock. The door swung open and he blinked at the light of a torch which shone into his eyes. A young subaltern in a neat white uniform stood there between the sergeant and the sentry.

'Qu'est-ce-que monsieur désire?' he asked – he at least understood French, even if he spoke it badly. Hornblower fumbled to express himself in an unfamiliar tongue.

'I want to see!' he stammered. 'I want to see the battle! Let me go on to the walls.'

The young officer shook his head reluctantly; like the other officers of the garrison, he felt a kindly feeling towards the English captain who – so rumour said – was so shortly to be conducted to Paris and shot.

'It is forbidden,' he said.

'I will not escape,' said Hornblower; desperate excitement was loosening his tongue now. 'Word of honour – I swear it! Come with me, but let me see! I want to see!'

The officer hesitated.

'I cannot leave my post here,' he said.

'Then let me go alone. I swear I will stay on the walls. I will not try to escape.'

'Word of honour?' asked the subaltern.

'Word of honour. Thank you, sir.'

The subaltern stood aside, and Hornblower dashed out of his room, down the short corridor to the courtyard, and up the ramp which led to the seaward bastion. As he reached it, the forty-two-pounder mounted there went off with a deafening roar, and the long tongue of orange flame nearly blinded him. In the darkness the bitter powder smoke engulfed him. Nobody in the groups bending over the guns noticed him, and he ran down the steep staircase to the curtain wall, where, away from the guns, he could see without being blinded.

Rosas Bay was all a-sparkle with gun flashes. Then, five times in regular succession, came the brilliant red glow of a broadside, and each glow lit up a stately ship gliding in rigid line ahead past the anchored French ships. The *Pluto* was there; Hornblower saw her three decks, her ensign at the peak, her admiral's flag at the mizzen, her topsails set and her other canvas furled. Leighton would be there, walking his quarterdeck – thinking of Barbara, perhaps. And that next astern was the *Caligula*. Bolton would be stumping about her deck revelling in the crash of her broadsides. She was firing rapidly and well – Bolton was a good captain, although a badly educated man. The words 'Oderint dum metuant' – the Caesar Caligula's maxim – picked out in letters of gold across the *Caligula*'s stern had meant nothing to Bolton until Hornblower translated and explained them to him. At this very moment, perhaps, those letters were being defaced and battered by the French shot.

But the French squadron was firing back badly and irregularly. There was no sudden glow of broadsides where they lay anchored, but only an irregular and intermittent sparkle as the guns were loosed off anyhow. In a night action like this, and after a sudden surprise, Hornblower would not have trusted even an English seaman with independent fire. He doubted if as many as one-tenth of the French guns were being properly served and pointed. As for the heavy guns pealing away beside him from the fortress, he was quite certain they were doing no good to the French cause and possibly some harm. Firing at half a mile in the darkness, even from a steady platform and with large calibre guns, they were as likely to hit friend as foe. It had well repaid Admiral Martin to send in Leighton and his ships in the moonless hours of the night, risking all the navigational perils of the bay.

Hornblower choked with emotion and excitement as his imagination called up the details of what would be going on in the English ships – the leadsman chanting the soundings with disciplined steadiness, the heave of the ship to the deafening crash of the broadside, the battle lanterns glowing dimly in the smoke of the lower decks, the squeal and rattle of the gun trucks as the guns were run up again, the steady orders of the officers in charge of sections of guns, the quiet voice of the captain addressing the helmsmen. He leaned far over the parapet in the darkness, peering down into the bay.

A whiff of wood smoke came to his nostrils, sharply

distinct from the acrid powder smoke which was drifting by from the guns. They had lit the furnaces for heating shot, but the commandant would be a fool if he allowed his guns to fire red-hot shot in these conditions. French ships were as inflammable as English ones, and just as likely to be hit in a close battle like this. Then his grip tightened on the stonework of the parapet, and he stared and stared again with aching eyes towards what had attracted his notice. It was the tiniest, most subdued little red glow in the distance. The English had brought in fire ships in the wake of their fighting squadron. A squadron at anchor like this was the best possible target for a fire ship, and Martin had planned his attack well in sending in his ships of the line first to clear away guard boats and beat down the French fire and occupy the attention of the crews. The red glow suddenly increased, grew brighter and brighter still, revealing the hull and masts and rigging of a small brig; still brighter it grew as the few daring spirits who remained on board flung open hatches and gunports to increase the draught. The tongues of flame which soared up were visible even to Hornblower on the ramparts, and they revealed to him, too, the form of the *Turenne* alongside her – the one French ship which had emerged from the previous battle with all her masts. Whoever the young officer in command of the fire ship might be, he was a man with a cool head and determined will, thus to select the most profitable target of all.

Hornblower saw points of fire begin to ascend the rigging of the *Turenne* until she was outlined in red like some setpiece in a firework display. Sudden jets of flame showed where powder charges on her deck were taking fire; and then the whole setpiece suddenly swung round and began to drift before the gentle wind as the burnt cables gave way. A mast fell in an upwards torrent of sparks, strangely reflected in the black water all round. At once the sparkle of gunfire in the other French ships began to die away as the crews were called from their guns to deal with the drifting menace, and a slow movement of the shadowy forms lit by the flames revealed that their cables had been cut by officers terrified of death by fire.

Then suddenly Hornblower's attention was distracted to a point closer in to shore, where the abandoned wreck of the *Sutherland* lay beached. There, too, a red glow could be seen, growing and spreading momentarily. Some daring party from the British squadron had boarded her and set her on fire, too, determined not to leave even so poor a trophy in the hands of the French. Farther out in the bay three red dots of light were soaring upwards slowly, and Hornblower gulped in sudden nervousness lest an English ship should have caught fire as well, but he realized next moment that it was only a signal – three vertical red lanterns – which was apparently the prearranged recall, for with their appearance the firing abruptly ceased. The blazing wrecks lit up now the whole of this corner of the bay with a lurid red in whose light could be distinctly seen the other French ships, drifting without masts or anchors towards the shore. Next came a blinding flash and a stunning explosion as the magazine of the *Turenne* took fire. For several seconds after the twenty tons of gunpowder had exploded Hornblower's eyes could not see nor his mind think; the blast of it had shaken him, like a child in the hands of an angry nurse, even where he stood.

He became aware that daylight was creeping into the bay, revealing the ramparts of Rosas in hard outlines, and dulling the flames from the wreck of the *Sutherland*. Far out in the bay, already beyond gunshot of the fortress, the five British ships of the line were standing out to sea in their rigid line-ahead. There was something strange about the appearance of the *Pluto*; it was only at his second glance that Hornblower realized that she had lost her main topmast – clear proof that one French shot at least had done damage. The other ships revealed no sign of having received any injury during one of the best managed affairs in the long history of the British Navy. Hornblower tore his gaze from his vanishing friends to study the field of battle. Of the *Turenne* and the fire ship there was no sign at all; of the *Sutherland* there only remained a few blackened timbers emerging from the water, with a wisp of smoke suspended above them. Two ships of the line were on the rocks to the westward of the fortress, and French seamanship would never make them seaworthy again. Only the three-decker was left, battered and mastless, swinging to the anchor which had checked her on the very edge of the surf. The next easterly gale would see her, too, flung ashore and useless. The British Mediterranean fleet would in the future have to dissipate none of its energies in a blockade of Rosas.

Here came General Vidal, the governor of the fortress, making his rounds with his staff at his heels, and just in time to save Hornblower from falling into a passion of despair at watching the English squadron disappear over the horizon.

'What are you doing here?' demanded the General, checking at the sight of him. Under the sternness of his expression could be read the kindly pity which Hornblower had noticed in the faces of all his enemies when they began to suspect that a firing party awaited him.

'The officer of the grand guard allowed me to come up here,' explained Hornblower in his halting French. 'I gave him my parole of honour not to try to escape. I will withdraw it again now, if you please.'

'He had no business to accept it, in any case,' snapped the General, but with that fateful kindliness still apparent. 'You wanted to see the battle, I suppose?'

'Yes, General.'

'A fine piece of work your companions have done.' The General shook his head sadly. 'It will not make the government in Paris feel any better disposed towards you, I fear, Captain.'

Hornblower shrugged his shoulders; he had already caught the infection of that gesture during his few days' sojourn among Frenchmen. He noted, with a lack of personal interest which seemed odd to him even then, that this was the first time that the Governor had hinted openly at danger threatening him from Paris.

'I have done nothing to make me afraid,' he said.

'No, no, of course not,' said the Governor hastily and out of countenance, like a parent denying to a child that a prospective dose of medicine would be unpleasant.

He looked round for some way of changing the subject, and fortunate chance brought one. From far below in the bowels of the fortress came a muffled sound of cheering – English cheers, not Italian screeches.

'That must be those men of yours, Captain,' said the General, smiling again. 'I fancy the new prisoner must have told them by now the story of last night's affair.'

'The new prisoner?' demanded Hornblower.

'Yes, indeed. A man who fell overboard from the admiral's ship – the *Pluto*, is it not? – and had to swim ashore. Ah, I suspected you would be interested, Captain. Yes, off you go and talk to him. Here, Dupont, take charge of the captain and escort him to the prison.'

Hornblower could hardly spare the time in which to thank his captor, so eager was he to interview the new arrival and hear what he had to say. Two weeks as a prisoner had already had their effect in giving him a thirst for news. He ran down the ramp, Dupont puffing beside him, across the cobbled court, in through the door which a sentry opened for him at a gesture from his escort, down the dark stairway to the iron-studded door where stood two sentries on duty. With a great clattering of keys the doors were opened for him and he walked into the room.

It was a wide low room – a disused storeroom, in fact – lit and ventilated only by a few heavily barred apertures opening into the fortress ditch. It stank of closely confined humanity and it was at present filled with a babel of sound as what was left of the crew of the *Sutherland* plied questions at someone hidden in the middle of the crowd. At Hornblower's entrance the crowd fell apart and the new prisoner came forward; he was naked save for his duck trousers and a long pigtail hung down his back.

'Who are you?' demanded Hornblower.

'Phillips, sir. Maintopman in the *Pluto*.'

His honest blue eyes met Hornblower's gaze without a sign of flinching. Hornblower could guess that he was neither a deserter nor a spy – he had borne both possibilities in mind.

'How did you come here?'

'We was settin' sail, sir, to beat out o' the bay. We'd just seen the old *Sutherland* take fire, an' Cap'n Elliott he says to us, he says, sir, "Now's the time, my lads. Top'sls and to'gar'ns." So up we went aloft, sir, an' I'd just taken the earring o' the main to'gar'n when down came the mast, sir, an' I was pitched off into the water. So was a lot o' my mates, sir, but just then the Frenchy which was burnin' blew up, an' I think the wreckage killed a lot of 'em, sir, 'cos I found I was alone, an' *Pluto* was gone away, an' so I swum for the shore, an' there was a lot of Frenchies what I think had swum from the burning Frenchy an' they took me to some sojers an' the sojers brought me here, sir. There was a orficer what arst me questions – it'd 'a made you laugh, sir, to hear him trying to speak English – but I wasn't sayin' nothin', sir. An' when they see that they puts me in here along with the others, sir. I was just telling 'em about the fight, sir. There was the old *Pluto*, an' *Caligula*, sir, an' –'

'Yes, I saw it,' said Hornblower, shortly. 'I saw that *Pluto* had lost her main topmast. Was she knocked about much?'

'Lor' bless you, sir, no, sir. We hadn't had half a dozen shot come aboard, an' they didn't do no damage, barrin' the one that wounded the Admiral.'

'The Admiral!' Hornblower reeled a little as he stood, as though he had been struck. 'Admiral Leighton, d'you mean?'

'Admiral Leighton, sir.'

'Was – was he badly hurt?'

'I dunno, sir. I didn't see it meself, o' course, sir, seein' as how I was on the main deck at the time. Sailmaker's mate, he told me, sir, that the Admiral had been hit by a splinter. Cooper's mate told *him*, sir, what helped to carry him below.'

Hornblower could say no more for the present. He could only stare at the kindly stupid face of the sailor before him. Yet even in that moment he could take note of the fact that the sailor was not in the least moved by the wounding of his Admiral. Nelson's death had put the whole fleet into mourning, and he knew of half a dozen other flag officers whose death or whose wounding would have brought tears into the eyes of the men serving under him. If it had been one of those, the man would have told of the accident to him before mentioning his own misadventures. Hornblower had known before that Leighton was not beloved by his officers, and here was a clear proof that he was not beloved by his men either. But perhaps Barbara had loved him. She had at least married him. Hornblower forced himself to speak, to bear himself naturally.

'That will do,' he said, curtly, and then looked round to catch his coxswain's eye. 'Anything to report, Brown?'

'No, sir. All well, sir.'

Hornblower rapped on the door behind him to be let out of prison, to be conducted by his guard back to his room again, where he could walk up and down, three steps each way, his brain seething like a pot on a fire. He only knew enough to unsettle him, to make him anxious. Leighton had been wounded, but that did not mean that he would die. A splinter wound – that might mean much or little. Yet he had been carried below. No admiral would have allowed that, if he had been able to resist – not in the heat of a fight, at any rate. His face might be lacerated or his belly torn open – Hornblower, shuddering, shook his mind free from the memories of all the horrible wounds he had seen received on board ship during twenty years' service. But, coldbloodedly, it was an even chance that Leighton would die – Hornblower had signed too many casualty lists to be unaware of the chances of a wounded man's recovery.

If Leighton were to die, Barbara would be free again. But what had that to do with him, a married man – a married man whose wife was pregnant? She would be no nearer to him, not while Maria lived. And yet it assuaged his jealousy to think of her as a widow. But then perhaps she would marry again, and he would have to go once more through all the torment he had endured when he had first heard of her marriage to Leighton. In that case he would rather Leighton lived – a cripple, perhaps mutilated or impotent; the implications of that train of thought drove him into a paroxysm of too-rapid thinking from which he only emerged after a desperate struggle for sanity.

In the cold reaction which followed he sneered at himself for a fool. He was the prisoner of a man whose empire extended from the Baltic to Gibraltar. He told himself he would be an old man, that his child and Maria's would be grown up before he regained his liberty. And then with a sudden shock he remembered that he might soon be dead – shot for violation of the laws of war. Strange how he could forget that possibility.

Sneering, he told himself that he had a coward's mind which could leave the imminence of death out of its calculations because the possibility was too monstrous to bear contemplation.

There was something else he had not reckoned upon lately, too. If Bonaparte did not have him shot, if he regained his freedom, even then he still had to run the gauntlet of a court martial for the loss of the *Sutherland*. A court martial might decree for him death or disgrace or ruin; the British public would not hear lightly of a British ship of the line surrendering, however great the odds against her. He would have liked to ask Phillips, the seaman from the *Pluto*, about what had been said in the fleet regarding the *Sutherland*'s action, whether the general verdict had been one of approval or not. But of course it would be impossible to ask; no captain could ask a seaman what the fleet thought of him, even if there was a chance of hearing the truth – which, too, was doubtful. He was compassed about with uncertainties – the uncertainties of his imprisonment, of the possibility of his trial by the French, of his future court martial, of Leighton's wound. There was even an uncertainty regarding Maria; she was pregnant – would the child be a girl or a boy, would he ever see it, would anyone raise a finger to help her, would she be able to educate the child properly without his supervision?

Once more the misery of imprisonment was borne in upon him. He grew sick with longing for his liberty, for his freedom, for Barbara and for Maria.

3

Hornblower was walking next day upon the ramparts again; the sentries with their loaded muskets stood one each end of the sector allotted to him, and the subaltern allotted to guard him sat discreetly against the parapet so as not to break in upon the thoughts which preoccupied him. But he was too tired to think much now – all day and nearly all night yesterday he had paced his room, three paces up and three paces back, with his mind in a turmoil. Exhaustion was saving him now, he could think no more.

He welcomed as a distraction a bustle at the main gate, the turning out of the guard, the opening of the gate, and the jingling entrance of a coach drawn by six fine horses. He stood and watched the proceedings with all the interest of a captive. There was an escort of fifty mounted men in the cocked hats and blue-and-red uniforms of Bonaparte's gendarmerie, coachmen and servants on the box, an officer dismounting hurriedly to open the door. Clearly the new arrival must be a man of importance. Hornblower experienced a faint feeling of disappointment when there climbed out of the coach not a Marshal with plumes and feathers, but just another officer of gendarmerie. A youngish man with a bullet black head, which he revealed as he held his cocked hat in his hand while stooping to descend; the star of the Legion of Honour on his breast; high black boots with spurs. Hornblower wondered idly why a colonel of gendarmerie who was obviously not crippled should arrive in a coach instead of on horseback. He watched him go clinking across the courtyard to the Governor's headquarters.

Hornblower's walk was nearly finished when one of the young French aides-de-camp of the Governor approached him on the ramparts and saluted.

'His Excellency sends you his compliments, sir, and he would be glad if you could spare him a few minutes of your time as soon as it is convenient to you.'

Addressed to a prisoner, as Hornblower told himself bitterly, these words might as well have been 'Come at once.'

'I will come now, with the greatest of pleasure,' said Hornblower, maintaining the solemn farce.

Down in the Governor's office the colonel of gendarmerie was standing conversing alone with His Excellency; the Governor's expression was sad.

'I have the honour of presenting to you, Captain,' he said, turning, 'Colonel Jean-Baptiste Caillard, Grand Eagle of the Legion of Honour, and one of His Imperial Majesty's personal aides-de-camp. Colonel, this is Captain Horatio Hornblower, of His Britannic Majesty's Navy.'

The Governor was clearly worried and upset. His hands were fluttering and he stammered a little as he spoke, and he made a pitiful muddle of his attempt on the aspirates of Hornblower's name. Hornblower bowed, but as the colonel remained unbending he stiffened to attention. He could recognize that type of man at once – the servant of a tyrant, and in close personal association with him, modelling his conduct not on the tyrant's, but on what he fancied should be the correct behaviour of a tyrant, far out-Heroding Herod in arbitrariness and cruelty. It might be merely a pose – the man might be a kind husband and the loving father of a family – but it was a pose which might have unpleasant results for anyone in his power. His victims would suffer in his attempt to prove, to himself as well as to others, that he could be more stern, more unrelenting – and therefore naturally more able – than the man who employed him.

Caillard ran a cold eye over Hornblower's appearance.

'What is he doing with that sword at his side?' he asked of the Governor.

'The Admiral returned it to him on the day of the battle,' explained the Governor hastily. 'He said –'

'It doesn't matter what he said,' interrupted Caillard. 'No criminal as guilty as he can be allowed a weapon. And a sword is the emblem of a gentleman of honour, which he most decidedly is not. Take off that sword, sir.'

Hornblower stood appalled, hardly believing he had understood. Caillard's face wore a fixed mirthless smile which showed white teeth, below the black moustache which lay like a gash across his olive face.

'Take off that sword,' repeated Caillard, and then, as Hornblower made no movement, 'If Your Excellency will permit me to call in one of my gendarmes, I will have the sword removed.'

At the threat Hornblower unbuckled his belt and allowed the weapon to fall to the ground; the clatter rang loud in the silence. The sword of honour which the Patriotic Fund had awarded him ten years ago for his heading of the boarding party which took the *Castilla* lay on the floor, jerked half out of its scabbard. The hiltless tang and the battered places on the sheath where the gold had been torn off bore mute witness to the lust for gold of the Empire's servants.

'Good!' said Caillard. 'Now will Your Excellency have the goodness to warn this man of his approaching departure?'

'Colonel Caillard,' said the Governor, 'has come to take you and your first lieutenant, Mistaire – Mistaire Bush, to Paris.'

'Bush?' blazed out Hornblower, moved as not even the loss of his sword could move him. 'Bush? That is impossible. Lieutenant Bush is seriously wounded. It might easily be fatal to take him on a long journey at present.'

'The journey will be fatal to him in any case,' said Caillard, still with the mirthless smile and the gleam of white teeth.

The Governor wrung his hands.

'You cannot say that, Colonel. These gentlemen have still to be tried. The Military Commission has yet to give its verdict.'

'These gentlemen, as you call them, Your Excellency, stand condemned out of their own mouths.'

Hornblower remembered that he had made no attempt to deny, while the Admiral was questioning him and preparing his report, that he had been in command of the *Sutherland* the day she wore French colours and her landing party stormed the battery at

Llanza. He had known the ruse to be legitimate enough, but he had not reckoned on a French emperor determined upon convincing European opinion of the perfidy of England and cunning enough to know that a couple of resounding executions might well be considered evidence of guilt.

'The colonel,' said the Governor to Hornblower, 'has brought his coach. You may rely upon it that Mistaire Bush will have every possible comfort. Please tell me which of your men you would like to accompany you as your servant. And if there is anything which I can provide which will make the journey more comfortable, I will do so with the greatest pleasure.'

Hornblower debated internally the question of the servant. Polwheal, who had served him for years, was among the wounded in the casemate. Nor, he fancied, would he have selected him in any case; Polwheal was not the man for an emergency – and it was just possible that there might be an emergency. Latude had escaped from the Bastille. Was not there a faint chance that he might escape from Vincennes? Hornblower thought of Brown's bulging muscles and cheerful devotion.

'I would like to take my coxswain, Brown, if you please,' he said.

'Certainly. I will send for him and have your present servant pack your things with him. And with regard to your needs for the journey?'

'I need nothing,' said Hornblower. At the same time as he spoke he cursed himself for his pride. If he were ever to save himself and Bush from the firing party in the ditch at Vincennes he would need gold.

'Oh, I cannot allow you to say that,' protested the

Governor. 'There may be some few comforts you would like to buy when you are in France. Besides, you cannot deprive me of the pleasure of being of assistance to a brave man. Please do me the favour of accepting my purse. I beg you to, sir.'

Hornblower fought down his pride and took the proffered wallet. It was of surprising weight and gave out a musical chink as he took it.

'I must thank you for your kindness,' he said. 'And for all your courtesy while I have been your prisoner.'

'It has been a pleasure to me, as I said,' replied the Governor. 'I want to wish you the – the very best of luck on your arrival in Paris.'

'Enough of this,' said Caillard. 'My orders from His Majesty call for the utmost expedition. Is the wounded man in the courtyard?'

The Governor led the way out, and the gendarmes closed up round Hornblower as they walked towards the coach. Bush was lying there on a stretcher, strangely pale and strangely wasted out there in the bright light. He was feebly trying to shield his eyes from the sun; Hornblower ran and knelt beside him.

'They're going to take us to Paris, Bush,' he said.

'What, you and me, sir?'

'Yes.'

'It's a place I've often wanted to see.'

The Italian surgeon who had amputated Bush's foot was plucking at Hornblower's sleeve and fluttering some sheets of paper. These were instructions, he explained in faulty Italian French, for the further treatment of the stump. Any surgeon in France would understand them. As soon as the ligatures came away the wound would heal at once. He had put a parcel of dressings into the coach for use on the journey. Hornblower tried to thank him, but was interrupted when the surgeon turned away to supervise the lifting of Bush, stretcher and all, into the coach. It was an immensely long vehicle, and the stretcher just fitted in across one door, its ends on the two seats.

Brown was there now, with Hornblower's valise in his hand. The coachman showed him how to put it into the boot. Then a gendarme opened the other door and stood waiting for Hornblower to enter. Hornblower looked up at the ramparts towering above him; no more than half an hour ago he had been walking there, worn out with doubt. At least one doubt was settled now. In a fortnight's time perhaps they would all be settled, after he had faced the firing party at Vincennes. A spurt of fear welled up within him at the thought, destroying the first momentary feeling almost of pleasure. He did not want to be taken to Paris to be shot; he wanted to resist. Then he realized that resistance would be both vain and undignified, and he forced himself to climb into the coach, hoping that no one had noticed his slight hesitation.

A gesture from the sergeant of gendarmerie brought Brown to the door as well, and he came climbing in to sit apologetically with his officers. Caillard was mounting a big black horse, a spirited, restless creature which champed at its bit and passaged feverishly about. When he had settled himself in the saddle the word was given, and the horses were led round the courtyard, the coach jolting and heaving over the cobbles, out through the gate and down to the road which wound under the guns of the fortress. The mounted gendarmerie closed up round the coach, a whip cracked, and they were off at a slow trot, to the jingling of the harness and the clattering of the hoofs and the creaking of the leather-work.

Hornblower would have liked to have looked out of the windows at the houses of Rosas village going by – after three weeks' captivity the change of scene allured him – but first he had to attend to his wounded lieutenant.

'How is it going, Bush?' he asked, bending over him.

'Very well, thank you, sir,' said Bush.

There was sunlight streaming in through the coach windows now, and here a succession of tall trees by the roadside threw flickering shadows over Bush's face. Fever and loss of blood had made Bush's face less craggy and gnarled, drawing the flesh tight over the bones so that he looked unnaturally younger, and he was pale instead of being the mahogany brown to which Hornblower was accustomed. Hornblower thought he saw a twinge of pain cross Bush's expression as the coach lurched on the abominable road.

'Is there anything I can do?' he asked, trying hard to keep the helplessness out of his voice.

'Nothing, thank you, sir,' whispered Bush.

'Try and sleep,' said Hornblower.

Bush's hand which lay outside the blanket twitched and stirred and moved towards him; he took it and he felt a gentle pressure. For a few brief seconds Bush's hand stroked his feebly, caressing it as though it was a woman's. There was a glimmer of a smile on Bush's drawn face with its closed eyes. During all the years they had served together it was the first sign of affection either had shown for the other. Bush's head turned on the pillow, and he lay quite still, while Hornblower sat not daring to move for fear of disturbing him.

The coach had slowed to a walk – it must be breasting the long climb which carried the road across the roots of the peninsula of Cape Creux. Yet even at that speed the coach lurched and rolled horribly; the surface of the road must be utterly uncared for. The sharp ringing of the hoofs of the escorts' horses told that they were travelling over rock, and the irregularity of the sound was a dear indication of the way the horses were picking their way among the holes. Framed in the windows Hornblower could see the gendarmes in their blue uniforms and cocked hats jerking and swaying about with the rolling of the coach. The presence of fifty gendarmes as an escort was not a real indication of the political importance of himself and Bush, but only a proof that even here, only twenty miles from France, the road was unsafe for small parties – a little band of Spanish guerilleros was to be found on every inaccessible hilltop.

But there was always a chance that Claros or Rovira with their Catalan miqueletes a thousand strong might come swooping down on the road from their Pyrenean fastnesses. Hornblower felt hope surging up within him at the thought that at any moment, in that case, he might find himself a free man again. His pulse beat faster and he crossed and uncrossed his knees restlessly – with the utmost caution so as not to disturb Bush. He did not want to be taken to Paris to face a mockery of a trial. He did not want to die. He was beginning to fret himself into a fever, when common sense came to his rescue and he compelled himself to sink into a stolid indifference.

Brown was sitting opposite him, primly upright with his arms folded. Hornblower almost grinned, sympathetically, at sight of him. Brown was actually self-conscious. He had never in his life before, presumably, had to be at such close quarters with a couple of officers. Certainly he must be feeling awkward at having to sit in the presence of two such lofty individuals as a captain and a first lieutenant. For that matter, it was at least a thousand to one that Brown had never been inside a coach before, had never sat on leather upholstery with a carpet under his feet. Nor had he had any experience in gentlemen's service, his duties as captain's coxswain being mainly disciplinary and executive. There was something comic about seeing Brown, with the proverbial adaptability of the British seaman, aping what he thought should be the manners of the gentleman's gentleman, and sitting there as if butter would not melt in his mouth.

The coach lurched again, quickening its pace and the horses broke from a walk into a trot. They must be at the top of the long hill now, with a long descent before them, which would bring them back to the seashore somewhere near Llanza, where he had stormed the battery under protection of the tricolour flag. It was an exploit he had been proud of – still was, for that matter. He had never dreamed for one moment that it would lead him to Paris and a firing party. Through the window on Bush's side he could see the rounded brown slopes of the Pyrenees soaring upwards; on the other side, as the coach swung sickeningly round a bend, he caught a glimpse of the sea far below, sparkling in the rays of the afternoon sun. He craned his neck to look at it, the sea which had played him so many scurvy tricks and which he loved. He thought, with a little catch in his throat, that this would be the last day on which he would ever see it. Tonight they would cross the frontier; tomorrow they would plunge into France, and in ten days, a fortnight, he would be rotting in his grave at Vincennes. It would be hard to leave this life, even with all its doubts and uncertainties, to lose the sea with its whims and its treacheries, Maria and the child, Lady Barbara –

Those were white cottages drifting past the windows, and on the side towards the sea, perched on the grassy cliff, was the battery of Llanza. He could see a sentry dressed in blue and white; stooping and looking upwards he could see the French flag at the top of the flagstaff – Bush, here, had hauled it down not so many weeks ago. He heard the coachman's whip crack and the horses quickened their pace; it was still eight miles or so to the frontier and Caillard must be anxious to cross before dark. The mountains, bristling here with pines, were hemming the road in close between them and the sea. Why did not Claros or Rovira come to save him? At every turn of the road there was an ideal site for an ambush. Soon they would be in France and it would be too late. He had to struggle again to remain passive. The prospect of crossing into France seemed to make his fate far more certain and imminent.

It was growing dark fast – they could not be far now from the frontier. Hornblower tried to visualize the charts he had often handled, so as to remember the name of the French frontier town, but his mind was not sufficiently under control to allow it. The coach was coming to a standstill; he heard footsteps outside, heard Caillard's metallic voice saying, 'In the name of the Emperor,' and an unknown voice say, 'Passez, passez, monsieur.' The coach lurched and accelerated again; they were in France now. Now the horses' hoofs were ringing on cobblestones. There were houses, one or two lights to be seen. Outside the houses there were men in all kinds of uniforms, and a few women picking their way among them, dressed in pretty costumes with caps on their heads. He could hear laughter and joking. Then abruptly the coach swerved to the right and drew up in the courtyard of an inn. Lights were appearing in plenty in the fading twilight. Someone opened the door of the coach and drew down the steps for him to descend.

4

Hornblower looked round the room to which the innkeeper and the sergeant of gendarmerie had jointly conducted them. He was glad to see a fire burning there, for he was stiff and chilled with his long inactivity in the coach. There was a truckle bed against one wall, a table with a white cloth already spread. A gendarme appeared at the door, stepping slowly and heavily – he was the first of the two who were carrying the stretcher. He looked round to see where to lay it down, turned too abruptly, and jarred it against the jamb of the wall.

'Careful with that stretcher!' snapped Hornblower, and then, remembering he had to speak French, 'Attention! Mettez le brancard là. Doucement!'

Brown came and knelt over the stretcher.

'What is the name of this place?' asked Hornblower of the innkeeper.

'Cerbére. Hôtel Iéna, monsieur,' answered the innkeeper, fingering his leather apron.

'Monsieur is allowed no speech with anyone whatever,' interposed the sergeant. 'He will be served, but he must address no speech to the inn servants. If he has any wishes, he will speak to the sentry outside his door. There will be another sentry outside his window.'

A gesture of his hand called attention to the cocked hat and the musket barrel of a gendarme, darkly visible through the glass.

'You are too amiable, monsieur,' said Hornblower.

'I have my orders. Supper will be served in half an hour.'

'I would be obliged if Colonel Caillard would give orders for a surgeon to attend Lieutenant Bush's wounds at once.'

'I will ask him, sir,' said the sergeant, escorting the innkeeper from the room.

Bush, when Hornblower bent over him, seemed somehow a little better than in the morning. There was a little colour in his cheeks and more strength in his movements.

'Is there anything I can do, Bush?' asked Hornblower.

'Yes –'

Bush explained the needs of sick-room nursing. Hornblower looked up at Brown, a little helplessly.

'I am afraid it'll call for two of you, sir, because I'm a heavy man,' said Bush apologetically. It was the apology in his tone which brought Hornblower to the point of action.

'Of course,' he said with all the cheerfulness he could bring into his voice. 'Come on, Brown. Lift him from the other side.'

After the business was finished, with no more than a single half-stifled groan from Bush, Brown displayed more of the astonishing versatility of the British seaman.

'I'll wash you, sir, shall I? An' you haven't had your shave today, have you, sir?'

Hornblower sat and watched in helpless admiration the deft movements of the burly sailor as he washed and shaved his first lieutenant. The towels were so well arranged that no single drop of water fell on the bedding.

'Thank 'ee, Brown, thank 'ee,' said Bush, sinking back on his pillow.

The door opened to admit a little bearded man in a semi-military uniform carrying a leather case.

'Good evening, gentlemen,' he said, sounding all his consonants in the manner which Hornblower was yet to discover was characteristic of the Midi. 'I am the surgeon, if you please. And this is the wounded officer? And these are the hospital notes of my confrére at Rosas? Excellent. Yes, exactly. And how are you feeling, sir?'

Hornblower had to translate, limpingly, the surgeon's question to Bush, and the latter's replies. Bush put out his tongue, and submitted to having his pulse felt, and his temperature gauged by a hand thrust into his shirt.

'So,' said the surgeon. 'And now let us see the stump. Will you hold the candle for me here, if you please, sir?'

He turned back the blankets from the foot of the stretcher, revealing the little basket which guarded the stump, laid the basket on the floor and began to remove the dressings.

'Would you tell him, sir,' asked Bush, 'that my foot which isn't there tickles most abominably, and I don't know how to scratch it?'

The translation taxed Hornblower's French to the utmost, but the surgeon listened sympathetically.

'That is not at all unusual,' he said. 'And the itchings will come to a natural end in course of time. Ah, now here is the stump. A beautiful stump. A lovely stump.'

Hornblower, compelling himself to look, was vaguely reminded of the knuckle end of a roast leg of mutton; the irregular folds of flesh were caught in by half-healed scars, but out of the scars hung two ends of black thread.

'When Monsieur le Lieutenant begins to walk again,' explained the surgeon, 'he will be glad of an ample pad of flesh at the end of the stump. The end of the bone will not chafe –'

'Yes, exactly,' said Hornblower, fighting down his squeamishness.

'A very beautiful piece of work,' said the surgeon. 'As long as it heals properly and gangrene does not set in. At this stage the surgeon has to depend on his nose for his diagnosis.'

Suiting the action to the word the surgeon sniffed at the dressings and at the raw stump.

'Smell, monsieur,' he said, holding the dressings to Hornblower's face. Hornblower was conscious of the faintest whiff of corruption.

'Beautiful, is it not?' said the surgeon. 'A fine healthy wound and yet every evidence that the ligatures will soon free themselves.'

Hornblower realized that the two threads hanging out of the scars were attached to the ends of the two main arteries. When corruption inside was complete the threads could be drawn out and the wounds allowed to heal; it was a race between the rotting of the arteries and the onset of gangrene.

'I will see if the ligatures are free now. Warn your friend that I shall hurt him a little.'

Hornblower looked towards Bush to convey the message, and was shocked to see that Bush's face was distorted with apprehension.

'I know,' said Bush. 'I know what he's going to do – sir.'

Only as an afterthought did he say that 'sir'; which was the clearest proof of his mental preoccupation. He grasped the bedclothes in his two fists, his jaw set and his eyes shut.

'I'm ready,' he said through his clenched teeth.

The surgeon drew firmly on one of the threads and Bush writhed a little. He drew on the other.

'A-ah,' gasped Bush, with sweat on his face.

'Nearly free,' commented the surgeon. 'I could tell by the feeling of the threads. Your friend will soon be well. Now let us replace the dressings. So. And so.' His dexterous plump fingers rebandaged the stump, replaced the wicker basket, and drew down the bed coverings.

'Thank you, gentlemen,' said the surgeon, rising to his feet and brushing his hands one against the other. 'I will return in the morning.'

'Hadn't you better sit down, sir,' came Brown's voice to Hornblower's ears as though from a million miles away, after the surgeon had withdrawn. The room was veiled in grey mist which gradually cleared away as he sat, to reveal Bush lying back on his pillow and trying to smile, and Brown's homely honest face wearing an expression of acute concern.

'Rare bad you looked for a minute, sir. You must be hungry, I expect, sir, not having eaten nothing since breakfast, like.'

It was tactful of Brown to attribute this faintness to hunger, to which all flesh might be subject without shame, and not merely to weakness in face of wounds and suffering.

'That sounds like supper coming now,' croaked Bush from the stretcher, as though one of a conspiracy to ignore their captain's feebleness.

The sergeant of gendarmerie came clanking in, two women behind him bearing trays. The women set the table deftly and quickly, their eyes downcast, and withdrew without looking up, although one of them smiled at the corner of her mouth in response to a meaning cough from Brown which drew a gesture of irritation from the sergeant. The latter cast one searching glance round the room before shutting and locking the door with a clashing of keys.

'Soup,' said Hornblower, peering into the tureen which steamed deliciously. 'And I fancy this is stewed veal.'

The discovery confirmed him in his notion that Frenchmen lived exclusively on soup and stewed veal – he put no faith in the more vulgar notions regarding frogs and snails.

'You will have some of this broth, I suppose, Bush?' he continued. He was talking desperately hard now to conceal the feeling of depression and unhappiness which was overwhelming him. 'And a glass of this wine? It has no label – let's hope for the best.'

'Some of their rotgut claret, I suppose,' grunted Bush. Eighteen years of war with France had given most Englishmen men the notion that the only wines fit for men to drink were port and sherry and Madeira, and that Frenchmen only drank thin claret which gave the unaccustomed drinker the bellyache.

'We'll see,' said Hornblower as cheerfully as he could. 'Let's get you propped up first.'

With his hand behind Bush's shoulders he heaved him up a little; as he looked round helplessly, Brown came to his rescue with pillows taken from the bed, and between them they settled Bush with his head raised and his arms free and a napkin under his chin. Hornblower brought him a plate of soup and a piece of bread.

'M'm,' said Bush, tasting. 'Might be worse. Please, sir, don't let yours get cold.'

Brown brought a chair for his captain to sit at the table, and stood in an attitude of attention beside it; there was another place laid, but his action proclaimed as loudly as words how far it was from his mind to sit with his captain. Hornblower ate, at first with a distaste and then with increasing appetite.

'Some more of that soup, Brown,' said Bush. 'And my glass of wine, if you please.'

The stewed veal was extraordinarily good, even to a man who was accustomed to meat he could set his teeth in.

'Dash my wig,' said Bush from the bed. 'Do you think I could have some of that stewed veal, sir? This travelling has given me an appetite.'

Hornblower had to think about that. A man in a fever should be kept on a low diet, but Bush could not be said to be in a fever now, and he had lost a great deal of blood which he had to make up. The yearning look on Bush's face decided him.

'A little will do you no harm,' he said. 'Take this plate to Mr Bush, Brown.'

Good food and good wine – the fare in the *Sutherland* had been repulsive, and at Rosas scanty – tended to loosen their tongues and make them more cheerful. Yet it was hard to unbend beyond a certain unstated limit. The awful majesty surrounding a captain of a ship of the line lingered even after the ship had been destroyed; more than that, the memory of the very strict reserve which Hornblower had maintained during his command acted as a constraint. And to Brown a first lieutenant was in a position nearly as astronomically lofty as a captain; it was awesome to be in the same room as the two of them, even with the help of making-believe to be their old servant. Hornblower had finished his cheese by now, and the moment which Brown had been dreading had arrived.

'Here, Brown,' he said rising, 'sit down and eat your supper while it's still hot.'

Brown, now at the age of twenty-eight, had served His Majesty in His Majesty's ships from the age of eleven, and during that time he had never made use at table of other instruments than his sheath knife and his fingers; he had never eaten off china, nor had he drunk from a wineglass. He experienced a nightmare sensation as if his officers were watching him with four eyes as large as footballs the while he nervously picked up a spoon and addressed himself to this unaccustomed task. Hornblower realized his embarrassment in a clairvoyant flash. Brown had thews and sinews which Hornblower had often envied; he had a stolid courage in action which Hornblower could never hope to rival. He could knot and splice, hand, reef and steer, cast the lead or pull an oar, all of them far better than his captain. He could go aloft on a black night in a howling storm without thinking twice about it, but the sight of a knife and fork made his hands tremble. Hornblower thought about how Gibbon would have pointed the moral epigrammatically in two vivid antithetical sentences.

Humiliation and nervousness never did any good to a man – Hornblower knew that if anyone ever did. He took a chair unobtrusively over beside Bush's stretcher and sat down with his back almost turned to the table, and plunged desperately into conversation with his first lieutenant while the crockery clattered behind him.

'Would you like to be moved into the bed?' he asked, saying the first thing which came into his head.

'No thank you, sir,' said Bush. 'Two weeks now I've slept in the stretcher. I'm comfortable enough, sir, and it'd be painful to move me, even if – if –'

Words failed Bush to describe his utter determination not to sleep in the only bed and leave his captain without one.

'What are we going to Paris for, sir?' asked Bush.

'God knows,' said Hornblower. 'But I have a notion that Boney himself wants to ask us questions.'

That was the answer he had decided upon hours before in readiness for this inevitable question; it would not help Bush's convalescence to know the fate awaiting him.

'Much good will our answers do him,' said Bush, grimly. 'Perhaps we'll drink a dish of tea in the Tuileries with Maria Louisa.'

'Maybe,' answered Hornblower. 'And maybe he wants lessons in navigation from you. I've heard he's weak at mathematics.'

That brought a smile. Bush notoriously was no good

with figures and suffered agonies when confronted with a simple problem in spherical trigonometry. Hornblower's acute ears heard Brown's chair scrape a little; presumably his meal had progressed satisfactorily.

'Help yourself to the wine, Brown,' he said, without turning round.

'Aye aye, sir,' said Brown cheerfully.

There was a whole bottle of wine left as well as some in the other. This would be a good moment for ascertaining if Brown could be trusted with liquor. Hornblower kept his back turned to him and struggled on with his conversation with Bush. Five minutes later Brown's chair scraped again more definitely, and Hornblower looked round.

'Had enough, Brown?'

'Aye aye, sir. A right good supper.'

The soup tureen and the dish of stew were both empty; the bread had disappeared all save the heel of the loaf; there was only a morsel of cheese left. But one bottle of wine was still two-thirds full – Brown had contented himself with a half bottle at most, and the fact that he had drunk that much and no more was the clearest proof that he was safe as regards alcohol.

'Pull the bellrope, then.'

The distant jangling brought in time the rattling of keys to the door, and in came the sergeant and the two maids; the latter set about clearing the tables under the former's eye.

'I must get something for you to sleep on, Brown,' said Hornblower.

'I can sleep on the floor, sir.'

'No, you can't.'

Hornblower had decided opinions about that; there had been occasions as a young officer when he had slept on the bare planks of a ship's deck, and he knew their unbending discomfort.

'I want a bed for my servant,' he said to the sergeant.

'He can sleep on the floor.'

'I will not allow anything of the kind. You must find a mattress for him.'

Hornblower was surprised to find how quickly he was acquiring the ability to talk French; the quickness of his mind enabled him to make the best use of his limited vocabulary and his retentive memory had stored up all sorts of words, once heard, and was ready to produce them from the subconscious part of his mind as soon as the stimulus of necessity was applied.

The sergeant had shrugged his shoulders and rudely turned his back.

'I shall report your insolence to Colonel Caillard tomorrow morning,' said Hornblower hotly. 'Find a mattress immediately.'

It was not so much the threat that carried the day as long-ingrained habits of discipline. Even a sergeant of French gendarmerie was accustomed to yielding deference to gold lace and epaulettes and an authoritative manner. Possibly the obvious indignation of the maids at the suggestion that so fine a man should be left to sleep on the floor may have weighed with him too. He called to the sentry at the door and told him to bring a mattress from the stables where the escort were billeted. It was only a palliasse of straw when it came, but it was something infinitely more comfortable than bare and draughty boards, all the same. Brown looked his gratitude to Hornblower as the mattress was spread out in the corner of the room.

'Time to turn in,' said Hornblower, ignoring it, as the door was locked behind the sergeant. 'Let's make you comfortable, first, Bush.'

It was some obscure self-conscious motive which made Hornblower select from his valise the embroidered nightshirt over which Maria's busy fingers had laboured lovingly – the nightshirt which he had brought with him from England for use should it happen that he should dine and sleep at a Governor's or on board the flagship. All the years he had been a captain he had never shared a room with anyone save Maria, and it was a novel experience for him to prepare for bed in sight of Bush and Brown, and he was ridiculously self-conscious about it, regardless of the fact that Bush, white and exhausted, was already lying back on his pillow with drooping eyelids, while Brown modestly stripped off his trousers with downcast eyes, wrapped himself in the cloak which Hornblower insisted on his using, and curled himself up on his palliasse without a glance at his superior.

Hornblower got into bed.

'Ready?' he asked, and blew out the candle; the fire had died down to embers which gave only the faintest red glow in the room. It was the beginning of one of those wakeful nights which Hornblower had grown by now able to recognize in advance. The moment he blew out the candle and settled his head on the pillow he knew he would not be able to sleep until just before dawn. In his ship he would have gone up on deck or walked his stern gallery; here he could only lie grimly immobile. Sometimes a subdued crackling told how Brown was turning over on his straw mattress; once or twice Bush moaned a little in his feverish sleep.

Today was Wednesday. Only sixteen days ago and Hornblower had been captain of a seventy-four, and absolute master of the happiness of five hundred seamen. His least word directed the operations of a gigantic engine of war; the blows it had dealt had caused an imperial throne to totter. He thought regretfully of night-time aboard his ship, the creaking of the timbers and the singing of the rigging, the impassive quartermaster at the wheel in the faint light of the binnacle and the officer of the watch pacing the quarterdeck.

Now he was a nobody; where once he had minutely regulated five hundred men's lives he was reduced to chaffering for a single mattress for the only seaman left to him; police sergeants could insult him with impunity; he had to come and to go at the bidding of someone he despised. Worse than that – Hornblower felt the hot blood running under his skin as the full realization broke upon him again – he was being taken to Paris as a criminal. Very soon indeed, in some cold dawn, he would be led out into the ditch at Vincennes to face a firing party. Then he would be dead. Hornblower's vivid imagination pictured the impact of the musket bullets upon his breast, and he wondered how long the pain would last before oblivion came upon him. It was not the oblivion that he feared, he told himself – indeed in his present misery he almost looked forward to it. Perhaps it was the finality of death, the irrevocableness of it.

No, that was only a minor factor. Mostly it was instinctive fear of a sudden and drastic change to something completely unknown. He remembered the night he had spent as a child in the inn at Andover, when he was going to join his ship next day and enter upon the unknown life of the Navy. That was the nearest comparison – he had been frightened then, he remembered, so frightened he had been unable to sleep; and yet 'frightened' was too strong a word to describe the state of mind of someone who was quite prepared to face the future and could not be readily blamed for this sudden acceleration of heartbeat and prickling of sweat!

A moaning sigh from Bush, loud in the stillness of the room, distracted him from his analysis of his fear. They were going to shoot Bush, too. Presumably they would lash him to a stake to have a fair shot at him – curious how, while it was easy to order a party to shoot an upright figure, however helpless, every instinct revolted against shooting a helpless man prostrate on a stretcher. It would be a monstrous crime to shoot Bush, who, even supposing his captain were guilty, could have done nothing except obey orders. But Bonaparte would do it. The necessity of rallying Europe round him in his struggle against England was growing ever more pressing. The blockade was strangling the Empire of the French as Antaeus had been strangled by Hercules. Bonaparte's unwilling allies – all Europe, that was to say, save Portugal and Sicily – were growing restive and thinking about defection; the French people themselves, Hornblower shrewdly guessed, were by now none too enamoured of this King Stork whom they had imposed on themselves. It would not be sufficient for Bonaparte merely to say that the British fleet was the criminal instrument of a perfidious tyranny; he had said that for a dozen years. The mere announcement that British naval officers had violated the laws of war would carry small enough weight, too. But to try a couple of officers and shoot them would be a convincing gesture, and the perverted statement of facts issued from Paris might help to sustain French public opinion – European public opinion as well – for another year or two in its opposition to England.

But it was bad luck that the victims should be Bush and he. Bonaparte had had a dozen British naval captains in his hands during the last few years, and he could have trumped up charges against half of them. Presumably it was destiny which had selected Hornblower and Bush to suffer. Hornblower told himself that for twenty years he had been aware of a premonition of sudden death. It was certain and inevitable now. He hoped he would meet it bravely, go down with colours flying; but he mistrusted his own weak body. He feared that his cheeks would be pale and his teeth would chatter, or worse still, that his heart would weaken so that he would faint before the firing party had done their work. That would be a fine opportunity for a mordant couple of lines in the *Moniteur Universel* – fine reading for Lady Barbara and Maria.

If he had been alone in the room he would have groaned aloud in his misery and turned over restlessly. But as it was he lay grimly rigid and silent. If his subordinates were awake they would never be allowed to guess that he was awake, too. To divert his mind from his approaching execution he cast round in search of something else to think about, and new subjects presented themselves in swarms. Whether Admiral

Leighton were alive or dead, and whether, if the latter were the case, Lady Barbara Leighton would think more often or less often about Hornblower, her lover; how Maria's pregnancy was progressing; what was the state of British public opinion regarding the loss of the *Sutherland*, and, more especially, what Lady Barbara thought about his surrendering – there were endless things to think and worry about; there was endless flotsam bobbing about in the racing torrent of his mind. And the horses stampeded in the stable, and every two hours he heard the sentries being changed outside window and door.

5

Dawn was not fully come, the room was only faintly illuminated by the grey light, when a clash of keys and a stamping of booted feet outside the door heralded the entrance of the sergeant of gendarmerie.

'The coach will leave in an hour's time,' he announced. 'The surgeon will be here in half an hour. You gentlemen will please be ready.'

Bush was obviously feverish; Hornblower could see that at his first glance as he bent over him, still in his embroidered silk nightshirt. But Bush stoutly affirmed that he was not ill.

'I'm well enough, thank you, sir,' he said; but his face was flushed and yet apprehensive, and his hands gripped his bedclothes. Hornblower suspected that the mere vibration of the floor as he and Brown walked about the room was causing pain to the unhealed stump of his leg.

'I'm ready to do anything you want done,' said Hornblower.

'No, thank you, sir. Let's wait till the doctor comes, if you don't mind, sir.'

Hornblower washed and shaved in the cold water in the wash-stand jug; during the time which had elapsed since he had left the *Sutherland* he had never been allowed hot. But he yearned for the cold shower bath he had been accustomed to take under the jet of the wash-deck pump; his skin seemed to creep when he stopped to consider it, and it was a ghoulish business to make shift with washing glove and soap, wetting a few inches at a time. Brown dressed himself unobtrusively in his own corner of the room, scurrying out like a mouse to wash when his captain had finished.

The doctor arrived with his leather satchel.

'And how is he this morning?' he asked, briskly; Hornblower saw a shade of concern pass over his face as he observed Bush's evident fever.

He knelt down and exposed the stump, Hornblower beside him. The limb jerked nervously as it was grasped with firm fingers; the doctor took Hornblower's hand and laid it on the skin above the wound.

'A little warm,' said the doctor. It was hot to Hornblower's touch. 'That may be a good sign. We shall know now.'

He took hold of one of the ligatures and pulled at it. The thing came gliding out of the wound like a snake.

'Good!' said the doctor. 'Excellent!'

He peered closely at the debris entangled in the knot, and then bent to examine the trickle of pus which had followed the ligature out of the wound.

'Excellent,' repeated the doctor.

Hornblower went back in his mind through the numerous reports which surgeons had made to him regarding wounded men, and the verbal comments with which they had amplified them. The words 'laudable pus' came up in his mind; it was important to distinguish between the drainage from a wound struggling to heal itself and the stinking ooze of a poisoned limb. This was clearly laudable pus, judging by the doctor's comments.

'Now for the other one,' said the doctor. He pulled at the remaining ligature, but all he got was a cry of pain from Bush – which seemed to go clean through Hornblower's heart – and a convulsive writhing of Bush's tortured body.

'Not quite ready,' said the doctor. 'I should judge that it will only be a matter of hours, though. Is your friend proposing to continue his journey today?'

'He is under orders to continue it,' said Hornblower in his limping French. 'You would consider such a course unwise?'

'Most unwise,' said the doctor. 'It will cause him a great deal of pain and may imperil the healing of the wound.'

He felt Bush's pulse and rested his hand on his forehead.

'Most unwise,' he repeated.

The door opened behind him to reveal the gendarmerie sergeant.

'The carriage is ready.'

'It must wait until I have bandaged this wound. Get outside,' said the doctor testily.

'I will go and speak to the Colonel,' said Hornblower.

He brushed past the sergeant who tried too late to intercept him, into the main corridor of the inn, and out into the courtyard where stood the coach. The horses were being harnessed up, and a group of gendarmes were saddling their mounts on the farther side. Chance dictated that Colonel Caillard should be crossing the courtyard, too, in his blue and red uniform and his gleaming high boots, the star of the Legion of Honour dancing on his breast.

'Sir,' said Hornblower.

'What is it now?' demanded Caillard.

'Lieutenant Bush must not be moved. He is very badly wounded and a crisis approaches.'

The broken French came tumbling disjointedly from Hornblower's lips.

'I can do nothing in contravention of my orders,' said Caillard. His eyes were cold and his mouth hard.

'You were not ordered to kill him,' protested Hornblower.

'I was ordered to bring you and him to Paris with the utmost dispatch. We shall start in five minutes.'

'But, sir – cannot you wait even today?'

'Even as a pirate you must be aware of the impossibility of disobeying orders,' said Caillard.

'I protest against those orders in the name of humanity.'

That was a melodramatic speech, but it was a melodramatic moment, and in his ignorance of French Hornblower could not pick and choose his words. A sympathetic murmur in his ear attracted his notice, and, looking round, he saw the two aproned maids and a fat woman and the innkeeper all listening to the conversation with obvious disapproval of Caillard's point of view. They shut themselves away behind the kitchen door as Caillard turned a terrible eye upon them, but they had granted Hornblower a first momentary insight into the personal unpopularity which Imperial harshness was causing to develop in France.

'Sergeant,' said Caillard abruptly. 'Put the prisoners into the coach.'

There was no hope of resistance. The gendarmes

carried Bush's stretcher into the courtyard and perched it up on the seats, with Brown and Hornblower running round it to protect it from unnecessary jerks. The surgeon was scribbling notes hurriedly at the foot of the sheaf of notes regarding Bush's case which Hornblower had brought from Rosas. One of the maids came clattering across the courtyard with a steaming tray which she passed in to Hornblower through the open window. There was a platter of bread and three bowls of a black liquid which Hornblower was later to come to recognize as coffee – what blockaded France had come to call coffee. It was no pleasanter than the infusion of burnt crusts which Hornblower had sometimes drunk on shipboard during a long cruise without the opportunity of renewing cabin stores, but it was warm and stimulating at that time in the morning.

'We have no sugar, sir,' said the maid apologetically.

'It doesn't matter,' answered Hornblower, sipping thirstily.

'It is a pity the poor wounded officer has to travel,' she went on. 'These wars are terrible.'

She had a snub nose and a wide mouth and big black eyes – no one could call her attractive, but the sympathy in her voice was grateful to a man who was a prisoner. Brown was propping up Bush's shoulders and holding a bowl to his lips. He took two or three sips and turned his head away. The coach rocked as two men scrambled up on to the box.

'Stand away, there!' roared the sergeant.

The coach lurched and rolled and wheeled round out of the gates, the horses' hoofs clattering loud on the cobbles, and the last Hornblower saw of the maid was the slight look of consternation on her face as she realized that she had lost the breakfast tray for good.

The road was bad, judging by the way the coach lurched; Hornblower heard a sharp intake of breath from Bush at one jerk. He remembered what the swollen and inflamed stump of Bush's leg looked like; every jar must be causing him agony. He moved up the seat to the stretcher and caught Bush's hand.

'Don't you worry yourself, sir,' said Bush. 'I'm all right.'

Even while he spoke Hornblower felt him grip tighter as another jolt caught him unexpectedly.

'I'm sorry, Bush,' was all he could say; it was hard for the captain to speak at length to the lieutenant on such personal matters as his regret and unhappiness.

'We can't help it, sir,' said Bush, forcing his peaked features into a smile.

That was the main trouble, their complete helplessness. Hornblower realized that there was nothing he could say, nothing he could do. The leather-scented stuffiness of the coach was already oppressing him, and he realized with horror that they would have to endure this jolting prison of theirs for another twenty days, perhaps, before they should reach Paris. He was restless and fidgety at the thought of it, and perhaps his restlessness communicated itself by contact to Bush, who gently withdrew his hand and turned his head to one side, leaving his captain free to fidget within the narrow confines of the coach.

Still there were glimpses of the sea to be caught on one side, and of the Pyrenees on the other. Putting his head out of the window Hornblower ascertained that their escort was diminished today. Only two troopers rode ahead of the coach, and four clattered behind at the heels of Caillard's horse. Presumably their entry into France made any possibility of a rescue far less likely. Standing thus, his head awkwardly protruding through the window, was less irksome than sitting in the stuffiness of the carriage. There were the vineyards and the stubble field to be seen, and the swelling heights of the Pyrenees receding into the blue distance. There were people, too – nearly all women, Hornblower noted – who hardly looked up from their hoeing to watch the coach and its escort bowling along the road. Now they were passing a party of uniformed soldiers – recruits and convalescents, Hornblower guessed, on their way to their units in Catalonia – shambling along the road more like sheep than soldiers. The young officer at their head saluted the glitter of the star on Caillard's chest and eyed the coach curiously at the same time.

Strange prisoners had passed along that road before him; Alvarez, the heroic defender of Gerona, who died on a wheelbarrow – the only bed granted him – in a dungeon on his way to trial, and Toussaint l'Ouverture, the Negro hero of Haiti, kidnapped from his sunny island and sent to die, inevitably, of pneumonia in a rocky fortress in the Jura; Palafox of Zaragoza, young Mina from Navarre – all victims of the tyrant's Corsican rancour. He and Bush would only be two more items in a list already notable. D'Enghien who had been shot in Vincennes six years ago was of the blood-royal, and his death had caused a European sensation, but Bonaparte had murdered plenty more. Thinking of all those who had preceded him made Hornblower gaze more yearningly from the carriage window, and breathe more deeply of the free air.

Still in sight of sea and hills – Mount Canigou still dominating the background – they halted at a posting inn beside the road to change horses. Caillard and the escort took new mounts; four new horses were harnessed up to the coach, and in less than a quarter of an hour they were off again, breasting the steep slopes before them with renewed strength. They must be averaging six miles to the hour at least, thought Hornblower, his mind beginning to make calculations. How far Paris might be he could only guess – five or six hundred miles, he fancied. From seventy to ninety hours of travel would bring them to the capital, and they might travel eight, twelve, fifteen hours a day. It might be five days, it might be twelve, days, before they reached Paris – vague enough figures. He might be dead in a week's time, or he might still be alive in three weeks. Still alive! As Hornblower thought those words he realized how greatly he desired to live; it was one of those moments when the Hornblower whom he observed so dispassionately and with faint contempt suddenly blended with the Hornblower who was himself, the most important and vital person in the whole world. He envied the bent old shepherd in the distance with the plaid rug over his shoulders, hobbling over the hillside bent over his stick.

Here was a town coming – there were ramparts, a frowning citadel, a lofty cathedral. They passed through a gateway and the horses' hoofs rang loudly on cobblestones as the coach threaded its way through narrow streets. Plenty of soldiers here, too; the streets were filled with variegated uniforms. This must be Perpignan, of course, the French base for the invasion of Catalonia. The coach stopped with a jerk in a wider street where an avenue of plane trees and a flagged quay bordered a little river, and, looking upward, Hornblower read the sign 'Hôtel de la Poste et du Perdrix. Route Nationale 9. Paris 849'. With a rush and bustle the horses were changed, Brown and Hornblower were grudgingly allowed to descend and stretch their stiff legs before returning to attend to Bush's wants – they were few enough in his present fever. Caillard and the gendarmes were snatching a hasty meal – the latter at tables outside the inn, the former visible through the windows of the front room. Someone brought the prisoners a tray with slices of cold meat, bread, wine, and cheese. It had hardly been handed into the coach when the escort climbed upon their horses again, the whip cracked and they were off. The coach heaved and dipped like a ship at sea as it mounted first one hump-backed bridge and then another, before the horses settled into a steady trot along the wide straight road bordered with poplars.

'They waste no time,' said Hornblower, grimly.

'No, sir, that they don't!' agreed Brown.

Bush would eat nothing, shaking his head feebly at the offer of bread and meat. All they could do for him was to moisten his lips with wine, for he was parched and thirsty; Hornblower made a mental note to remember to ask for water at the next posting house, and cursed himself for forgetting anything so obvious up to now. He and Brown shared the food, eating with their fingers and drinking turn and turn about from the bottle of wine, Brown apologetically wiping the bottle's mouth with the napkin after drinking. And as soon as the food was finished Hornblower was on his feet again craning through the carriage window, watching the countryside drifting by. A thin chill rain began, soaking his scanty hair as he stood there, wetting his face and even running in trickles down his neck, but still he stood there, staring out at freedom.

The sign of the inn where they stopped at nightfall read 'Hôtel de la Poste de Sigean. Route Nationale 9. Paris 805. Perpignan 44'. This place Sigean was no more than a sparse village, straggling for miles along the high road, and the inn was a tiny affair, smaller than the posting stables round the other three sides of the courtyard. The staircase to the upper rooms was too narrow and winding for the stretcher to be carried up them; it was only with difficulty that the bearers were able to turn with it into the salon which the innkeeper reluctantly yielded to them. Hornblower saw Bush wincing as the stretcher jarred against the sides of the door.

'We must have a surgeon at once for the lieutenant,' he said to the sergeant.

'I will inquire for one.'

The innkeeper here was a surly brute with a squint; he was ungracious about clearing his best sitting room of its spindly furniture, and bringing beds for Hornblower and Brown, and producing the various articles they asked for to help make Bush comfortable. There were no wax candles nor lamps; only tallow dips which stank atrociously.

'How's the leg feeling?' asked Hornblower, bending over Bush.

'All right, sir,' said Bush, stubbornly, but he was so

obviously feverish and in such obvious pain that Hornblower was anxious about him.

When the sergeant escorted in the maid with the dinner he asked, sharply:

'Why has the surgeon not come?'

'There is no surgeon in this village.'

'No surgeon? The lieutenant is seriously ill. Is there no – no apothecary?'

Hornblower used the English word in default of French.

'The cow-doctor went across the hills this afternoon and will not be back tonight. There is no one to be found.'

The sergeant went out of the room, leaving Hornblower to explain the situation to Bush.

'All right,' said the latter, turning his head on the pillow with the feeble gesture which Hornblower dreaded. Hornblower nerved himself.

'I'd better dress that wound of yours myself,' he said. 'We might try cold vinegar on it, as they do in our service.'

'Something cold,' said Bush, eagerly.

Hornblower pealed at the bell, and when it was eventually answered he asked for vinegar and obtained it. Not one of the three had a thought for their dinner cooling on the side table.

'Now,' said Hornblower.

He had a saucer of vinegar beside him, in which lay the soaking lint, and the clean bandages which the surgeon at Rosas had supplied were at hand. He turned back the bedclothes and revealed the bandaged stump. The leg twitched nervously as he removed the bandages;

it was red and swollen and inflamed, hot to the touch for several inches above the point of amputation.

'It's pretty swollen here, too, sir,' whispered Bush. The glands in his groin were huge.

'Yes,' said Hornblower.

He peered at the scarred end, examined the dressings he had removed, with Brown holding the light. There had been a slight oozing from the point where the ligature had been withdrawn yesterday; much of the rest of the scar was healed and obviously healthy. There was only the other ligature which could be causing this trouble; Hornblower knew that if it were ready to come out it was dangerous to leave it in. Cautiously he took hold of the silken thread. The first gentle touch of it conveyed to his sensitive fingers a suggestion that it was free. It moved distinctly for a quarter of an inch, and judging by Bush's quiescence, it caused him no sudden spasm of pain. Hornblower set his teeth and pulled; the thread yielded very slowly, but it was obviously free, and no longer attached to the elastic artery. He pulled steadily against a yielding resistance. The ligature came slowly out of the wound, knot and all. Pus followed it in a steady trickle, only slightly tinged with blood. The thing was done.

The artery had not burst, and clearly the wound was in need of the free drainage open to it now with the withdrawal of the ligature.

'I think you're going to start getting well now,' he said, aloud, making himself speak cheerfully, 'How does it feel?'

'Better,' said Bush. 'I think it's better, sir.'

Hornblower applied the soaking lint to the scarred

surface. He found his hands trembling, but he steadied them with an effort as he bandaged the stump – not an easy job, this last, but one which he managed to complete in adequate fashion. He put back the wicker shield, tucked in the bedclothes, and rose to his feet. The trembling was worse than ever now, and he was shaken and sick, which surprised him.

'Supper, sir?' asked Brown. 'I'll give Mr Bush his.'

Hornblower's stomach resisted a protest at the suggestion of food. He would have liked to refuse, but that would have been too obvious a confession of weakness in front of a subordinate.

'When I've washed my hands,' he said loftily.

It was easier to eat than he had expected, when he sat down to force himself. He managed to choke down enough mouthfuls to make it appear as if he had eaten well, and with the passage of the minutes the memory of the revolting task on which he had been engaged became rapidly less clear. Bush displayed none of the appetite nor any of the cheerfulness which had been noticeable last night; that was the obvious result of his fever. But with free drainage to his wound it could be hoped that he would soon recover. Hornblower was tired now, as a result of his sleepless night the night before, and his emotions had been jarred into a muddle by what he had had to do; it was easier to sleep tonight, waking only at intervals to listen to Bush's breathing, and to sleep again reassured by the steadiness and tranquillity of the sound.

6

After that day the details of the journey became more blurred and indistinct – up to that day they had had all the unnatural sharpness of a landscape just before rain. Looking back at the journey, what was easiest to remember was Bush's convalescence – his steady progress back to health from the moment that the ligature was withdrawn from his wound. His strength began to come back fast, so that it would have been astonishing to anyone who did not know of his iron constitution and of the Spartan life he had always led. The transition was rapid between the time when his head had to be supported to allow him to drink and the time when he could sit himself up by his own unaided strength.

Hornblower could remember those details when he tried to, but all the rest was muddled and vague. There were memories of long hours spent at the carriage window, when it always seemed to be raining, and the rain wetted his face and hair. Those were hours spent in a sort of melancholy; Hornblower came to look back on them afterwards in the same way as someone recovered from insanity must look back on the blank days in the asylum. All the inns at which they stayed and the doctors who had attended to Bush were confused in his mind. He could remember the relentless regularity with which the kilometre figures displayed at the posting stations indicated the dwindling distance between them and Paris – Paris 525, Paris 383, Paris 287; somewhere at that point they changed from Route Nationale No. 9 to Route Nationale No. 7. Each day was bringing them nearer to Paris and death, and each day he sank farther into apathetic melancholy. Issoire, Clermont-Ferrand, Moulins; he read the names of the towns through which they passed without remembering them.

Autumn was gone now, left far behind down by the Pyrenees. Here winter had begun. Cold winds blew in melancholy fashion through the long avenues of leafless trees, and the fields were brown and desolate. At night he was sleeping heavily, tormented by dreams which he could not remember in the morning; his days he spent standing at the carriage window staring with sightless eyes over a dreary landscape where the chill rain fell. It seemed as if he had spent years consecutively in the leathery atmosphere of the coach, with the clatter of the horses' hoofs in his ears, and, visible in the tail of his eye, the burly figure of Caillard riding at the head of the escort close to the offside hind wheel.

During the bleakest afternoon they had yet experienced it did not seem as if Hornblower would be roused from his stupor even by the sudden unexpected stop which to a bored traveller might provide a welcome break in the monotony of travel. Dully, he watched Caillard ride up to ask the reason; dully, he gathered from the conversation that one of the coach horses had lost a shoe and gone dead lame. He watched with indifference the unharnessing of the unfortunate brute, and heard without interest the unhelpful answers of a passing travelling salesman with a pack-mule of whom

Caillard demanded the whereabouts of the nearest smith. Two gendarmes went off at a snail's pace down a side track, leading the crippled animal; with only three horses the coach started off again towards Paris.

Progress was slow, and the stage was a long one. Only rarely before had they travelled after dark, but here it seemed that night would overtake them long before they could reach the next town. Bush and Brown were talking quite excitedly about this remarkable mishap – Hornblower heard their cackle without noticing it, as a man long resident beside a waterfall no longer hears the noise of the fall. The darkness which was engulfing them was premature. Low black clouds covered the whole sky, and the note of the wind in the trees carried with it something of menace. Even Hornblower noted that, nor was it long before he noticed something else, that the rain beating upon his face was changing to sleet, and then from sleet to snow; he felt the big flakes upon his lips, and tasted them with his tongue. The gendarme who lit the lamps beside the driver's box revealed to them through the windows the front of his cloak caked thick with snow, shining faintly in the feeble light of the lamp. Soon the sound of the horses' feet was muffled and dull, the wheels could hardly be heard, and the pace of the coach diminished still further as it ploughed through the snow piling in the road. Hornblower could hear the coachman using his whip mercilessly upon his weary animals – they were heading straight into the piercing wind, and were inclined to take every opportunity to flinch away from it.

Hornblower turned back from the window to his subordinates inside the coach – the faint light which the glass front panel allowed to enter from the lamps was no more than enough to enable him just to make out their shadowy forms. Bush was lying huddled under all his blankets; Brown was clutching his cloak round him, and Hornblower for the first time noticed the bitter cold. He shut the coach window without a word, resigning himself to the leathery stuffiness of the interior. His dazed melancholy was leaving him without his being aware of it.

'God help sailors,' he said cheerfully, 'on a night like this.'

That drew a laugh from the others in the darkness – Hornblower just caught the note of pleased surprise in it which told him that they had noticed and regretted the black mood which had gripped him during the last few days, and were pleased with this first sign of his recovery. Resentfully he asked himself what they expected of him. They did not know, as he did, that death awaited him and Bush in Paris. What was the use of thinking and worrying, guarded as they were by Caillard and six gendarmes? With Bush a hopeless cripple, what chance was there of escape? They did not know that Hornblower had put aside all thought of escaping by himself. If by a miracle he had succeeded, what would they think of him in England when he arrived there with the news that he had left his lieutenant to die? They might sympathize with him, pity him, understand his motive – he hated the thought of any of that; better to face a firing party at Bush's side, never to see Lady Barbara again, never to see his child. And better to spend his last few days in apathy than in fretting. Yet the present circumstances, so different from the monotony of the rest of the journey, had stimulated him. He laughed and chatted with the others as he had not done since they had left Béziers.

The coach crawled on through the darkness with the wind shrieking overhead. Already the windows on one side were opaque with the snow which was plastered upon them – there was not warmth enough within the coach to melt it. More than once the coach halted, and Hornblower, putting his head out, saw that they were having to clear the horses' hoofs of the snow balled into ice under their shoes.

'If we're more than two miles from the next post house,' he announced, sitting back again, 'we won't reach it until next week.'

Now they must have topped a small rise, for the horses were moving quicker, almost trotting, with the coach swaying and lurching over the inequalities of the road. Suddenly from outside they heard an explosion of shouts and yells.

'Hé, hé, hé!'

The coach swung round without warning, lurching frightfully, and came to a halt leaning perilously over to one side. Hornblower sprang to the window and looked out. The coach was poised perilously on the bank of a river; Hornblower could see the black water sliding along almost under his nose. Two yards away a small rowing boat, moored to a post, swayed about under the influence of wind and stream. Otherwise there was nothing to be seen in the blackness. Some of the gendarmes had run to the coach horses' heads; the animals were plunging and rearing in their fright at the sudden apparition of the river before them.

Somehow in the darkness the coach must have got off the road and gone down some side track leading to the river here; the coachman had reined his horses round only a fraction of a second before disaster threatened. Caillard was sitting his horse blaring sarcasms at the others.

'A fine coachman you are, God knows. Why didn't you drive straight into the river and save me the trouble of reporting you to the sous-chef of the administration? Come along, you men. Do you want to stay here all night? Get the coach back on the road, you fools.'

The snow came driving down in the darkness, the hot lamps sizzling continuously as the flakes lighted on them. The coachman got his horses under control again, the gendarmes stood back, and the whip cracked. The horses plunged and slipped, pawing for a footing, and the coach trembled without stirring from the spot.

'Come along, now!' shouted Caillard. 'Sergeant, and you, Pellaton, take the horses. You other men get to the wheels! Now, altogether. Heave! Heave!'

The coach lurched a scant yard before halting again. Caillard cursed wildly.

'If the gentlemen in the coach would descend and help,' suggested one of the gendarmes, 'it would be better.'

'They can, unless they would rather spend the night in the snow,' said Caillard; he did not condescend to address Hornblower directly. For a moment Hornblower thought of telling him that he would see him damned first – there would be some satisfaction in that – but on the other hand he did not want to condemn

Bush to a night of discomfort merely for an intangible self-gratification.

'Come on, Brown,' he said, swallowing his resentment, and he opened the door and they jumped down into the snow.

Even with the coach thus lightened, and with five men straining at the spokes of the wheels, they could make no progress. The snow had piled up against the steep descent to the river, and the exhausted horses plunged uselessly in the deep mass.

'God, what a set of useless cripples!' raved Caillard. 'Coachman, how far is it to Nevers?'

'Six kilometres, sir.'

'You mean you think it's six kilometres. Ten minutes ago you thought you were on the right road and you were not. Sergeant, ride into Nevers for help. Find the mayor, and bring every able-bodied man in the name of the Emperor. You, Ramel, ride with the sergeant as far as the high road, and wait there until he returns. Otherwise they'll never find us. Go on, sergeant, what are you waiting for? And you others, tether your horses and put your cloaks on their backs. You can keep warm digging the snow away from that bank. Coachman, come off that box and help them.'

The night was incredibly dark. Two yards from the carriage lamps nothing was visible at all, and with the wind whistling by they could not hear, as they stood by the coach, the movements of the men in the snow. Hornblower stamped about beside the coach and flogged himself with his arms to get his circulation back. Yet this snow and this icy wind were strangely refreshing. He felt no desire at the moment for the cramped stuffiness of the coach. And as he swung his arms an idea came to him, which checked him suddenly in his movements, until, ridiculously afraid of his thoughts being guessed, he went on stamping and swinging more industriously than ever. The blood was running hot under his skin now, as it always did when he was making plans – when he had outmanoeuvred the *Natividad*, for instance, and when he had saved the *Pluto* in the storm off Cape Creux.

There had been no hope of escape without the means of transporting a helpless cripple; now, not twenty feet from him, there was the ideal means – the boat which rocked to its moorings at the river bank. On a night like this it was easy to lose one's way altogether – except in a boat on a river; in a boat one had only to keep shoving off from shore to allow the current to carry one away faster than any horse could travel in these conditions. Even so, the scheme was utterly harebrained. For how many days would they be able to preserve their liberty in the heart of France, two able-bodied men and one on a stretcher? They would freeze, starve – possibly even drown. But it was a chance, and nothing nearly as good would present itself (as far as Hornblower could judge from his past observations) between now and the time when the firing party at Vincennes would await them. Hornblower observed with mild interest that his fever was abating as he formed his resolve; and he was sufficiently amused at finding his jaw set in an expression of fierce resolution to allow his features to relax into a grim smile. There was always something laughable to him in being involved in heroics.

Brown came stamping round the coach and Hornblower addressed him, contriving with great effort to keep his voice low and yet matter of fact.

'We're going to escape down the river in that boat, Brown,' he said.

'Aye, aye, sir,' said Brown, with no more excitement in his voice than if Hornblower had been speaking of the cold. Hornblower saw his head in the darkness turn towards the nearly visible figure of Caillard, pacing restlessly in the snow beside the coach.

'That man must be silenced,' said Hornblower.

'Aye, aye, sir.' Brown meditated for a second before continuing. 'Better let me do that, sir.'

'Very good.'

'Now, sir?'

'Yes.'

Brown took two steps towards the unsuspecting figure.

'Here,' he said. 'Here, you.'

Caillard turned and faced him, and as he turned he received Brown's fist full on his jaw, in a punch which had all Brown's mighty fourteen stone behind it. He dropped in the snow, with Brown leaping upon him like a tiger, Hornblower behind him.

'Tie him up in his cloak,' whispered Hornblower. 'Hold on to his throat while I get it unbuttoned. Wait. Here's his scarf. Tie his head up in that first.'

The sash of the Legion of Honour was wound round and round the wretched man's head. Brown rolled the writhing figure over and with his knee in the small of his back tied his arms behind him with his neckcloth. Hornblower's handkerchief sufficed for his ankles –

Brown strained the knot tight. They doubled the man in two and bundled him into his cloak, tying it about him with his swordbelt. Bush, lying on his stretcher in the darkness of the coach, heard the door open and a heavy load drop upon the floor.

'Mr Bush,' said Hornblower – the formal 'Mr' came naturally again now the action had begun again – 'We are going to escape in the boat.'

'Good luck, sir,' said Bush.

'You're coming too. Brown, take that end of the stretcher. Lift. Starboard a bit. Steady.'

Bush felt himself lifted out of the coach, stretcher and all, and carried down through the snow.

'Get the boat close in,' snapped Hornblower. 'Cut the moorings. Now, Bush, let's get these blankets round you. Here's my cloak, take it as well. You'll obey orders, Mr Bush. Take the other side, Brown. Lift him into the sternsheets. Lower away. Bow thwart, Brown. Take the oars. Right. Shove off. Give way.'

It was only six minutes from the time when Hornblower had first conceived the idea. Now they were free, adrift on the black river, and Caillard was gagged and tied into a bundle on the floor of the coach. For a fleeting moment Hornblower wondered whether Caillard would suffocate before being discovered, and he found himself quite indifferent in the matter. Bonaparte's personal aides-de-camp, especially if they were colonels of gendarmerie as well, must expect to run risks while doing the dirty work which their situation would bring them. Meanwhile he had other things to think about.

'Easy!' he hissed at Brown. 'Let the current take her.'

The night was absolutely black; seated on the stern

thwart he could not even see the surface of the water overside. For that matter, he did not know what river it was. But every river runs to the sea. The sea! Hornblower writhed in his seat in wild nostalgia at a vivid recollection of sea breezes in the nostrils and the feel of a heaving deck under his feet. Mediterranean or Atlantic, he did not know which, but if they had fantastic luck they might reach the sea in this boat by following the river far enough, and the sea was England's and would bear them home, to life instead of death, to freedom instead of imprisonment, to Lady Barbara, to Maria and his child.

The wind shrieked down on them, driving snow down his neck – thwarts and bottom boards were thick with snow. He felt the boat swing round under the thrust of the wind, which was in his face now instead of on his cheek.

'Turn her head to wind, Brown,' he ordered, 'and pull slowly into it.'

The surest way of allowing the current a free hand with them was to try to neutralize the effect of the wind – a gale like this would soon blow them on shore, or even possibly blow them upstream; in this blackness it was impossible to guess what was happening to them.

'Comfortable, Mr Bush?' he asked.

'Aye, aye, sir.'

Bush was faintly visible now, for the snow had driven up already against the grey blankets that swathed him and could just be seen from where Hornblower sat, a yard away.

'Would you like to lie down?'

'Thank you, sir, but I'd rather sit.'

Now that the excitement of the actual escape was over, Hornblower found himself shivering in the keen wind without his cloak. He was about to tell Brown that he would take one of the sculls when Bush spoke again.

'Pardon, sir, but d'you hear anything?'

Brown rested on his oars, and they sat listening.

'No,' said Hornblower. 'Yes, I do, by God!'

Underlying the noise of the wind there was a distant monotonous roaring.

'H'm,' said Hornblower, uneasily.

The roar was growing perceptibly louder; now it rose several notes in the scale, suddenly, and they could distinguish the sound of running water. Something appeared in the darkness beside the boat; it was a rock nearly covered, rendered visible in the darkness by the boiling white foam round it. It came and was gone in a flash, the clearest proof of the speed with which the boat was travelling.

'Jesus!' said Brown in the bows.

Now the boat was spinning round, lurching, jolting. All the water was white overside, and the bellowing of the rapid was deafening. They could do no more than sit and cling to their seat as the boat heaved and jerked. Hornblower shook himself free from his dazed helplessness, which seemed to have lasted half an hour and probably lasted no more than a couple of seconds.

'Give me a scull,' he snapped at Brown. 'You fend off port side. I'll take starboard.'

He groped in the darkness, found a scull, and took it from Brown's hand; the boat spun, hesitated, plunged again. All about them was the roar of the rapid. The starboard side of the boat caught on a rock; Hornblower felt icy water deluge his legs as it poured in over the side behind him. But already he was thrusting madly and blindly with his scull against the rock, he felt the boat slip and swing, he thrust so that the swing was accentuated, and next moment they were clear, wallowing sluggishly with the water up to the thwarts. Another rock slid hissing past, but the roar of the fall was already dwindling.

'Christ!' said Bush, in a mild tone contrasting oddly with the blasphemy. 'We're through!'

'D'you know if there's a bailer in the boat, Brown?' demanded Hornblower.

'Yessir, there was one at my feet when I came on board.'

'Find it and get this water out. Give me your other scull.'

Brown splashed about in the icy water in a manner piteous to hear as he groped for the floating wooden basin.

'Got it, sir,' he reported, and they heard the regular sound of the water being scooped overside as he began work.

In the absence of the distraction of the rapids they were conscious of the wind again now, and Hornblower turned the boat's bows into it and pulled slowly at the sculls. Past experience appeared to have demonstrated conclusively that this was the best way to allow the current a free hand to take the boat downstream and away from pursuit. Judging by the speed with which the noise of the rapid was left behind the current of this river was very fast indeed – that was only to be expected, too, for all the rain of the past few days must have brought up every river brim full. Hornblower wondered vaguely again what river this was, here in the heart of France. The only one with whose name he was acquainted and which it might possibly be was the Rhône, but he felt a suspicion that the Rhône was fifty miles or so farther eastward. This river presumably had taken its origin in the gaunt Cevennes whose flanks they had turned in the last two days' journey. In that case it would run northward, and must presumably turn westward to find the sea – it must be the Loire or one of its tributaries. And the Loire fell into the Bay of Biscay below Nantes, which must be at least four hundred miles away. Hornblower's imagination dallied with the idea of a river four hundred miles long, and with the prospect of descending it from source to mouth in the depth of winter.

A ghostly sound as if from nowhere brought him back to earth again. As he tried to identify it it repeated itself more loudly and definitely, and the boat lurched and hesitated. They were gliding over a bit of rock which providence had submerged to a depth sufficient just to scrape their keel. Another rock, foam covered, came boiling past them dose overside. It passed them from stern to bow, telling him what he had no means of discovering in any other way in the blackness, that in this reach the river must be running westward, for the wind was in the east and he was pulling into it.

'More of those to come yet, sir,' said Bush – already they could hear the growing roar of water among rocks.

'Take a scull and watch the port side, Brown,' said Hornblower.

'Aye aye, sir. I've got the boat nearly dry,' volunteered Brown, feeling for the scull.

The boat was lurching again now, dancing a little in the madness of the river. Hornblower felt bow and stem lift successively as they dropped over what felt like a downward step in the water; he reeled as he stood, and the water remaining in the bottom of the boat surged and splashed against his ankles. The din of the rapid in the darkness round them was tremendous; white water was boiling about them on either side. The boat swung and pitched and rolled. Then something invisible struck the port side amidships with a splinter crash. Brown tried unavailingly to shove off, and Hornblower swung round and with his added strength forced the boat clear. They plunged and rolled again; Hornblower, feeling in the darkness, found the gunwale stove in, but apparently only the two upper stakes were damaged – chance might have driven that rock through below the water line as easily as it had done above it. Now the keel seemed to have caught; the boat heeled hideously, with Bush and Hornblower falling on their noses, but she freed herself and went on through the roaring water. The noise was dying down again and they were through another rapid.

'Shall I bail again, sir?' asked Brown.

'Yes. Give me your scull.'

'Light on the starboard bow, sir' interjected Bush.

Hornblower craned over his shoulder. Undoubtedly it was a light, with another close beside it, and another farther on, barely visible in the driving snow. That must be a village on the river bank, or a town – the town of Nevers, six kilometres, according to the coachman, from where they had embarked. They had come four miles already.

'Silence now!' hissed Hornblower. 'Brown, stop bailing.'

With those lights to guide him in the darkness, stable, permanent things in this insane world of infinite indefiniteness, it was marvellous how he felt master of his fate once more. He knew again which was upstream and which was down – the wind was still blowing downstream. With a touch of the sculls he turned the boat downstream, wind and current sped her along fast and the lights were gliding by rapidly. The snow stung his face – it was hardly likely there would be anyone in the town to observe them on a night like this. Certainly the boat must have come down the river faster than the plodding horses of the gendarmes whom Caillard had sent ahead. A new roaring of water caught his ear, different in timbre from the sound of a rapid. He craned round again to see the bridge before them silhouetted in white against the blackness by reason of the snow driven against the arches. He tugged wildly, first at one scull and then at both, heading for the centre of an arch; he felt the bow dip and the stern heave as they approached – the water was banked up above the bridge and rushed down through the arches in a long sleek black slope. As they whirled under Hornblower bent to his sculls, to give the boat sufficient way to carry her through the eddies which his seaman's instinct warned him would await them below the piers. The crown of the arch brushed his head as he pulled – the floods had risen as high as that. The sound of rushing water echoed strangely under the stonework for a second, and then they were through, with Hornblower tugging madly at the sculls.

One more light on the shore, and then they were in utter blackness again, their sense of direction lost.

'Christ!' said Bush again, this time with utter solemnity, as Hornblower rested on his sculls. The wind shrieked down upon them, blinding them with snow. From the bows came a ghostly chuckle.

'God help sailors,' said Brown, 'on a night like this.'

'Carry on with the bailing, Brown, and save your jokes for afterwards,' snapped Hornblower. But he giggled, nevertheless, even despite of the faint shock he experienced at hearing the lower deck cracking jokes to a captain and a first lieutenant. His ridiculous habit of laughing insanely in the presence of danger or hardship was already ready to master him, and he giggled now, while he dragged at the oars and fought against the wind – he could tell by the way the blades dragged through the water that the boat was making plenty of leeway. He only stopped giggling when he realized with a shock that it was hardly more than two hours back that he had first uttered the prayer about God helping sailors on a night like this. It seemed like a fortnight ago at least that he had last breathed the leathery stuffiness of the inside of the coach.

The boat grated heavily over gravel, caught, freed itself, bumped again, and stuck fast. All Hornblower's shoving with the sculls would not get her afloat again.

'Nothing to do but shove her off,' said Hornblower, laying down his sculls.

He stepped over the side into the freezing water, slipping on the stones, with Brown beside him. Between them they ran her out easily, scrambled on board, and Hornblower made haste to seize the sculls and pull her into the wind. Yet a few seconds later they were aground again. It was the beginning of a nightmare period. In the darkness Hornblower could not guess whether their difficulties arose from the action of the wind in pushing them against the bank, or from the fact that the river was sweeping round in a great bend here, or whether they had strayed into a side channel with scanty water. However it was, they were continually having to climb out and shove the boat off. They slipped and plunged over the invisible stones; they fell waist deep into unseen pools, they cut themselves and bruised themselves in this mad game of blind man's buff with the treacherous river. It was bitterly cold now; the sides of the boat were glazed with ice. In the midst of his struggles with the boat Hornblower was consumed with anxiety for Bush, bundled up in cloak and blankets in the stern.

'How is it with you, Bush?' he asked.

'I'm doing well, sir,' said Bush.

'Warm enough?'

'Aye aye, sir. I've only one foot to get wet now, you know, sir.'

He was probably being deceitfully cheerful, thought Hornblower, standing ankle deep in rushing water and engaged in what seemed to be an endless haul of the boat through invisible shallows. Blankets or no blankets, he must be horribly cold and probably wet as well, and he was a convalescent who ought to have been kept in bed. Bush might die out here this very night. The boat came free with a run, and Hornblower staggered back waist deep in the chill water. He swung himself in over the swaying gunwale while Brown, who apparently had been completely submerged, came spluttering in over the other side. Each of them grabbed a scull in their anxiety to have something to do while the wind cut them to the bone.

The current whirled them away. Their next contact with the shore was among trees – willows, Hornblower guessed in the darkness. The branches against which they scraped volleyed snow at them, scratched them and whipped them, held the boat fast until by feeling round in the darkness they found the obstruction and lifted it clear. By the time they were free of the willows Hornblower had almost decided that he would rather have rocks if he could choose and he giggled again, feebly, with his teeth chattering. Naturally, they were among rocks again quickly enough; at this point apparently there was a sort of minor rapid down which the river rolled among rocks and banks of stones.

Already Hornblower was beginning to form a mental picture of the river – long swift reaches alternating with narrow and rock-encumbered stretches, looped back and forth at the whim of the surrounding country. This boat they were in had probably been built close to the spot where they had found her, had been kept there as a ferry boat, probably by farming people, on the clear reach where they had started, and had probably never been more than half a mile from her moorings before. Hornblower, shoving off from a rock, decided that the odds were heavily against her ever seeing her moorings again.

Below the rapid they had a long clear run – Hornblower had no means of judging how long. Their eyes were quick now to pick out the snow-covered shore when it was a yard or more away, and they kept the boat clear. Every glimpse gave them a chance to guess at the course of the river compared with the direction of the wind, so that they could pull a few lusty strokes without danger of running aground as long as there was no obstructions in mid-channel. In fact, it had almost stopped snowing – Hornblower guessed that what little snow was being flung at them by the wind had been blown from branches or scooped from drifts. That did not make it any warmer; every part of the boat was coated with ice – the floorboards were slippery with it except where his heels rested while rowing.

Ten minutes of this would carry them a mile or more – more for certain. He could not guess at all how long they had been travelling, but he could be sure that with the countryside under thick snow they were well ahead of any possible pursuit, and the longer this wonderful rock-free reach endured the safer they would be. He tugged away fiercely, and Brown in the bows responded, stroke for stroke.

'Rapids ahead, sir,' said Bush at length.

Resting on his oar Hornblower could hear, far ahead, the familiar roar of water pouring over rocks; the present rate of progress had been too good to last, and soon they would be whirling down among rocks again, pitching and heaving.

'Stand by to fend off on the port side, Brown,' he ordered.

'Aye aye, sir.'

Hornblower sat on his thwart with his scull poised; the water was sleek and black overside. He felt the boat swing round. The current seemed to be carrying her over to one side, and he was content to let her go. Where the main mass of water made its way was likely to be the clearest channel down the rapid. The roar of the fall was very loud now.

'By God!' said Hornblower in sudden panic, standing up to peer ahead.

It was too late to save themselves – he had noticed the difference in the sound of the fall only when they were too close to escape. Here there was no rapid like those they had already descended, not even one much worse. Here there was a rough dam across the river – a natural transverse ledge, perhaps, which had caught and retained the rocks rolled down in the bed, or else something of human construction. Hornblower's quick brain turned these hypotheses over even as the boat leaped at the drop. Along its whole length water was brimming over the obstruction; at this particular point it surged over in a wide swirl, sleek at the top, and plunging into foaming chaos below. The boat heaved sickeningly over the summit and went down the slope like a bullet. The steep steady wave at the foot was as unyielding as a brick wall as they crashed into it.

Hornblower found himself strangling under the water, the fall still roaring in his ears, his brain still racing. In nightmare helplessness he was scraped over the rocky bottom. The pressure in his lungs began to hurt him. It was agony – agony. Now he was breathing again – one single gulp of air like fire in his throat as he went under again, and down to the rocks at the bottom until his breast was hurting worse than before. Then another quick breath – it was as painful to breathe as it was to strangle. Over and down, his ears roaring and his head swimming. The grinding of the rocks of the river bed over which he was scraped was louder than any clap of thunder he had ever heard. Another gulp of air – it was as if he had been anticipating it, but he had to force himself to make it, for he felt as if it would be easier not to, easier to allow this agony in his breast to consume him.

Down again, to the roar and torment below the surface. His brain, still working like lightning, guessed how it was with him. He was caught in the swirl below the dam, was being swept downstream on the surface, pushed into the undertow and carried up again along the bottom, to be spewed up and granted a second in which to breathe before being carried round again. He was ready this time to strike out feebly, no more than three strokes, sideways, at his next breathing space. When he was next sucked down the pain in his breast was inconceivably greater and blending with that agony was another just as bad of which he now became conscious – the pain of the cold in his limbs. It called for every scrap of his resolution to force himself to take another breath and to continue his puny effort sideways when the time came for it. Down again; he was ready to die, willing, anxious to die, now, so that this pain would stop. A bit of board had come into his hand, with nails protruding from one end. That must be a plank from the boat, shattered to fragments and whirling round and round with him, eternally. Then his resolution flickered up once more. He caught a gulp of air as he rose to the surface, striking out for the shore, waiting in apprehension to be dragged down. Marvellous; he had time for a second breath, and a third. Now he wanted to live, so heavenly were these painless breaths he was taking. But he was so tired, and so sleepy. He got to his feet, fell as the water swept his legs away again from under him, splashed and struggled in mad panic, scrambling through the shallows on his hands and knees. Rising, he took two more steps, before falling with his face in the snow and his feet still trailing in the rushing water.

He was roused by a human voice bellowing apparently in his ear. Lifting his head he saw a faint dark figure a yard or two away, bellowing with Brown's voice.

'Ahoy! Cap'n, Cap'n! Oh, Cap'n!'

'I'm here,' moaned Hornblower, and Brown came and knelt over him.

'Thank God, sir,' he said, and then, raising his voice, 'The cap'n's here, Mr Bush.'

'Good!' said a feeble voice five yards away.

At that Hornblower fought down his nauseating weakness and sat up. If Bush were still alive he must be looked after at once. He must be naked and wet, exposed in the snow to this cutting wind. Hornblower reeled to his feet, staggered, clutched Brown's arm, and stood with his brain whirling.

'There's a light up there, sir,' said Brown, hoarsely. 'I was just goin' to it if you hadn't answered my hail.'

'A light?'

Hornblower passed his hands over his eyes and peered up the bank. Undoubtedly it was a light shining faintly, perhaps a hundred yards away. To go there meant surrender – that was the first reaction of Hornblower's mind. But to stay here meant death. Even if by a miracle they could light a fire and survive the night here they would be caught next morning – and Bush would be dead for certain. There had been a faint chance of life when he planned the escape from the coach, and now it was gone.

'Well carry Mr Bush up,' he said.

'Aye aye, sir.'

They plunged through the snow to where Bush lay.

'There's a house just up the bank, Bush. We'll carry you there.'

Hornblower was puzzled by his ability to think and to speak while he felt so weak; the ability seemed unreal, fictitious.

'Aye aye, sir.'

They stooped and lifted him up between them, linking hands under his knees and behind his back. Bush put his arms round their necks; his flannel nightshirt dripped a further stream of water as they lifted him. Then they started trudging, knee deep in the snow, up the bank towards the distant light.

They stumbled over obstructions hidden in the snow. They slipped and staggered. Then they slid down a bank and fell, all together, and Bush gave a cry of pain.

'Hurt, sir?' asked Brown.

'Only jarred my stump. Captain, leave me here and send down help from the house.'

Hornblower could still think. Without Bush to burden them they might reach the house a little quicker, but he could imagine all the delays that would ensue after they had knocked at the door – the explanations which would have to be made in his halting French, the hesitation and the time wasting before he could get a carrying party started off to find Bush – who meanwhile would be lying wet and naked in the snow. A quarter of an hour of it would kill Bush, and he might be exposed for twice as long as that. And there was the chance that there would be no one in the house to help carry him.

'No,' said Hornblower cheerfully. 'It's only a little way. Lift, Brown.'

They reeled along through the snow towards the light. Bush was a heavy burden – Hornblower's head was swimming with fatigue and his arms felt as if they were being dragged out of their sockets. Yet somehow within the shell of his fatigue the inner kernel of his brain was still active and restless.

'How did you get out of the river?' he asked, his voice sounding flat and unnatural in his ears.

'Current took us to the bank at once, sir,' said Bush, faintly surprised. 'I'd only just kicked my blankets off when I touched a rock, and there was Brown beside me hauling me out.'

'Oh,' said Hornblower.

The whim of a river in flood was fantastic; the three of them had been within a yard of each other when they entered the water, and he had been dragged under while the other two had been carried to safety. They could not guess at his desperate struggle for life, and they would never know of it, for he would never be able to tell them about it. He felt for the moment a bitter sense of grievance against them, resulting from his weariness and his weakness. He was breathing heavily, and he felt as if he would give a fortune to lay down his burden and rest for a couple of minutes; but his pride forbade, and they went on through the snow, stumbling over the inequalities below the surface. The light was coming near at last.

They heard a faint inquiring bark from a dog.

'Give 'em a hail, Brown,' said Hornblower.

'Ahoy!' roared Brown. 'House ahoy!' Instantly two dogs burst into a clamorous barking.

'Ahoy!' yelled Brown again, and they staggered on. Another light flashed into view from another part of the house. They seemed to be in some kind of garden now; Hornblower could feel plants crushing under his feet in the snow, and the thorns of a rose tree tore at his trouser leg. The dogs were barking furiously. Suddenly a voice came from a dark upper window.

'Who is there?' it asked in French.

Hornblower prodded at his weary brain to find words to reply.

'Three men,' he said. 'Wounded.'

That was the best he could do.

'Come nearer,' said the voice, and they staggered forward, slipped down an unseen incline, and halted in the square of light cast by the big lighted window in the ground floor, Bush in his nightshirt resting in the arms of the bedraggled other two.

'Who are you?'

'Prisoners of war,' said Hornblower.

'Wait one moment, if you please,' said the voice politely.

They stood shuddering in the snow until a door opened near the lighted window, showing a bright rectangle of light and some human silhouettes.

'Come in, gentlemen,' said the polite voice.

7

The door opened into a stone flagged hall; a tall thin man in a blue coat with a glistening white cravat stood there to welcome them, and at his side was a young woman, her shoulders bare in the lamplight. There were three others, too – maidservants and a butler, Hornblower fancied vaguely, as he advanced into the hall under the burden of Bush's weight. On a side table the lamplight caught the ivory butts of a pair of pistols, evidently laid there by their host on his deciding that his nocturnal visitors were harmless. Hornblower and Brown halted again for a moment, ragged and dishevelled and daubed with snow, and water began to trickle at once to the floor from their soaking garments; and Bush was between them, one foot in a grey worsted sock slicking out under the hem of his flannel nightshirt. Hornblower's constitutional weakness almost overcame him again and he had to struggle hard to keep himself from giggling as he wondered how these people were explaining to themselves the arrival of a nightshirted cripple out of a snowy night.

At least his host had sufficient self-control to show no surprise.

'Come in, come in,' he said. He put his hand to a door beside him and then withdrew it. 'You will need a better fire than I can offer you in the drawing room. Felix, show the way to the kitchen – I trust you gentlemen will pardon my receiving you there? This way, sirs. Chairs, Felix, and send the maids away.'

It was a vast low-ceilinged room, stone-flagged like the hall. Its grateful warmth was like Paradise; in the hearth glowed the remains of a fire and all round them kitchen utensils winked and glittered. The woman without a word piled fresh billets of wood upon the fire and set to work with bellows to work up a blaze. Hornblower noticed the glimmer of her silk dress; her piled-up hair was golden, nearly auburn.

'Cannot Felix do that, Marie, my dear? Very well, then. As you will,' said their host. 'Please sit down, gentlemen. Wine, Felix.'

They lowered Bush into a chair before the fire. He sagged and wavered in his weakness, and they had to support him; their host clucked in sympathy.

'Hurry with those glasses, Felix, and then attend to the beds. A glass of wine, sir? And for you, sir? Permit me.'

The woman he had addressed as 'Marie' had risen from her knees, and withdrew silently; the fire was crackling bravely amid its battery of roasting spits and cauldrons. Hornblower was shivering uncontrollably, nevertheless, in his dripping clothes. The glass of wine he drank was of no help to him; the hand he rested on Bush's shoulder shook like a leaf.

'You will need dry clothes,' said their host. 'If you will permit me, I will –'

He was interrupted by the re-entrance of the butler and Marie, both of them with their arms full of clothes and blankets.

'Admirable!' said their host. 'Felix, you will attend these gentlemen. Come, my dear.'

The butler held a silken nightshirt to the blaze while Hornblower and Brown stripped Bush of his wet clothes and chafed him with a towel.

'I thought I should never be warm again,' said Bush, when his head came out through the collar of the nightshirt. 'And you, sir? You shouldn't have troubled about me. Won't you change your clothes now, sir? I'm all right.'

'We'll see you comfortable first,' said Hornblower. There was a fierce perverse pleasure in neglecting himself to attend to Bush. 'Let me look at that stump of yours.'

The blunt seamed end still appeared extraordinarily healthy. There was no obvious heat or inflammation when Hornblower took it in his hand, no sign of pus exuding from the scars. Felix found a cloth in which Hornblower bound it up, while Brown wrapped him about in a blanket.

'Lift him now, Brown. We'll put him into bed.'

Outside in the flagged hall they hesitated as to which way to turn, when Marie suddenly appeared from the left hand door.

'In here,' she said; her voice was a harsh contralto. 'I have had a bed made up on the ground floor for the wounded man. I thought it would be more convenient.'

One maid – a gaunt old woman, rather – had just taken a warming pan from between the sheets; the other was slipping a couple of hot bottles into the bed. Hornblower was impressed by Marie's practical forethought. He tried with poor success to phrase his thanks in French while they lowered Bush into bed, and covered him up.

'God, that's good, thank you, sir,' said Bush.

They left him with a candle burning at his bedside – Hornblower was in a perfect panic now to strip off his wet clothes before that roaring kitchen fire. He towelled himself with a warm towel and slipped into a warm woollen shirt; standing with his bare legs toasting before the blaze he drank a second glass of wine. Fatigue and cold fell away from him, and he felt exhilarated and lightheaded as a reaction. Felix crouched before him tendering him a pair of trousers, and he stepped into them and suffered Felix to tuck in his shirt tails and button him up – it was the first time since childhood that he had been helped into his trousers, but this evening it seemed perfectly natural. Felix crouched again to put on his socks and shoes, stood to buckle his stock and help him on with waistcoat and coat.

'Monsieur le Comte and Madame la Vicomtesse await monsieur in the drawing room,' said Felix – it was odd how, without a word of explanation, Felix had ascertained that Brown was of a lower social level. The very clothes he had allotted to Brown indicated that.

'Make yourself comfortable here, Brown,' said Hornblower.

'Aye aye, sir,' said Brown, standing at attention with his black hair in a rampant mass – only Hornblower had had an opportunity so far of using a comb.

Hornblower stepped in to look at Bush, who was already asleep, snoring faintly at the base of his throat. He seemed to have suffered no ill effects from his immersion and exposure – his iron frame must have grown accustomed to wet and cold during twenty-five years at sea. Hornblower blew out the candle and softly closed the door, motioning to the butler to precede him. At the drawing-room door Felix asked Hornblower his name, and when he announced him Hornblower was oddly relieved to hear him make a sad hash of the pronunciation – it made Felix human again.

His host and hostess were seated on either side of the fire at the far end of the room, and the Count rose to meet him.

'I regret,' he said, 'that I did not quite hear the name which my majordomo announced.'

'Captain Horatio Hornblower, of His Britannic Majesty's ship *Sutherland*,' said Hornblower.

'It is the greatest pleasure to meet you, Captain,' said the Count, sidestepping the difficulty of pronunciation with the agility to be expected of a representative of the old régime. 'I am Lucien Antoine de Ladon, Comte de Graçay.'

The men exchanged bows.

'May I present you to my daughter-in-law? Madame la Vicomtesse de Graçay.'

'Your servant, ma'am,' said Hornblower, bowing again, and then felt like a graceless lout because the English formula had risen to his lips by the instinct the action prompted. He hurriedly racked his brains for the French equivalent, and ended in a shamefaced mumble of 'Enchanté.'

The Vicomtesse had black eyes in the maddest contrast with her nearly auburn hair. She was stoutly – one might almost say stockily – built, and was somewhere near thirty years of age, dressed in black silk which left sturdy white shoulders exposed. As she curtseyed her eyes met his in complete friendliness.

'And what is the name of the wounded gentleman

whom we have the honour of entertaining?' she asked; even to Hornblower's unaccustomed ear her French had a different quality from the Count's.

'Bush,' said Hornblower, grasping the import of the question with an effort. 'First Lieutenant of my ship. I have left my servant, Brown, in the kitchen.'

'Felix will see that he is comfortable,' interposed the Count. 'What of yourself, Captain? Some food? A glass of wine?'

'Nothing, thank you,' said Hornblower. He felt in no need of food in this mad world, although he had not eaten since noon.

'Nothing, despite the fatigues of your journey?'

There could hardly be a more delicate allusion than that to Hornblower's recent arrival through the snow, drenched and battered.

'Nothing, thank you,' repeated Hornblower.

'Will you not sit down, Captain?' asked the Vicomtesse. They all three found themselves chairs.

'You will pardon us, I hope,' said the Count, 'if we continue to speak French. It is ten years since I last had occasion to speak English, and even then I was a poor scholar, while my daughter-in-law speaks none.'

'Bush,' said the Vicomtesse. 'Brown. I can say those names. But your name, Captain, is difficult. Orrenblor – I cannot say it.'

'Bush! Orrenblor!' exclaimed the Count, as though reminded of something. 'I suppose you are aware, Captain, of what the French newspapers have been saying about you recently?'

'No,' said Hornblower. 'I should like to know, very much.'

'Pardon me, then.'

The Count took up a candle and disappeared through a door; he returned quickly enough to save Hornblower from feeling too self-conscious in the silence that ensued.

'Here are recent copies of the *Moniteur,*' said the Count. 'I must apologize in advance, Captain, for the statements made in them.'

He passed the newspapers over to Hornblower, indicating various columns in them. The first one briefly announced that a dispatch by semaphore just received from Perpignan informed the Ministry of Marine that an English ship of the line had been captured at Rosas. The next was the amplification. It proclaimed in triumphant detail that the hundred-gun ship *Sutherland* which had been committing acts of piracy in the Mediterranean had met a well-deserved fate at the hands of the Toulon fleet directed by Admiral Cosmao. She had been caught unawares and overwhelmed, and had 'pusillanimously hauled down the colours of perfidious Albion under which she had committed so many dastardly crimes.' The French public was assured that her resistance had been of the poorest, it being advanced in corroboration that only one French ship had lost a topmast during the cannonade. The action took place under the eyes of thousands of the Spanish populace, and would be a salutory lesson to those few among them who, deluded by English lies or seduced by English gold, still cherished notions of resistance to their lawful sovereign King Joseph.

Another article announced that the infamous Captain Hornblower and his equally wicked lieutenant Bush had surrendered in the *Sutherland*, the latter being one of the few wounded in the encounter. All those peace-loving

French citizens who had suffered as a result of their piratical depredations could rest assured that a military court would inquire immediately into the crimes these two had committed. Too long had the modern Carthage sent forth her minions to execute her vile plans with impunity! Their guilt would soon be demonstrated to a world which would readily discriminate between the truth and the vile lies which the poisoned pens in Canning's pay so persistently poured forth.

Yet another article declared that as a result of Admiral Cosmao's great victory over the *Sutherland* at Rosas English naval action on the coasts of Spain had ceased, and the British army of Wellington, so imprudently exposed to the might of the French arms, was already suffering seriously from a shortage of supplies. Having lost one vile accomplice in the person of the detestable Hornblower, perfidious Albion was about to lose another on Wellington's inevitable surrender.

Hornblower read the smudgy columns in impotent fury. 'A hundred-gun ship', forsooth, when the *Sutherland* was only a seventy-four and almost the smallest of her rate in the list! 'Resistance of the poorest!' 'One topmast lost!' The *Sutherland* had beaten three bigger ships into wrecks and had disabled a fourth before surrendering. 'One of the few wounded!' Two-thirds of the *Sutherland*'s crew had given life or limb, and with his own eyes he had seen the blood running from the scuppers of the French flagship. 'English naval action had ceased!' There was not a hint that a fortnight after the capture of the *Sutherland* the whole French squadron had been destroyed in the night attack on Rosas Bay.

His professional honour had been impugned; the circumstantial lies had been well told, too – that subtle touch about only one topmast being lost had every appearance of verisimilitude. Europe might well believe that he was a poltroon as well as a pirate, and he had not the slightest chance of contradicting what had been said. Even in England such reports must receive a little credit – most of the *Moniteur*'s bulletins, especially the naval ones, were reproduced in the English press. Lady Barbara, Maria, his brother captains, must all be wondering at the present moment just how much credence should be given to the *Moniteur*'s statements. Accustomed as the world might be to Bonaparte's exaggerations people could hardly be expected to realize that in this case everything said – save for the bare statement of his surrender – had been completely untrue. His hands shook a little with the passion that consumed him, and he was conscious of the hot flush in his cheeks as he looked up and met the eyes of the others.

It was hard to grope for his few French words while he was so angry.

'He is a liar!' he spluttered at length. 'He dishonours me!'

'He dishonours everyone,' said the Count, quietly.

'But this – but this,' said Hornblower, and then gave up the struggle to express himself in French. He remembered that while he was in captivity in Rosas he had realized that Bonaparte would publish triumphant bulletins regarding the capture of the *Sutherland*, and it was only weakness to be enraged by them now that he was confronted by them.

'Will you forgive me,' asked the Count, 'if I change

the subject and ask you a few personal questions?'

'Certainly.'

'I presume you have escaped from an escort which was taking you to Paris?'

'Yes,' said Hornblower.

'Where did you escape?'

Hornblower tried to explain that it was at a point where a by-road ran down to the river's edge, six kilometres on the farther side of Nevers. Haltingly, he went on to describe the conditions of his escape, the silencing of Colonel Caillard, and the wild navigation of the river in the darkness.

'That must have been about six o'clock, I presume?' asked the Count.

'Yes.'

'It is only midnight now, and you have come twenty kilometres. There is not the slightest chance of your escort seeking you here for some time. That is what I wanted to know. You will be able to sleep in tranquillity tonight, Captain.'

Hornblower realized with a shock that he had long taken it for granted that he would sleep in tranquillity, at least as far as immediate recapture was concerned; the atmosphere of the house had been too friendly for him to feel otherwise. By way of reaction, he began to feel doubts.

'Are you going to – to tell the police we are here?' he asked; it was infernally difficult to phrase that sort of thing in a foreign language and avoid offence.

'On the contrary,' said the Count. 'I shall tell them, if they ask me, that you are not here. I hope you will consider yourself among friends in this house, Captain, and that you will make your stay here as long as is convenient to you.'

'Thank you, sir. Thank you very much,' stammered Hornblower.

'I may add,' went on the Count, 'that circumstances – it is too long a story to tell you – make it quite certain that the authorities will accept my statement that I know nothing of your whereabouts. To say nothing of the fact that I have the honour to be mayor of this commune and so represent the government, even though my *adjoint* does all the work of the position.'

Hornblower noticed his wry smile as he used the word 'honour', and tried to stammer a fitting reply, to which the Count listened politely. It was amazing, now Hornblower came to think about it, that chance should have led him to a house where he was welcomed and protected, where he might consider himself safe from pursuit, and sleep in peace. The thought of sleep made him realize that he was desperately tired, despite his excitement. The impassive face of the Count, and the friendly face of his daughter-in-law, gave no hint as to whether or not they too were tired; for a moment Hornblower wrestled with the problem which always presents itself the first evening of one's stay in a strange house – whether the guest should suggest going to bed or wait for a hint from his host. He made his resolve, and rose to his feet.

'You are tired,' said the Vicomtesse – the first words she had spoken for some time.

'Yes,' said Hornblower.

'I will show you your room, sir. Shall I ring for your servant? No?' said the Count.

Out in the hall, after Hornblower had bowed good night, the Count indicated the pistols still lying on the side table.

'Perhaps you would care to have those at your bedside?' he asked politely. 'You might feel safer?'

Hornblower was tempted, but finally he refused the offer. Two pistols would not suffice to save him from Bonaparte's police should they come for him.

'As you will,' said the Count, leading the way with a candle. 'I loaded them when I heard your approach because there was a chance that you were a party of réractaires – young men who evade the conscription by hiding in the woods and mountains. Their number has grown considerably since the latest decree anticipating the conscription. But I quickly realized that no gang meditating mischief would proclaim its proximity with shouts. Here is your room, sir. I hope you will find here everything you require. The clothes you are wearing appear to fit so tolerably that perhaps you will continue to wear them tomorrow? Then I shall say good night. I hope you will sleep well.'

The bed was deliciously warm as Hornblower slid into it and closed the curtains. His thoughts were pleasantly muddled; disturbing memories of the appalling swoop of the little boat down the long black slope of water at the fall, and of his agonized battle for life in the water, were overridden by mental pictures of the Count's long, mobile face and of Caillard bundled in his cloak and dumped down upon the carriage floor. He did not sleep well, but he could hardly be said to have slept badly.

8

Felix entered the next morning bearing a breakfast tray, and he opened the bed curtains while Hornblower lay dazed in his bed. Brown followed Felix, and while the latter arranged the tray on the bedside table he applied himself to the task of gathering together the clothes which Hornblower had flung down the night before, trying hard to assume the unobtrusive deference of a gentleman's servant. Hornblower sipped gratefully at the steaming coffee, and bit into the bread; Brown recollected another duty and hurried across to open the bedroom curtains.

'Gale's pretty nigh dropped, sir,' he said. 'I think what wind there's left is backing southerly, and we might have a thaw.'

Through the deep windows of the bedroom Hornblower could see from his bed a wide landscape of dazzling white, falling steeply away down to the river which was black by contrast, appearing like a black crayon mark on white paper. Trees stood out starkly through the snow where the gale had blown their branches bare; down beside the river the willows there – some of them stood in the flood, with white foam at their feet – were still domed with white. Hornblower fancied he could hear the rushing of water, and was certain that he could hear the regular droning of the fall, the tumbling water at whose foot was just visible over the shoulder of the bank. Far beyond the river could be seen the snow-covered roofs of a few small houses.

'I've been in to Mr Bush already, sir,' said Brown – Hornblower felt a twinge of remorse at being too interested in the landscape to have a thought to spare for his lieutenant – 'and he's all right an' sends you his best respects, sir. I'm goin' to help him shave after I've attended to you, sir.'

'Yes,' said Hornblower.

He felt deliciously languorous. He wanted to be idle and lazy. The present was a moment of transition between the miseries and dangers of yesterday and the unknown activities of today, and he wanted that moment to be prolonged on and on indefinitely; he wanted time to stand still, the pursuers who were seeking him on the other side of Nevers to be stilled into an enchanted rigidity while he lay here free from danger and responsibility. The very coffee he had drunk contributed to his ease by relieving his thirst without stimulating him to activity. He sank imperceptibly and delightfully into a vague daydream; it was hateful of Brown to recall him to wakefulness again by a respectful shuffling of his feet.

'Right,' said Hornblower resigning himself to the inevitable.

He kicked off the bedclothes and rose to his feet, the hard world of the matter-of-fact closing round him, and his daydreams vanishing like the cloud-colours of a tropical sunrise. As he shaved and washed in the absurdly small basin in the corner, he contemplated grimly the prospect of prolonged conversation in French with his hosts. He grudged the effort it would involve, and he envied Bush his complete inability to speak any other tongue than English. Having to exert himself today loomed as large to his self-willed mind as the fact that he was doomed to death if he were caught again. He listened absentmindedly to Bush's garrulity when he went in to visit him, and did nothing at all to satisfy his curiosity regarding the house in which they had found shelter, and the intentions of their hosts. Nor was his mood relieved by his pitying contempt for himself at thus working off his ill temper on his unoffending lieutenant. He deserted Bush as soon as he decently could and went off in search of his hosts in the drawing room.

The Vicomtesse alone was there, and she made him welcome with a smile.

'M. de Graçay is at work in his study,' she explained. 'You must be content with my entertaining you this morning.'

To say even the obvious in French was an effort for Hornblower, but he managed to make the suitable reply, which the lady received with a smile. But conversation did not proceed smoothly, with Hornblower having laboriously to build up his sentences beforehand and to avoid the easy descent into Spanish which was liable to entrap him whenever he began to think in a foreign tongue. Nevertheless, the opening sentences regarding the storm last night, the snow in the fields, and the flood, elicited for Hornblower one interesting fact – that the river whose roar they could hear was the Loire, four hundred miles or more from its mouth in the Bay of Biscay. A few miles upstream lay the town of Nevers; a little way downstream the large tributary, the Allier, joined the Loire, but there was hardly a house and no village on the river in that direction for twenty miles as far as Pouilly – from whose vineyards had come the wine they had drunk last night.

'The river is only as big as this in winter,' said the Vicomtesse. 'In summer it dwindles away to almost nothing. There are places where one can walk across it, from one bank to the other. Then it is blue, and its banks are golden, but now it is black and ugly.'

'Yes,' said Hornblower.

He felt a peculiar tingling sensation down his thighs and calves as the words recalled his experience of the night before, the swoop over the fall and the mad battle in the flood. He and Bush and Brown might easily all be sodden corpses now, rolling among the rocks at the bottom of the river until the process of corruption should bring them to the surface.

'I have not thanked you and M. de Graçay for your hospitality,' he said, picking his words with care. 'It is very kind of the Count.'

'Kind? He is the kindest man in the whole world. I can't tell you how good he is.'

There was no doubting the sincerity of the Count's daughter-in-law as she made this speech; her wide humorous mouth parted and her dark eyes glowed.

'Really?' said Hornblower – the word 'vraiment' slipped naturally from his lips now that some animation had come into the conversation.

'Yes, really. He is good all the way through. He is sweet and kind, by nature and not – not as a result of experience. He has never said a word to me, not once, not a word, about the disappointment I have caused him.'

'You, madame?'

'Yes. Oh, isn't it obvious? I am not a great lady – Marcel should not have married me. My father is a Normandy peasant, on his own land, but a peasant all the same, while the Ladons, Counts of Graçay, go back to – to Saint Louis, or before that. Marcel told me how disappointed was the Count at our marriage, but I should never have known of it otherwise – not by word or by action. Marcel was the eldest son then, because Antoine had been killed at Austerlitz. And Marcel is dead, too – he was wounded at Aspern – and I have no son, no child at all, and the Count has never reproached me, never.'

Hornblower tried to make some kind of sympathetic noise.

'And Louis-Marie is dead as well now. He died of fever in Spain. He was the third son, and M. de Graçay is the last of the Ladons. I think it broke his heart, but he has never said a bitter word.'

'The three sons are all dead?' said Hornblower.

'Yes, as I told you. M. de Graçay was an émigré – he lived in your town of London with his children for years after the Revolution. And then the boys grew up and they heard of the fame of the Emperor – he was First Consul then – and they all wanted to share in the glory of France. It was to please them that the Count took advantage of the amnesty and returned here – this is all that the Revolution has left of his estates. He never went to Paris. What would he have in common with the Emperor? But he allowed his sons to join the army, and now they are all dead, Antoine and Marcel and Louis-Marie. Marcel married me when his regiment was billeted in our village, but the others never married. Louis-Marie was only eighteen when he died.'

'Terrible!' said Hornblower.

The banal words did not express his sense of the pathos of the story, but it was all he could think of. He understood now the Count's statement of the night before that the authorities would be willing to accept his bare word that he had seen nothing of any escaped prisoners. A great gentleman whose three sons had died in the Imperial service would never be suspected of harbouring fugitives.

'Understand me,' went on the Vicomtesse. 'It is not because he hates the Emperor that he makes you welcome here. It is because he is kind, because you needed help – I have never known him to deny help to anyone. Oh, it is hard to explain, but I think you understand.'

'I understand,' said Hornblower, gently.

His heart warmed to the Vicomtesse. She might be lonely and unhappy; she was obviously as hard as her peasant upbringing would make her, and yet her first thought was to impress upon this stranger the goodness and virtue of her father-in-law. With her nearly-red hair and black eyes she was a striking-looking woman, and her skin had a thick creaminess which enhanced her looks; only a slight irregularity of feature and the wideness of her mouth prevented her from being of dazzling beauty. No wonder the young subaltern in the Hussars – Hornblower took it for granted that the dead Vicomte de Graçay had been a subaltern of Hussars – had fallen in love with her during the dreary routine of training, and had insisted on marrying her despite his father's opposition. Hornblower thought he would not find it hard to fall in love with her himself if he were mad enough to allow such a thing to happen while his life was in the hands of the Count.

'And you?' asked the Vicomtesse. 'Have you a wife in England? Children?'

'I have a wife,' said Hornblower.

Even without the handicap of a foreign language it was difficult to describe Maria to a stranger; he said that she was short and dark, and he said no more. Her red hands and dumpy figure, her loyalty to him which cloyed when it did not irritate – he could not venture on a fuller description lest he should betray the fact that he did not love her, and he had never betrayed it yet.

'So that you have no children either?' asked the Vicomtesse again.

'Not now,' said Hornblower.

This was torment. He told of how little Horatio and little Maria had died of smallpox in a Southsea lodging, and then with a gulp he went on to say that there was another child due to be born in January next.

'Let us hope you will be home with your wife then,' said the Vicomtesse. 'Today you will be able to discuss plans of escape with my father-in-law.'

As if this new mention of his name had summoned him, the Count came into the room on the tail of this sentence.

'Forgive my interrupting you,' he said, even while he returned Hornblower's bow, 'but from my study window I have just seen a gendarme approaching this house from a group which was riding along the river bank. Would it be troubling you too much, Captain, to ask you to go into Monsieur Bush's room for a time? I shall send your servant in to you, too, and perhaps then you would be good enough to lock the door. I shall interview the gendarme myself, and you will only be detained for a few minutes, I hope.'

A gendarme! Hornblower was out of the room and was crossing over to Bush's door before this long speech was finished, while M. de Graçay escorted him thither, unruffled, polite, his words unhurried. Bush was sitting up in bed as Hornblower entered, but what he began to say was broken off by Hornblower's abrupt gesture demanding silence. A moment later Brown tapped at the door and was admitted, Hornblower carefully locking the door after him.

'What is it, sir?' whispered Bush, and Hornblower whispered an explanation, still standing with his hand on the handle, stooping to listen.

He heard a knocking on the outer door, and the rattling of chains as Felix went to open it. Feverishly he tried to hear the ensuing conversation, but he could not understand it. But the gendarme was speaking with respect, and Felix in the flat passionless tones of the perfect butler. He heard the tramp of booted feet and the ring of spurs as the gendarme was led into the hall, and then all the sounds died away with the closing of a door upon them. The minutes seemed like hours as he waited. Growing aware of his nervousness he forced himself to turn and smile at the others as they sat with their ears cocked, listening.

The wait was too long for them to preserve their tension; soon they relaxed, and grinned at each other, not with hollow mirth as Hornblower's had been at the start. At last a renewed burst of sound from the hall keyed them up again, and they stayed rigid listening to the penetrating voices. And then they heard the clash of the outside door shutting, and the voices ceased. Still it was a long time before anything more happened – five minutes – ten minutes, and then a tap on the door startled them as though it were a pistol shot.

'Can I come in, Captain?' said the Count's voice.

Hurriedly Hornblower unlocked the door to admit him, and even then he had to stand and wait in feverish patience, translating awkwardly while the Count apologized to Bush for intruding upon him, and made polite inquiries about his health and whether he slept well.

'Tell him I slept nicely, if you please, sir,' said Bush.

'I am delighted to hear it,' said the Count 'Now in the matter of this gendarme –'

Hornblower brought forward a chair for him. He would not allow it to be thought that his impatience overrode his good manners.

'Thank you, Captain, thank you. You are sure I will not be intruding if I stay? That is good of you. The gendarme came to tell me –'

The narrative was prolonged by the need for interpreting to Bush and Brown. The gendarme was one of those posted at Nevers; every available man in that town had been turned out shortly before midnight by a furious Colonel Caillard to search for the fugitives. In the darkness they had been able to do little, but with the coming of the dawn Cailliard had begun a systematic search of both banks of the river, seeking for traces of the prisoners and making inquiries at every house and cottage along the banks. The visit of the gendarme had been merely one of routine – he had come to ask if anything had been seen of three escaped Englishmen, and to give warning that they might be in the vicinity. He had been perfectly satisfied with the Count's assurance upon the point. In fact, the gendarme had no expectation of finding the Englishmen alive. The search had already revealed a blanket, one of those which had been used by the wounded Englishman, lying on the bank down by the Bec d'Allier, which seemed a sure indication that their boat had capsized, in which case, with the river in flood, there could be no doubt that they had been drowned. Their bodies would be discovered somewhere along the course of the river during the next few days. The gendarme appeared to be of the opinion that the boat must have upset somewhere in the first rapid they had encountered, before they had gone a mile, so madly was the river running.

'I hope you will agree with me, Captain, that this information is most satisfactory,' added the Count.

'Satisfactory!' said Hornblower. 'Could it be better?'

If the French should believe them to be dead there would be an end to the pursuit. He turned and explained the situation to the others in English, and they endeavoured with nods and smiles to indicate to the Count their gratification.

'Perhaps Bonaparte in Paris will not be satisfied with this bald story,' said the Count. 'In fact I am sure he will not, and will order a further search. But it will not trouble us.'

'Thank you, sir,' said Hornblower, and the Count made a deprecatory gesture.

'It only remains,' he said, 'to make up our minds

about what you gentlemen would find it best to do in the future. Would it be officious of me to suggest that it might be inadvisable for you to continue your journey while Lieutenant Bush is still unwell?'

'What does he say, sir?' asked Bush – the mention of his name had drawn all eyes on him. Hornblower explained.

'Tell his lordship, sir,' said Bush, 'that I can make myself a jury leg in two shakes, an' this time next week I'll be walking as well as he does.'

'Excellent!' said the Count, when this had been translated and expurgated for him. 'And yet I cannot see that the construction of a wooden leg is going to be of much assistance in our problem. You gentlemen might grow beards, or wear disguises. It was in my mind that by posing as German officers in the Imperial service you might, during your future journey, provide an excuse for your ignorance of French. But a missing foot cannot be disguised; for months to come the arrival of a stranger without a foot will recall to the minds of inquisitive police officers the wounded English officer who escaped and was believed to be drowned.'

'Yes,' said Hornblower. 'Unless we could avoid all contact with police officers.'

'That is quite impossible,' said the Count with decision. 'In this French Empire there are police officers everywhere. To travel you will need horses certainly, a carriage very probably. In a journey of a hundred leagues horses and a carriage will bring you for certain to the notice of the police. No man can travel ten miles along a road without having his passport examined.'

The Count pulled in perplexity at his chin; the deep

parentheses at the corners of his mobile mouth were more marked than ever.

'I wish,' said Hornblower, 'that our boat had not been destroyed last night. On the river, perhaps –'

The idea came up into his mind fully formed and as it did so his eyes met the Count's. He was conscious afresh of a strange sympathy between him and the Count. The same idea was forming in the Count's mind, simultaneously – it was not the first time that he had noticed a similar phenomenon.

'Of course!' said the Count, 'the river! How foolish of me not to think of it. As far as Orleans the river is unnavigable; because of the winter floods the banks are practically deserted save at the towns, and there are few of those, which you could pass at night if necessary, as you did at Nevers.'

'Unnavigable, sir?'

'There is no commercial traffic. There are fishermen's boats here and there, and there are a few others engaged in dredging sand from the river bed. That is all. From Orleans to Nantes Bonaparte has been making efforts to render the river available to barges, but I understand he has had small success. And above Briare the new lateral canal carries all the traffic, and the river is deserted.'

'But could we descend it, sir?' persisted Hornblower.

'Oh, yes,' said the Count, meditatively. 'You could do so in summer in a small rowing boat. There are many places where it would be difficult, but never dangerous.'

'In summer!' exclaimed Hornblower.

'Why, yes. You must wait until the lieutenant here is well, and then you must build your boat – I suppose you sailors can build you own boat? You cannot hope to start for a long time. And then in January the river usually freezes, and in February come the floods, which last until March. Nothing could live on the river then – especially as it would be too cold and wet for you. It seems to be quite necessary that you should give me the pleasure of your company until April, Captain.'

This was something entirely unexpected, this prospect of waiting for four months the opportunity to start. Hornblower was taken by surprise; he had supposed that a few days, three or four weeks at most, would see them on their way towards England again. For ten years he had never been as long as four months consecutively in the same place – for that matter during those ten years he had hardly spent four months on shore altogether. His mind sought unavailingly for alternatives. To go by road undoubtedly would involve horses, carriages, contact with all sorts of people. He could not hope to bring Bush and Brown successfully through. And if they went by river they obviously would have to wait; in four months Bush could be expected to make a complete recovery, and with the coming of summer they would be able to dispense with the shelter of inns or houses, sleeping on the river bank, avoiding all intercourse with Frenchmen, drifting downstream until they reached the sea.

'If you have fishing rods with you,' supplemented the Count, 'anyone observing you as you go past the towns will look on you as a fishing party out for the day. For some reason which I cannot fully analyse a freshwater fisherman can never be suspected of evil intent – except possibly by the fish.'

Hornblower nodded. It was odd that at that very moment he too had been visualizing the boat drifting downstream, with rods out, watched by incurious eyes from the bank. It was the safest way of crossing France which he could imagine.

And yet – April? His child would be born. Lady Barbara might have forgotten that he ever existed.

'It seems monstrous,' he said, 'that you should be burdened with us all through the winter.'

'I assure you, Captain, your presence will give the greatest pleasure both to Madame la Vicomtesse and myself.'

He could only yield to circumstances.

9

Lieutenant Bush was watching Brown fastening the last strap of his new wooden leg, and Hornblower, from across the room, was watching the pair of them.

''Vast heaving,' said Bush. 'Belay.'

Bush sat on the edge of his bed and moved his leg tentatively.

'Good,' he said. 'Give me your shoulder. Now, heave and wake the dead.'

Hornblower saw Bush rise and stand; he watched his lieutenant's expression change to one of hurt wonderment as he clung to Brown's burly shoulders.

'God!' said Bush feebly, 'how she heaves!'

It was the giddiness only to be expected after weeks of lying and sitting. Evidently to Bush the floor was pitching and tossing, and, judging by the movement of his eyes, the walls were circling round him. Brown stood patiently supporting him as Bush confronted this unexpected phenomenon. Hornblower saw Bush set his jaw, his expression hardening as he battled with his weakness.

'Square away,' said Bush to Brown. 'Set a course for the captain.'

Brown began walking slowly towards Hornblower, Bush clinging to him, the leather-tipped end of the wooden leg falling with a thump on the floor at each effort to take a stride with it – Bush was swinging it too high, while his sound leg sagged at the knee in its weakness.

'God!' said Bush again. 'Easy! Easy!'

Hornblower rose in time to catch him and to lower him into the chair, where Bush sat and gasped. His big white face, already unnaturally pale through long confinement, was whiter than ever. Hornblower remembered with a pang the old Bush, burly and self-confident, with a face which might have been rough-hewn from a solid block of wood; the Bush who feared nothing and was prepared for anything. This Bush was frightened of his weakness. It had not occurred to him that he would have to learn to walk again – and that walking with a wooden leg was another matter still.

'Take a rest,' said Hornblower, 'before you start again.'

Desperately anxious as Bush had been to walk, weary as he was of helplessness, there were times during the next few days when Hornblower had to give him active encouragement while he was learning to walk. All the difficulties that arose had been unforeseen by him, and depressed him out of proportion to their importance. It was a matter of some days before he mastered his giddiness and weakness, and then as soon as he was able to use the wooden leg effectively they found all manner of things wrong with it. It was none too easy to find the most suitable length, and they discovered to their surprise that it was a matter of some importance to set the leather tip at exactly the right angle to the shaft – Brown and Hornblower between them, at a work-table in the stable yard, made and remade that wooden leg half a dozen times. Bush's bent knee, on which his weight rested when he walked, grew sore and inflamed; they had to pad the kneecap and remake the socket to fit, more than once, while Bush had to take his exercise in small amounts until the skin over his kneecap grew calloused and more accustomed to its new task. And when he fell – which was often – he caused himself frightful agony in his stump, which was hardly healed; with his knee bent at right angles the stump necessarily bore the brunt of practically any fall, and the pain was acute.

But teaching Bush to walk was one way of passing the long winter days, while orders from Paris turned out the conscripts from every depot round, and set them searching once more for the missing English prisoners. They came on a day of lashing rain, a dozen shivering boys and a sergeant, wet through, and made only the poorest pretence at searching the house and its stabling – Hornblower and Bush and Brown were safe enough behind the hay in an unobtrusive loft. The conscripts were given in the kitchen a better meal by the servants than they had enjoyed for some time, and marched off to prosecute their inquiries elsewhere – every house and village for miles round was at least visited.

After that the next occurrence out of the ordinary was the announcement in Bonaparte's newspapers that the English captain and lieutenant, Hornblower and Bush, had met a well-deserved fate by being drowned in the Loire during an attempt to escape from an escort which was conducting them to their trial; undoubtedly (said the bulletin) this had saved the miscreants from the firing party which awaited them for the purpose of exacting the penalty of their flagrant piracy in the Mediterranean.

Hornblower read the announcement with mixed feelings when the Count showed it to him; not every man has the privilege of reading his own obituary. His first reaction was that it would make their escape considerably easier, seeing that the police would no longer be on the watch for them. But that feeling of relief was swamped by a wave of other feelings. Maria in England would think herself a widow, at this very moment when their child was about to be born. What would it mean to her? Hornblower knew, only too acutely, that Maria loved him as dearly as a woman could love a man, although he only admitted it to himself at moments like this. He could not guess what she would do when she believed him dead. It would be the end of everything she had lived for. And yet she would have a pension, security, a child to cherish. She might set herself, unconsciously, to make a new life for herself. In a clairvoyant moment Hornblower visualized Maria in deep mourning, her mouth set in prim resignation, the coarse red skin of her cheeks wet with tears, and her red hands nervously clasping and unclasping. She had looked like that the summer day when little Horatio and little Maria had been buried in their common grave.

Hornblower shuddered away from the recollection. Maria would at least be in no need of money; the British press would see that the government did its duty there. He could guess at the sort of articles which would be appearing in reply to this announcement of Bonaparte's, the furious indignation that a British officer should be accused of piracy, the openly expressed suspicions that he had been murdered in cold blood and had not died while attempting to escape, the clamour for reprisals.

To this day a British newspaper seldom discussed Bonaparte without recalling the death of another British naval captain, Wright, who was said to have committed suicide in prison in Paris. Everyone in England believed that Bonaparte had had him murdered – they would believe the same in this case. It was almost amusing that nearly always the most effective attacks on the tyrant were based on actions on his part which were either trivial or innocent. The British genius for invective and propaganda had long discovered that it paid better to exploit trivialities rather than inveigh broadly against policies and principles; the newspapers would give more space to a condemnation of Bonaparte for causing the death of a single naval officer than to a discussion of the criminal nature of, say, the invasion of Spain, which had resulted in the wanton slaughter of some hundreds of thousands of innocent people.

And Lady Barbara would read that he was dead, too. She would be sorry – Hornblower was prepared to believe that – but how deep her sorrow would be he could not estimate at all. The thought called up all the flood of speculations and doubts which lately he had been trying to forget – whether she cared for him at all or not, whether or not her husband had survived his wound, and what he could do in the matter in any event.

'I am sorry that this announcement seems to cause you so much distress,' said the Count, and Hornblower realized that his expression had been anxiously studied during the whole reading. He had for once been caught off his guard, but he was on guard again at once. He made himself smile.

'It will make our journey through France a good deal easier,' he said.

'Yes. I thought the same as soon as I read it. I can congratulate you, Captain.'

'Thank you,' said Hornblower.

But there was a worried look in the Count's face; he had something more to say and was hesitating to say it.

'What are you thinking about, sir?' asked Hornblower.

'Only this – Your position is in one way more dangerous now. You have been pronounced dead by a government which does not admit mistakes – cannot afford to admit them. I am afraid in case I have done you a disservice in so selfishly accepting the pleasure of your company. If you are recaptured you *will* be dead; the government will see that you die without further attention being called to you.'

Hornblower shrugged his shoulders with a carelessness quite unassumed for once.

'They were going to shoot me if they caught me. This makes no difference.'

He dallied with the notion of a modern government dabbling in secret murder, for a moment was inclined to put it aside as quite impossible, as something one might believe of the Turks or perhaps even of the Sicilians, but not of Bonaparte, and then he realized with a shock that it was not at all impossible, that a man with unlimited power and much at stake, with underlings on whose silence he could rely, could not be expected to risk appearing ridiculous in the eye of his public when a mere murder would save him. It was a sobering thought, but he made himself smile again, bravely.

'You have all the courage characteristic of your

nation, Captain,' said the Count. 'But this news of your death will reach England. I fear that Madame Orrenblor will be distressed by it?'

'I am afraid she will.'

'I could find means of sending a message to England – my bankers can be trusted. But whether it would be advisable is another matter.'

If it were known in England that he was alive it would be known in France, and a stricter search would be instituted for him. It would be terribly dangerous. Maria would draw small profit from the knowledge that he was alive if that knowledge were to cause his death.

'I think it would not be advisable,' said Hornblower.

There was a strange duality in his mind; the Hornblower for whom he could plan so coolly, and whose chances of life he could estimate so closely, was a puppet of the imagination compared with the living, flesh and blood Hornblower whose face he had shaved that morning. He knew by experience now that only when a crisis came, when he was swimming for his life in a whirlpool, or walking a quarterdeck in the heat of action, that the two blended together – that was the moment when fear came.

'I hope, Captain,' said the Count, 'that this news has not disturbed you too much?'

'Not at all, sir,' said Hornblower.

'I am delighted to hear it. And perhaps you will be good enought to give Madame la Vicomtesse and myself the pleasure of your company again tonight at whist, you and Mr Bush?'

Whist was the regular way of passing the evening. The Count's delight in the game was another bond of sympathy between him and Hornblower. He was not a player of the mathematical variety, as was Hornblower. Rather did he rely upon a flair, an instinctive system of tactics. It was marvellous how often his blind leads found his partner's short suit and snatched tricks from the jaws of the inevitable, how often he could decide intuitively upon the winning play when confronted by a dilemma. There were rare evenings when this faculty would desert him, and when he would sit with a rueful smile losing rubber after rubber to the remorseless precision of his daughter-in-law and Hornblower. But usually his uncanny telepathic powers would carry him triumphantly through, to the exasperation of Hornblower if they had been opponents, and to his intense satisfaction if they had been partners – exasperation at the failure of his painstaking calculations, or satisfaction of their complete vindication.

The Vicomtesse was a good well-taught player of no brilliance whose interest in the game, Hornblower suspected, was entirely due to her devotion to her father-in-law. It was Bush to whom these evenings of whist were a genuine penance. He disliked card games of any sort – even the humble vingt-et-un – and in the supreme refinement of whist he was hopelessly at a loss. Hornblower had cured him of some of his worst habits – of asking, for instance, 'What are trumps?' halfway through every hand – had insisted on his counting the cards as they fell, on his learning the conventional leads and discards, and by so doing had made of him a player whose presence three good players could just tolerate rather than miss their evening's amusement; but the evenings to him were periods of agonized, hard-breathing concentration, of flustered mistakes and shamefaced apology – misery made no less acute by the fact that conversation was carried on in French in which he could never acquire any facility. Bush mentally classed together French, whist, and spherical trigonometry as subjects in which he was too old ever to make any further progress, and which he would be content, if he were allowed, to leave entirely to his admired captain.

For Hornblower's French was improving rapidly, thanks to the need for continual use of the language. His defective ear would never allow him to catch the trick of the accent – he would always speak with the tonelessness of the foreigner – but his vocabulary was widening and his grammar growing more certain and he was acquiring a fluency in the idiom which more than once earned him a pretty compliment from his host. Hornblower's pride was held in check by the astonishing fact that below stairs Brown was rapidly acquiring the same fluency. He was living largely with French people, too – with Felix and his wife the housekeeper, and their daughter Louise the maid, and, living over the stables across the yard, the family of Bertrand, who was Felix's brother and incidentally the coachman; Bertrand's wife was the cook, with two daughters to help her in the kitchen, while one of her young sons was footman under Felix and the other two worked in the stables under their father.

Hornblower had once ventured to hint to the Count that the presence of himself and the others might well be betrayed to the authorities by one of all these servants, but the Count merely shook his head with a serene confidence that could not be shaken.

'They will not betray me,' he said, and so intense was his conviction on the point that it carried conviction to Hornblower – and the better he came to know the Count the more obvious it became that no one who knew him well would ever betray him. And the Count added with a wry smile –

'You must remember, too, Captain, that here I *am* the authorities.'

Hornblower could allow his mind to subside into security and sloth again after that – a sense of security with a fantastic quality about it that savoured of a nightmare. It was unreal to be mewed for so long within four walls, deprived of the wide horizons and the endless variety of the sea. He could spend his mornings tramping up and down the stable yard, as though it were a quarterdeck and as though Bertrand and his sons chattering about their duties were a ship's crew engaged on their morning's deck-washing. The smell of the stables and the land winds which came in over the high walls were a poor substitute for the keen freshness of the sea. He spent hours in a turret window of the house, with a spyglass which the Count found for him, gazing round the countryside; the desolate vineyards in their winter solitude, the distant towers of Nevers – the ornate Cathedral tower and the graceful turrets of the Gonzaga palace; the rushing black river, its willows half submerged – the ice which came in January and the snow which three times covered the blank slopes that winter were welcome variations of the monotonous landscape; there were the distant hills and the nearby slopes; the trace of the valley of the Loire winding off into the unknown, and of the valley of the Allier coming down to meet it – to a landman's eye the prospect from the turret window would have been delightful, even perhaps in the lashing rain that fell so often, but to a seaman and a prisoner it was revolting. The indefinable charm of the sea was wanting, and so were the mystery and magic and freedom of the sea. Bush and Brown, noting the black bad temper in which Hornblower descended from the turret window after a sitting with his spyglass, wondered why he spent his time in that fashion. He wondered why himself, but weakly he could not stop himself from doing so. Specially marked was his bad temper when the Count and his daughter-in-law went out riding, returning flushed and healthy and happy after some brisk miles of the freedom for which he craved – he was stupidly jealous, he told himself, angrily, but he was jealous all the same.

He was even jealous of the pleasure Bush and Brown took in the building of the new boat. He was not a man of his hands, and once the design of the boat had been agreed upon – its fifteen feet of length and four feet of beam and its flat bottom – he could contribute nothing towards the work except unskilled labour. His subordinates were far more expert with tools than he was, with plane and saw and drill, and characteristically found immense pleasure in working with them. Bush's childish delight in finding his hands, softened by a long period of convalescence, forming their distinguishing callouses again, irritated him. He envied them the simple creative pleasure which they found in watching the boat grow under their hands in the empty loft which they had adopted as a workshop – more still he envied Brown the accuracy of eye he displayed, working with a spokeshave shaping the sculls without any of the apparatus of templates and models and stretched strings which Hornblower would have found necessary.

They were black days, all that winter of confinement. January came, and with it the date when his child would be born; he was half mad with the uncertainty of it all, with his worry about Maria and the child, with the thought that Barbara would think him dead and would forget him. Even the Count's sweetness of temper and unvarying courtesy irritated him as soon as it began to cloy. He felt he would give a year of his life to hear him make a tart rejoinder to one of Bush's clumsy speeches; the impulse to be rude to the Count, to fire up into a quarrel with him even though – or perhaps because – he owed him his life, was sometimes almost irresistible, and the effort of self-control tried his temper still further. He was surfeited with the Count's unwearying goodness, even with the odd way in which their thoughts ran so frequently together; it was queer, even uncanny, to see in the Count so often what seemed like reflections of himself in a mirror. It was madder still to remember that he had felt similar ties of sympathy, sometimes with the wickedest man he had ever known – with el Supremo in Central America.

El Supremo had died for his crime on a scaffold at Panama; Hornblower was worried by the thought that the Count was risking the guillotine at Paris for his friend's sake – it was mad to imagine any parallelism between the careers of el Supremo and the Count, but Hornblower was in a mad mood. He was thinking too much and he had too little to do, and his overactive brain was racketing itself to pieces. There was insanity in indulging in ridiculous mystic speculations about spiritual relationships between himself and the Count and el Supremo, and he knew it. Only self-control and patience were necessary, he told himself, to come safely through these last few weeks of waiting, but his patience seemed to be coming to an end, and he was so weary of exerting self-control.

It was the flesh that saved him when his spirit grew weak. One afternoon, descending from a long and maddening sitting with his telescope in the turret, he met the Vicomtesse in the upper gallery. She was at her boudoir door, about to enter, and she turned and smiled at him as he approached. His head was whirling; somehow his exasperation and feverishness drove him into holding out both his hands to her, risking a rebuff, risking everything, in his longing for some kind of comfort, something to ease this unbearable strain. She put her hands in his, smiling still, and at the touch self-possession broke down. It was madness to yield to the torrent of impulses let loose, but madness was somehow sweet. They were inside the room now, and the door was closed. There was sweet, healthy, satisfying flesh in his arms. There were no doubts nor uncertainties; no mystic speculations. Now blind instinct could take charge, all the bodily urges of months of celibacy. Her lips were ripe and rich and ready, the breasts which he crushed against him were hillocks of sweetness. In his nostrils was the faint intoxicating scent of womanhood.

Beyond the boudoir was the bedroom; they were there now and she was yielding to him. Just as another man might have given way to drink, might have stupefied his brain in beastly intoxication, so Hornblower numbed his own brain with lust and passion. He forgot everything, and he cared for nothing, in this mad lapse from self-control.

And she understood his motives, which was strange, and she did not resent them, which was stranger still. As his passion ebbed away, he could see her face again clearly, and her expression was tender and detached and almost maternal. She was aware of his unhappiness as she had been aware of his lust for that splendid body of hers. She had given him her body because of his crying need for it, as she might have given a cup of water to a man dying of thirst. Now she held his head to her breast, and stroked his hair, rocking a little as though he were a child, and murmuring little soothing words to him. A tear fell from her eye on to Hornblower's temple. She had come to love this Englishman, but she knew only too well that it was not love which had brought him into her arms. She knew of the wife and child in England, she guessed at the existence of the other woman whom he loved. It was not the thought of them which brought the tears to her eyes; it was the knowledge that she was not any part of his real life, that this stay of his on the banks of the Loire was as unreal to him as a dream, something to be endured until he could escape again to the sea, into the mad world which to him was sanity, where every day he would encounter peril and discomfort. These kisses he was giving her meant nothing to him compared with the business of life, which was war – the same war which had killed her young husband, the wasteful, prodigal, beastly business which had peopled Europe with widows and disfigured it with wasted fields and burned villages. He was kissing her as a man might pat his dog's head during an exciting business deal.

Then Hornblower lifted his face to hers again, and read the tragedy in her eyes. The sight of her tears moved him inexpressibly. He stroked her cheek.

'Oh, my dear,' he said in English, and then began to try to find French words to express what he wanted to say. Tenderness was welling up within him. In a blinding moment of relevation he realized the love she bore him, and the motives which had brought her submissively into his arms. He kissed her mouth, he brushed away the splendid red hair from her pleading eyes. Tenderness reawoke passion; and under his caresses her last reserve broke down.

'I love you!' she sighed, her arms about him. She had not meant to admit it, either to him or to herself. She knew that if she gave herself to him with passion he would break her heart in the end, and that he did not love her, not even now, when tenderness had replaced the blind lust in his eyes. He would break her heart if she allowed herself to love him; for one more second she had that clairvoyance before she let herself sink into the self-deception which she knew in the future she would not believe to be self-deception. But the temptation to deceive herself into thinking he loved her was overwhelming. She gave herself to him passionately.

10

The affair thus consummated seemed, to Hornblower's mind at least, to clear the air like a thunderstorm. He had something more definite to think about now than mystic speculations; there was Marie's loving kindness to soothe him, and for counter-irritant there was the pricking of his conscience regarding his seduction of his host's daughter-in-law under his host's roof. His uneasiness lest the Count's telepathic powers should enable him to guess at the secret he shared with Marie, the fear lest someone should intercept a glance or correctly interpret a gesture, kept his mind healthily active.

And the love-affair while it ran its course brought with it a queer unexpected happiness. Marie was everything Hornblower could desire as a mistress. By marriage she was of a family noble enough to satisfy his liking for lords, and yet the knowledge that she was of peasant birth saved him from feeling any awe on that account. She could be tender and passionate, protective and yielding, practical and romantic; and she loved him so dearly, while at the same time she remained reconciled to his approaching departure and resolute to help it on in every way, that his heart softened towards her more and more with the passage of the days.

That departure suddenly became a much nearer and more likely possibility – by coincidence it seemed to come up over the horizon from the hoped-for into the expected only a day or two after Hornblower's meeting with Marie in the upper gallery. The boat was finished, and lay, painted and equipped, in the loft ready for them to use; Brown kept it filled with water from the well and proudly announced that it did not leak a drop. The plans for their journey to the sea were taking definite shape. Fat Jeanne the cook baked biscuit for them – Hornblower came triumphantly into his own then, as the only person in the house who knew how ship's biscuit should be baked, and Jeanne worked under his supervision.

Anxious debate between him and the Count had ended in his deciding against running the risk of buying food while on their way unless compelled; the fifty pounds of biscuit which Jeanne baked for them (there was a locker in the boat in which to store it) would provide the three of them with a pound of bread each day for seventeen days, and there was a sack of potatoes waiting for them, and another of dried peas; and there were long thin Arles sausages – as dry as sticks, and, to Hornblower's mind, not much more digestible, but with the merit of staying eatable for long periods – and some of the dry cod which Hornblower had come to know during his captivity at Ferrol, and a corner of bacon; taken all in all – as Hornblower pointed out to the Count who was inclined to demur – they were going to fare better on their voyage down the Loire than they had often fared in the ships of His Majesty King George. Hornblower, accustomed for so long to sea voyages, never ceased to marvel at the simplicity of planning a river trip thanks to the easy solution of the problem of water supply; overside they would have unlimited fresh water for drinking and washing and bathing – much better water, too, as he told the Count again, than the stinking green stuff, alive with animalculae, doled out at the rate of four pints a head a day, with which people in ships had to be content.

He could anticipate no trouble until they neared the sea; it was only with their entry into tidal waters that they would be in any danger. He knew how the French coast swarmed with garrisons and customs officers – as a lieutenant under Pellew he had once landed a spy in the salt marshes of Bourgneuf – and it would be under their noses that they would have to steal a fishing boat and make their way to sea. Thanks to the Continental system, and the fear of English descents, and precautions against espionage, tidal waters would be watched closely indeed. But he felt he could only trust to fortune – it was hard to make plans against contingencies which might take any shape whatever, and besides, those dangers were weeks away, and Hornblower's newly contented mind was actually too lazy to devote much thought to them. And as he grew fonder of Marie, too, it grew harder to make plans which would take him away from her. His attachment for her was growing even as strong as that.

It was left to the Count to make the most helpful suggestion of all.

'If you would permit me,' he said, one evening, 'I would like to tell you of an idea I have for simplifying your passage through Nantes.'

'It would give me pleasure to hear it, sir,' said Hornblower – the Count's long-winded politeness was infectious.

'Please do not think,' said the Count, 'that I wish to interfere in any way in the plans you are making, but it occurred to me that your stay on the coast might be made safer if you assumed the role of a high official of the customs service.'

'I think it would, sir,' said Hornblower, patiently, 'but I do not understand how I could do it.'

'You would have to announce yourself, if necessary, as a Dutchman,' said the Count. 'Now that Holland is annexed to France and King Louis Bonaparte has fled, it is to be presumed that his employés will join the Imperial service. I think it is extremely likely that, say, a colonel of Dutch douaniers should visit Nantes to learn how to perform his duties – especially as it was over the enforcement of customs regulations that Bonaparte and his brother fell out. Your very excellent French would be just what might be expected of a Dutch customs officer, even though – please pardon my frankness – you do not speak quite like a native Frenchman.'

'But – but –,' stammered Hornblower; it really seemed to him that the Count's customary good sense had deserted him '– it would be difficult, sir –'

'Difficult?' smiled the Count. 'It might be dangerous, but, if you will forgive my contradicting you so directly, it would hardly be difficult. In your English democracy you perhaps have had no opportunity of seeing how much weight an assured manner and a uniform carry with them in a country like this, which has already made the easy descent from an autocracy to a bureaucracy. A colonel of douaniers on the coast can go anywhere, command anything. He never has to account for himself – his uniform does that for him.'

'But I have no uniform, sir,' said Hornblower, and before the words were out of his mouth he guessed what the Count was going to say.

'We have half a dozen needlewomen in the house,' smiled the Count, 'from Marie here to little Christine the cook's daughter. It would be odd if between them they could not make uniforms for you and your assistants. I might add that Mr Bush's wound, which we all so much deplore, will be an actual advantage if you adopt the scheme. It is exactly consonant with Bonaparte's methods to provide for an officer wounded in his service by giving him a position in the customs. Mr Bush's presence with you would add a touch of – shall we say realism? – to the effect produced by your appearance.'

The Count gave a little bow to Bush, in apology for thus alluding to Bush's crippled condition, and Bush returned it awkwardly from his chair in bland ignorance of at least two thirds of what had been said.

The value of the suggestion was obvious to Hornblower at once, and for days afterwards the women in the house were at work cutting and stitching and fitting, until the evening came when the three of them paraded before the Count in their neat coats of blue piped with white and red, and their rakish képis – it was the making of these which had taxed Marie's ingenuity most, for the képi was still at that time an unusual headdress in the French government services. On Hornblower's collar glittered the eight-pointed stars of colonel's rank, and the top of his képi bore the gold-lace rosette; as the three of them rotated solemnly before the Count the latter nodded approvingly.

'Excellent,' he said, and then hesitated. 'There is only one addition which I can think of to add realism. Excuse me a moment.'

He went off to his study leaving the others looking at each other, but he was back directly with a little leather case in his hand which he proceeded to open. Resting on the silk was a glittering cross of white enamel, surmounted by a golden crown and with a gold medallion in the centre.

'We must pin this on you,' he said. 'No one reaches colonel's rank without the Legion of Honour.'

'Father!' said Marie – it was rare that she used the familiar mode of address with him – 'that was Louis-Marie's.'

'I know, my dear, I know. But it may make the difference between Captain Hornblower's success or – or failure.'

His hands trembled a little, nevertheless, as he pinned the scarlet ribbon to Hornblower's coat.

'Sir – sir, it is too good of you,' protested Hornblower.

The Count's long, mobile face, as he stood up, was sad, but in a moment he had twisted it into his usual wry smile.

'Bonaparte sent it to me,' he said, 'after – after my son's death in Spain. It was a posthumous award. To me of course it is nothing – the trinkets of the tyrant can never mean anything to a Knight of the Holy Ghost. But because of its sentimental value I should be grateful if you would endeavour to preserve it unharmed and return it to me when the war is over.'

'I cannot accept it, sir,' said Hornblower, bending to unpin it again, but the Count checked him.

'Please, Captain,' he said, 'wear it, as a favour to me. It would please me if you would.'

More than ever after his reluctant acceptance did Hornblower's conscience prick him at the thought that he had seduced this man's daughter-in-law while enjoying his hospitality, and later in the evening when he found himself alone with the Count in the drawing room the conversation deepened his sense of guilt.

'Now that your stay is drawing to an end, Captain,' said the Count, 'I know how much I shall miss your presence after you have gone. Your company has given me the very greatest pleasure.'

'I do not think it can compare with the gratitude I feel towards you, sir,' said Hornblower.

The Count waved aside the thanks which Hornblower was endeavouring awkwardly to phrase.

'A little while ago we mentioned the end of the war. Perhaps there will come an end some day, and although I am an old man perhaps I shall live to see it. Will you remember, me then, and this little house beside the Loire?'

'Of course, sir,' protested Hornblower. 'I could never forget.'

He looked round the familiar drawing room, at the silver candelabra, the old-fashioned Louis Seize furniture, the lean figure of the Count in his blue dress-coat.

'I could never forget you, sir,' repeated Hornblower.

'My three sons were all young when they died,' said the Count. 'They were only boys, and perhaps they would not have grown into men I could have been proud of. And already when they went off to serve Bonaparte they looked upon me as an old-fashioned reactionary for whose views they had only the smallest patience – that was only to be expected. If they had lived through the wars we might have become better friends later. But they did not, and I am the last Ladon. I am a lonely man, Captain, lonely under this present régime, and yet I fear that when Bonaparte falls and the reactionaries return to power I shall be as lonely still. But I have not been lonely this winter, Captain.'

Hornblower's heart went out to the lean old man with the lined face sitting opposite him in the uncomfortable armchair.

'But that is enough about myself, Captain,' went on the Count. 'I wanted to tell you of the news which has come through – it is all of it important. The salute which we heard fired yesterday was, as we thought, in honour of the birth of an heir to Bonaparte. There is now a King of Rome, as Bonaparte calls him, to sustain the Imperial throne. Whether it will be any support I am doubtful – there are many Bonapartists who will not, I fancy, be too pleased at the thought of the retention of power indefinitely in a Bonaparte dynasty. And the fall of Holland is undoubted – there was actual fighting between the troops of Louis Bonaparte and those of Napoleon Bonaparte over the question of customs enforcement. France now extends to the Baltic – Hamburg and Lubeck are French towns like Amsterdam and Leghorn and Trieste.'

Hornblower thought of the cartoons in the English newspapers which had so often compared Bonaparte with the frog who tried to blow himself up as big as an ox.

'I fancy it is symptomatic of weakness,' said the

Count. 'Perhaps you do not agree with me? You do? I am glad to have my suspicions confirmed. More than that; there is going to be war with Russia. Already troops are being transferred to the East, and the details of a new conscription were published at the same time as the proclamation of a King of Rome. There will be more refractories than ever hiding about the country now. Perhaps Bonaparte will find he has undertaken a task beyond his strength when he comes to grips with Russia.'

'Perhaps so,' said Hornblower. He had not a high opinion of Russian military virtues.

'But there is more important news still,' said the Count. 'There has at last been published a bulletin of the Army of Portugal. It was dated from Almeida.'

It took a second or two for Hornblower to grasp the significance of this comment, and it only dawned upon him gradually, along with the endless implications.

'It means,' said the Count, 'that your Wellington has beaten Bonaparte's Masséna. That the attempt to conquer Portugal has failed, and that the whole of the affairs of Spain are thrown into flux again. A running sore has been opened in the side of Bonaparte's empire, which may drain him of his strength – at what cost to poor France one can hardly imagine. But of course, Captain, you can form a more reliable opinion of the military situation than I can, and I have been presumptuous in commenting on it. Yet you have not the facilities which I have of gauging the moral effect of this news. Wellington has beaten Junot, and Victor, and Soult. Now he has beaten Masséna, the greatest of them all. There is only one man now against whom European opinion can measure him, and that is Bonaparte. It is not well for a tyrant to have rivals in prestige. Last year how many years of power would one have given Bonaparte if asked? Twenty? I think so. Now in 1811 we change our minds. Ten years, we think. In 1812 we may revise our estimate again, and say five. I myself do not believe the Empire as we know it will endure after 1814 – Empires collapse at a rate increasing in geometrical progression, and it will be your Wellington who will pull this one down.'

'I hope sincerely you are right, sir,' said Hornblower.

The Count was not to know how disturbing this mention of Wellington was to his audience; he could not guess that Hornblower was daily tormented by speculations as to whether Wellington's sister was widowed or not, whether Lady Barbara Leighton, née Wellesley, ever had a thought to devote to the naval captain who had been reported dead. Her brother's triumphs might well occupy her mind to the exclusion of everything else, and Hornblower feared that when at last he should reach England she would be far too great a lady to pay him any attention at all. The thought irked him.

He went to bed in a peculiarly sober mood, his mind busy with problems of the most varying nature – from speculations about the approaching fall of the French Empire to calculations regarding the voyage down the Loire which he was about to attempt. Lying awake, long after midnight, he heard his bedroom door quietly open and close; he lay rigid, instantly, conscious of a feeling of faint distaste at this reminder of the intrigue which he was conducting under a hospitable roof. Very gently, the curtains of his bed were drawn open, and in the darkness he could see, through half opened eyes, a shadowy ghost bending over him. A gentle hand found his cheek and stroked it; he could no longer sham sleep, and he pretended to wake with a start.

'It is Marie, 'Oratio,' said a voice, softly.

'Yes,' said Hornblower.

He did not know what he should say or do – for that matter he did not know what he wanted. Mostly he was conscious of Marie's imprudence in thus coming to his room, risking discovery and imperilling everything. He shut his eyes as though still sleepy, to gain time for consideration; the hand ceased to stroke his cheek. Hornblower waited for a second or two more, and was astonished to hear the slight click of the latch of the door again. He sat up with a jerk. Marie had gone, as silently as she had come. Hornblower continued to sit up, puzzling over the incident, but he could make nothing of it. Certainly he was not going to run any risks by going to seek Marie in her room and asking for explanations; he lay down again to think about it, and this time, with its usual capriciousness, sleep surprised him in the midst of his speculations, and he slept soundly until Brown brought him his breakfast coffee.

It took him half the morning to nerve himself for what he foresaw to be a very uncomfortable interview; it was only then that he tore himself away from a last inspection of the boat, in Bush's and Brown's company, and climbed the stairs to Marie's boudoir and tapped at the door. He entered when she called, and stood there in the room of so many memories – the golden chairs with their oval backs upholstered in pink and white, the windows looking out on the sunlit Loire, and Marie in the window-seat with her needlework.

'I wanted to say "good morning",' he said at length, as Marie did nothing to help him out.

'Good morning,' said Marie. She bent her head over her needlework – the sunshine through the windows lit her hair gloriously – and spoke with her face concealed. 'We only have to say "good morning" today, and tomorrow we shall say "goodbye".'

'Yes,' said Hornblower stupidly.

'If you loved me,' said Marie, 'it would be terrible for me to have you go, and to know that for years we should not meet again – perhaps for ever. But as you do not, then I am glad that you are going back to your wife and your child, and your ships, and your fighting. That is what you wanted, and I am pleased that you should have it all.'

'Thank you,' said Hornblower.

Still she did not look up.

'You are the sort of man,' she went on, 'whom women love very easily. I do not expect that I shall be the last. I don't think that you will ever love anybody, or know what it is to do so.'

Hornblower could have said nothing in English in reply to these two astonishing statements, and in French he was perfectly helpless. He could only stammer.

'Goodbye,' said Marie.

'Goodbye, madame,' said Hornblower, lamely.

His cheeks were burning as he came out into the upper hall, in a condition of mental distress in which humiliation only played a minor part. He was thoroughly conscious of having acted despicably, and of having been dismissed without dignity. But he was puzzled by the other remarks Marie had made. It had never occurred to him that women loved him easily. Maria – it was odd, that similarity of names, Maria and Marie – loved him, he knew; he had found it a little tiresome and disturbing. Barbara had offered herself to him, but he had never ventured to believe that she had loved him – and had she not married someone else? And Marie loved him; Hornblower remembered guiltily an incident of a few days ago, when Marie in his arms had whispered hotly, 'Tell me you love me,' and he had answered with facile kindness, 'I love you, dear.' 'Then I am happy,' answered Marie. Perhaps it was a good thing that Marie knew now that he was lying, and had made easy his retreat. Another woman with a word might have sent him and Bush to prison and death – there were women capable of it.

And this question of his never loving anyone; surely Marie was wrong about that. She did not know the miseries of longing he had been through on Barbara's account, how much he had desired her and how much he still desired her. He hesitated guiltily here, wondering whether his desire would survive gratification. That was such an uncomfortable thought that he swerved away from it in a kind of panic. If Marie had merely revengefully desired to disturb him she certainly had achieved her object; and if on the other hand she had wanted to win him back to her she was not far from success either. What with the torments of remorse and his sudden uneasiness about himself Hornblower would have returned to her if she had lifted a finger to him, but she did not.

At dinner that evening she appeared young and light-hearted, her eyes sparkling and her expression animated, and when the Count lifted his glass for the toast of 'a prosperous voyage home' she joined in with every appearance of enthusiasm. Hornblower was glum beneath his forced gaiety. Only now, with the prospect of an immediate move ahead of him, had he become aware that there were decided arguments in favour of the limbo of suspended animation in which he had spent the past months. Tomorrow he was going to leave all this certainty and safety and indifferent negativeness. There was physical danger ahead of him; that he could face calmly and with no more than a tightening of the throat, but besides that there was the resolution of all the doubts and uncertainties which had so troubled him.

Hornblower was suddenly aware that he did not so urgently desire his uncertainties to be resolved. At present he could still hope. If Leighton were to declare that Hornblower had fought at Rosas contrary to the spirit of his orders; if the court martial were to decide that the *Sutherland* had not been fought to the last gasp – and courts martial were chancy affairs; if – if – if. And there was Maria with her cloying sweetness awaiting him, and the misery of longing for Lady Barbara, all in contrast with the smoothness of life here with the Count's unruffled politeness and the stimulus of Marie's healthy animalism. Hornblower had to force a smile as he lifted his glass.

II

The big green Loire was shrinking to its summer level. Hornblower had seen its floods and its ice come and go, had seen the willows at its banks almost submerged, but now it was back safely in its wide bed, with a hint of golden-brown gravel exposed on either bank. The swift green water was clear now, instead of turbid, and under the blue sky the distant reaches were blue as well, in charming colour contrast with the springtime emerald of the valley and the gold of the banks.

The two sleek dun oxen, patient under the yoke, had dragged the travois-sledge down to the water's edge in the first early light of dawn, Brown and Hornblower walking beside to see that the precious boat balanced on it came to no harm, and Bush stumping breathlessly behind them. The boat slid gently into the water, and under Bush's supervision the stable hands loaded her with the bags of stores which they had carried down. The faint morning mist still lay in the valley, and wreathed over the surface of the water, awaiting the coming of the sun to drink it up. It was the best time for departure: the mist would shield them from inquisitive persons who might be unduly curious at the sight of the expedition starting off. Up at the house farewells had all been said – the Count as unruffled as ever, as though it were usual for him to rise at five in the morning, and Marie smiling and calm. In the stable yard and the kitchen there had been tears; all the women had lamented Brown's going, weeping unashamed and yet laughing through their tears as he laughed and joked in the voluble French which he had acquired, and as he smacked their broad posteriors. Hornblower wondered how many of them Brown had seduced that winter, and how many Anglo-French children would be born next autumn as a result.

'Remember your promise to return after the war,' the Count had said to Hornblower. 'Marie will be as delighted to see you as I shall be.'

His smile had conveyed no hint of a hidden meaning – but how much did he guess, or know? Hornblower gulped as he remembered.

'Shove off,' he rasped. 'Brown, take the sculls.'

The boat scraped over the gravel, and then floated free as the current took her, dancing away from the little group of stable hands and the stolid oxen, vague already in the mist. The rowlocks creaked and the boat swayed to Brown's pulls; Hornblower heard the noises, and felt Bush seated in the stern beside him, but for some seconds he saw nothing. There was a mist about him far denser than the reality.

The one mist cleared with the other, as the sun came breaking through, warm on Hornblower's back. High up the bank on the opposite side was the orchard at which Hornblower had often gazed from his window; it was marvellous now under its load of blossom. Looking back he saw the château shining in the sun. The turrets at the corners had been added, he knew, no more than fifty years ago by a Comte de Graçay with a rococo taste for the antique, but they looked genuine enough at a distance. It was like a fairy castle in the pearly light, a dream castle; and already the months he had spent there seemed like a dream too, a dream from which he regretted awakening.

'Mr Bush,' he said sharply. 'I'll trouble you to get out your rod and make an appearance of fishing. Take a slower stroke, Brown.'

They went drifting on down the noble river, blue in the distance and green overside, clear and transparent, so that they could actually see the bottom passing away below them. It was only a few minutes before they reached the confluence of the Allier, itself a fine river almost the size of the Loire, and the united stream was majestically wide, a hundred and fifty fathoms at least from bank to bank. They were a long musket shot from land, but their position was safer even than that implied, for from the water's edge on either side stretched an extensive no man's land of sand and willow which the periodic floods kept free from human habitations and which was only likely to be visited by fishermen and laundering housewives.

The mist had entirely vanished now, and the hot sun bore with all the promise of one of those splendid spring days of central France. Hornblower shifted in his seat to make himself more comfortable. The hierarchy of this, his new command, was top-heavy. A proportion of one seaman to one lieutenant and one captain was ludicrous. He would have to exercise a great deal of tact to keep them all three satisfied – to see that Brown was not made resentful by having all the work to do and yet that discipline was not endangered by a too democratic division of labour. In a fifteen-foot boat it would be difficult to keep up the aloof dignity proper to a captain.

'Brown,' he said. 'I've been very satisfied with you so far. Keep in my good books and I'll see you're properly rewarded when we get back to England. There'll be a warrant for you as master's mate if you want it.'

'Thank 'ee, sir. Thank 'ee very kindly. But I'm happy as I am, beggin' your pardon, sir.'

He meant he was happy in his rating as a coxswain, but the tone of his voice implied more than that. Hornblower looked at him as he sat with his face turned up to the sun, pulling slowly at the sculls. There was a blissful smile on his face – the man was marvellously happy. He had been well fed and well housed for months, with plenty of women's society, with light work and no hardship. Even now there was a long prospect ahead of him of food better than he had ever known before he entered France, of no harder work than a little gentle rowing, of no need ever to turn out on a blustering night to reef topsails. Twenty years of the lower deck in King George's Navy, Hornblower realized, must make any man form the habit of living only in the present. Tomorrow might bring a flogging, peril, sickness, death; certainly hardship and probably hunger, and all without the opportunity of lifting a finger to ward off any of these, for any lifting of a finger would make them all more certain. Twenty years of being at the mercy of the incalculable, and not merely in the major things of life but in the minor ones, must make a fatalist of any man who survived them. For a moment Hornblower felt a little twinge of envy of Brown, who would never know the misery of helplessness, or the indignity of indecision.

The river channel here was much divided by islands each bordered by a rim of golden gravel; it was

Hornblower's business to select what appeared to be the most navigable channel – no easy task. Shallows appeared mysteriously right in the centre of what had seemed to be the main stream; over these the clear green water ran faster and faster and shallower and shallower until the bottom of the boat was grating on the pebbles. Sometimes the bank would end there with astonishing abruptness, so that one moment they were in six inches of rushing water and the next in six feet of transparent green, but more than once now they found themselves stuck fast, and Brown and Hornblower, trousers rolled to the knee, had to get out and haul the boat a hundred yards over a barely covered bank before finding water deep enough. Hornblower thanked his stars that he had decided on having the boat built flat-bottomed – a keel would have been a hampering nuisance.

Then they came to a dam, like the one which had brought them disaster in the darkness during their first attempt to navigate the river. It was half natural, half artificial, roughly formed of lumps of rock piled across the river bed, and over it the river poured in fury at a few points.

'Pull over to the bank there, Brown,' snapped Hornblower as his coxswain looked to him for orders.

They ran the boat up on to the gravel just above the dam, and Hornblower stepped out and looked downstream. There was a hundred yards of turbulent water below the dam; they would have to carry everything down. It took three journeys on the part of Hornblower and Brown to carry all their stores to the point he chose for them to re-enter the river – Bush with his wooden leg could only just manage to stumble over the uneven surface unladen – and then they addressed themselves to the business of transporting the boat. It was not easy; there was a colossal difference between dragging the boat through shallows even an inch deep only and carrying her bodily. Hornblower contemplated the task glumly for some seconds before plunging at it. He stooped and got his hands underneath.

'Take the other side, Brown. Now – lift.'

Between them they could just raise it; they had hardly staggered a yard with it before all the strength was gone from Hornblower's wrists and fingers and the boat slipped to the ground again. He avoided Brown's eye and stooped again, exasperated.

'Lift!' he said.

It was impossible to carry the heavy boat that way. He had no sooner lifted it than he was compelled to drop it again.

'It's no go, sir,' said Brown gently. 'We'll have to get her upon our backs, sir. That's the only way.'

Hornblower heard the respectful murmur as if from a long distance.

'If you take the bows, beggin' your pardon, sir, I'll look after the stern. Here, sir, lift t'other way round. Hold it, sir, 'till I can get aft. Right, sir. Ready. Lift!'

They had the boat up on their backs now, stooping double under the heavy load. Hornblower, straining under the lighter bows, thought of Brown carrying the much heavier stern, and he set his teeth and vowed to himself that he would not rest until Brown asked to. Within five seconds he was regretting his vow. His breath was coming with difficulty and there were stabbing pains in his chest. It grew harder and harder to take the trouble to attend to the proper placing of his feet as he stumbled over the uneven surface. Those months in the Château de Graçay had done their work in making him soft and out of condition; for the last few yards of the portage he was conscious of nothing save the overwhelming weight on his neck and shoulders and his difficulty of breathing. Then he heard Bush's bluff voice.

'Right, sir. Let me get hold, sir.'

With the small but welcome help that Bush could afford he was able to disengage himself and lower the boat to the ground; Brown was standing over the stern gasping, and sweeping the sweat off his forehead with his forearm. Hornblower saw him open his mouth to make a remark, presumably regarding the weight of the boat, and then shut it again when he remembered that now he was under discipline again and must only speak when spoken to. And discipline, Hornblower realized, required that he himself should display no sign of weakness before his subordinates – it was bad enough that he should have had to receive advice from Brown as to how to lift the boat.

'Take hold again, Brown, and we'll get her into the water,' he said, controlling his breathing with a vast effort.

They slid the boat in, and heaved the stores on board again. Hornblower's head was swimming with the strain; he thought longingly of his comfortable seat in the stern, and then put the thought from him.

'I'll take the sculls, Brown,' he said.

Brown opened and shut his mouth again, but he could not question explicit orders. The boat danced out over the water, with Hornblower at the sculls happy in the rather baseless conviction that he had demonstrated that a captain in the King's Navy was the equal even in physical strength of any mere coxswain, however Herculean his thews.

Once or twice that day shallows caught them out in midstream which they were unable to pass without lightening the boat to a maximum extent. When Hornblower and Brown, ankle-deep in rushing water, could drag the boat no farther, Bush had to get out too, his wooden leg sinking in the sand despite its broad leather sole, and limp downstream to the edge of the shallows and wait until the others dragged the lightened boat up to him – once he had to stand holding the bag of bread and the roll of bedding before they could tug the boat over the shallows, and on that occasion they had to unstrap his wooden leg, help him in, and then tug the leg free from the sand, so deeply had it sunk. There was another portage to be made that day, fortunately not nearly such a long one as the first; altogether there was quite enough interest in the day's journey to keep them from growing bored.

On that big lonely river it was almost like travelling through an uninhabited country. For the greater part of the day there was hardly a soul in sight. Once they saw a skiff moored to the bank which was obviously used as a ferry-boat, and once they passed a big wagon ferry – a flat-bottomed scow which was moored so as to swing itself across the river by the force of the current, pendulum-fashion on long mooring ropes. Once they passed a small boat engaged in the task of dredging sand for building purposes from the river bed; there were two weather-beaten men on board, hard at work with small hand dredgers on poles, which they scraped over the bottom and emptied into the boat. It was a nervous moment as they approached them, Bush and Brown with their ornamental fishing rods out, Hornblower forcing himself to do no more with the sculls than merely keep the boat in midstream. He had thought, as they drifted down, of giving orders to Bush and Brown regarding the instant silencing of the two men if they appeared suspicious, but he checked himself. He could rely on their acting promptly without warning, and his dignity demanded that he should betray none of the apprehension which he felt.

But the apprehension was quite baseless. There was no curiosity in the glances which the two sand dredgers threw at them, and there was cordiality in their smiles and in their polite 'Bonjour, messieurs.'

'Bonjour,' said Hornblower and Brown – Bush had the sense to keep shut the mouth which would instantly have betrayed them, and devoted his attention instead to his rod. Clearly boats with fishing parties on board were just common enough on the Loire to escape comment; and, besides, the intrinsic innocence of fishing as a pastime shielded them from suspicion, as Hornblower and the Count had agreed long before. And nobody could ever dream that a small boat in the heart of France was manned by escaped prisoners of war.

The commonest sight of all along the river was the women washing clothes, sometimes singly, sometimes in little groups whose gossiping chatter floated out to them distinctly over the water. The Englishmen could hear the 'clop clop clop' of the wooden beaters smacking the wet clothes on the boards, and could see the kneeling women sway down and up as they rinsed them in the current; most of the women looked up from their work and gave them a glance as they drifted by, but it was never more than a long glance, and often not as much. In time of war and upheaval there were so many possible explanations for the women not to know the occupants of the boat that their inability did not trouble them.

Of the roaring rapids such as had nearly destroyed them once before, they saw nothing; the junction of the Allier, and the cessation of the winter floods, accounted for that. The rock-strewn sand bars represented the sites of winter rapids and were far easier to navigate, or rather to circumvent. In fact, there were no difficulties at all. Even the weather was benign, a lovely clear day of sunshine, comfortably warm, lighting up the changing panorama of gold and blue and green. Brown basked in it all unashamedly, and the hardbitten Bush took his ease whenever the peacefulness of it caught him napping; in Bush's stern philosophy mankind – naval mankind at least – was born to sorrow and difficulty and danger, and any variation from such a state of affairs must be viewed with suspicion and not enjoyed too much lest it should have to be paid for at compound interest. It was too good to be true, this delightful drifting down the river, as morning wore into noon and noon into prolonged and dreamy afternoon, with a delicious lunch to eat of a cold pâté (a parting gift from fat Jeanne) and a bottle of wine.

The little towns, or rather villages, which they passed were all perched up high on the distant banks beyond the flood limits; Hornblower, who already knew by heart the brief itinerary and table of distances which the Count had made out for him, was aware that the first town with a bridge was at Briare, which they could not reach until late evening. He had intended to wait above the town until nightfall and then to run through in the darkness, but as the day wore on his resolve steadily hardened to push on without waiting. He could not analyse his motives. He was aware that it was a very remarkable thing for him to do, to run into danger, even the slightest, when urged neither by the call of duty nor the thirst for distinction. Here the only benefit would be the saving of an hour or two's time. The Nelsonian tradition to 'lose not an hour' was grained deeply into him, but it was hardly that which influenced him.

Partly it was his innate cross-grainedness. Everything had gone so supremely well. Their escape from their escort had been almost miraculous, the coincidence which had brought them to the Château de Graçay, where alone in all France they could have found safety, was more nearly miraculous still. Now this voyage down the river bore every promise of easy success. His instinctive reaction to all this unnatural prosperity was to put himself into the way of trouble – there had been so much trouble in his life that he felt uneasy without it.

But partly he was being driven by devils. He was morose and cantankerous. Marie was being left behind, and he was regretting that more with every yard that divided them. He was tormented by the thought of the shameful part he had played, and by memories of the hours they had spent together; sentimentally he was obsessed with longing for her. And ahead of him lay England where they thought him dead, where Maria would by now have reconciled herself to her loss and would be doubly and painfully happy with him in consequence, and where Barbara would have forgotten him, and where a court martial to inquire into his conduct awaited him. He thought grimly that it might be better for everyone if he *were* dead; he shrank a little from the prospect of returning to England as one might shrink from a cold plunge, or as he shrank from the imminent prospect of danger. That was the ruling motive. He had always forced himself to face danger, to advance bravely to meet it. He had always gulped down any pill which life had presented to him, knowing that any hesitation would give him a contempt for himself more bitter still. So now he would accept no excuse for delay.

Briare was in sight now, down at the end of the long wide reach of the river. Its church tower was silhouetted against the evening sky, and its long straggling bridge stood out black against the distant silver of the water. Hornblower at the sculls looked over his shoulder and saw all this; he was aware of his subordinate's eye turned inquiringly upon him.

'Take the sculls, Brown,' he growled.

They changed places silently, and Bush handed over the tiller to him with a puzzled look – he had been well aware of the design to run past bridges only at night. There were two vast black shapes creeping over the surface of the river down there, barges being warped out of the lateral canal on one side and into the canal of Briare on the other by way of a channel across the river dredged for the purpose. Hornblower stared forward as they approached under the impulse of Brown's steady strokes. A quick examination of the water surface told him which arch of the bridge to select, and he was able to discern the tow-ropes and warps of the barges – there were teams of horses both on the bridge and on the banks, silhouetted clearly against the sky as they tugged at the ropes to drag the bulky barges across the rushing current.

Men were looking at them now from the bridge, and there was just sufficient gap left between the barges to enable the boat to slip between without the necessity to stop and make explanations.

'Pull!' he said to Brown, and the boat went careering headlong down the river. They slid under the bridge with a rush, and neatly rounded the stern of one of the barges; the burly old man at the tiller, with a little grandchild beside him, looked down at them with a dull curiosity as they shot by. Hornblower waved his hand gaily to the child – excitement was a drug which he craved, which always sent his spirits high – and looked up with a grin at the other men on the bridge and on the banks. Then they were past, and Briare was left behind.

'Easy enough, sir,' commented Bush.

'Yes,' said Hornblower.

If they had been travelling by road they certainly would have been stopped for examination of their passports; here on the unnavigable river such a proceeding occurred to no one. The sun was low now, shining right into his eyes as he looked forward, and it would be dark in less than an hour. Hornblower began to look out for a place where they could be comfortable for the night. He allowed one long island to slide past them before he saw the ideal spot – a tiny hummock of an island with three willow trees, the green of the central part surrounded by a broad belt of golden brown where the receding river had left the gravel exposed.

'We'll run the boat aground over there, Brown,' he announced. 'Easy. Pull starboard. Pull both. Easy.'

It was not a very good landing. Hornblower, despite his undoubted ability in handling big ships, had much to learn regarding the behaviour of flat-bottomed boats amid the shoals of a river. There was a black eddy, which swung them round; the boat had hardly touched bottom before the current had jerked her free again. Brown, tumbling over the bows, was nearly waist deep in water and had to grab the painter and brace himself against the current to check her. The tactful silence which ensued could almost be felt while Brown tugged the boat up to the gravel again – Hornblower, in the midst of his annoyance, was aware of Bush's restless movement and thought of how his first lieutenant would have admonished a midshipman guilty of such a careless piece of work. It made him grin to think of Bush bottling up his feelings, and the grin made him forget his annoyance.

He stepped out into the shallow water and helped Brown run the lightened boat farther up the bank, checking Bush when he made to step out too – Bush could never accustom himself to seeing his captain at work while he sat idle. The water was no more than ankle-deep by the time he allowed Bush to disembark; they dragged the boat up as far as she could go and Brown made fast the painter to a peg driven securely into the earth, as a precaution in case any unexpected rise in the water level should float the boat off. The sun had set now in the flaming west, and it was fast growing dark.

'Supper,' said Hornblower. 'What shall we have?'

A captain with strict ideas of discipline would merely have announced what they should eat, and would certainly not have called his subordinates into consultation, but Hornblower was too conscious of the top-heavy organization of his present ship's company to be able to maintain appearances to that extent. Yet Bush and Brown were still oppressed by a life-long experience of subordination and could not bring themselves to proffer advice to their captain; they merely fidgeted and stood silent, leaving it to Hornblower to decree that they should finish off the cold pâté with some boiled potatoes. Once the decision was made, Bush proceeded to amplify and interpret his captain's original order, just as a good first lieutenant should.

'I'll handle the fire here,' he said. 'There ought to be all the driftwood we need, Brown. Yes, an' I'll want some sheer-legs to hang the pan over the fire – cut me three off those trees, there.'

Bush felt it in his bones that Hornblower was meditating taking part in the preparation of supper, and could not bear the thought. He looked up at his captain half appealingly, half defiantly. A captain should not merely never be seen doing undignified work, but he should be kept in awful isolation, screened away in the mysterious recesses of his cabin. Hornblower left them to it, and wandered off round the tiny island, looking over at the distant banks and the far houses, fast disappearing in the growing twilight. It was a shock to discover that the pleasant green which carpeted most of the island was not the grass he had assumed it to be, but a bank of nettles, knee high already despite the earliness of the season. Judging by his language, Brown on the other side had just made the same discovery while seeking fuel with his feet bare.

Hornblower paced the gravel bank for a space, and on his return it was an idyllic scene which met his eyes.

Brown was tending the little fire which flickered under the pot swinging from its tripod, while Bush, his wooden leg sticking stiffly out in front of him, was peeling the last of the potatoes. Apparently Bush had decided that a first lieutenant could share menial work with the sole member of the crew without imperilling discipline. They all ate together, wordless but friendly, beside the dying fire; even the chill air of the evening did not cool the feeling of comradeship of which each was conscious in his own particular way.

'Shall I set a watch, sir?' asked Bush, as supper ended.

'No,' said Hornblower.

The minute additional security which would be conferred by one of them staying awake would not compare with the discomfort and inconvenience of everyone losing four hours' sleep each night.

Bush and Brown slept in cloak and blanket on the bare soil, probably, Hornblower anticipated, most uncomfortably. For himself there was a mattress of cut nettles cunningly packed under the boat cover which Brown had prepared for him on the most level part of the gravel spit, presumably at a grave cost in stings. He slept on it peacefully, the dew wetting his face and the gibbous moon shining down upon it from the starry sky. Vaguely he remembered, in a troubled fashion, the stories of the great leaders of men – Charles XII especially – who shared their men's coarse fare and slept like them on the bare ground. For a second or two he feared he should be doing likewise, and then his common sense overrode his modesty and told him that he did not need to have recourse to theatrical tricks to win the affections of Bush and Brown.

12

Those days on the Loire were pleasant, and every day was more pleasant than the one preceding. For Hornblower there was not merely the passive pleasure of a fortnight's picnic, but there was the far more active one of the comradeliness of it all. During his ten years as a captain his natural shyness had reinforced the restrictions surrounding his position, and had driven him more and more in upon himself until he had grown unconscious of his aching need for human companionship. In that small boat, living at close quarters with the others, and where one man's misfortune was everyone's, he came to know happiness. His keen insight made him appreciate more than ever the sterling good qualities of Bush, who was secretly fretting over the loss of his foot, and the inactivity to which that loss condemned him, and the doubtfulness of his future as a cripple.

'I'll see you posted as captain,' said Hornblower, on the only occasion on which Bush hinted at his troubles, 'if it's my last act on earth.'

He thought he might possibly contrive that, even if disgrace awaited him personally in England. Lady Barbara must still remember Bush and the old days in the *Lydia*, and must be aware of his good qualities as Hornblower was himself. An appeal to her, properly worded – even from a man broken by court martial – might have an effect, and might set turning the hidden wheels of Government patronage. Bush deserved post rank more than half the captains he knew on the list.

Then there was Brown with his unfailing cheerfulness. No one could judge better than Hornblower the awkwardness of Brown's position, living in such close proximity to two officers. But Brown always could find the right mixture of friendliness and deference; he could laugh gaily when he slipped on a rounded stone and sat down in the Loire, and he could smile sympathetically when the same thing happened to Hornblower. He busied himself over the jobs of work which had to be done, and never, not even after ten days' routine had established something like a custom, appeared to take it for granted that his officers would do their share. Hornblower could foresee a great future for Brown, if helped by a little judicious exertion of influence. He might easily end as a captain, too – Darby and Westcott had started on the lower deck in the same fashion. Even if the court martial broke him Hornblower could do something to help him. Elliott and Bolton at least would not desert him entirely, and would rate Brown as midshipman in their ships if he asked them to with special earnestness.

In making these plans for the future of his friends, Hornblower could bring himself to contemplate the end of the voyage and the inevitable court martial with something like equanimity; for the rest, during those golden days, he was able to avoid all thought of their approaching end. It was a placid journey through a placid limbo. He was leaving behind him in the past the shameful memory of his treatment of Marie, and the troubles to come were still in the future; for once in his life he was able to live in the lotus-eating present.

All the manifold little details of the journey helped towards this desirable end – they were so petty and yet temporarily so important. Selecting a course between the golden sandbanks of the river; stepping out overside to haul the boat over when his judgement was incorrect; finding a lonely island on which to camp at night, and cooking supper when one was found; drifting past the gravel dredgers and the rare fishing parties; avoiding conspicuous behaviour while passing towns; there were always trifles to occupy the mind. There were the two nights when it rained, and they all slept huddled together under the shelter of a blanket stretched between willow trees – there had been a ridiculous pleasure about waking up to find Bush snoring beside him with a protective arm across him.

There was the pageantry of the Loire – Gien with its château-fortress high on its terraces, and Sully with its vast rounded bastions, and Château-Neuf-sur-Loire, and Jargeau. Then for miles along the river they were in sight of the gaunt square towers of the cathedral of Orleans – Orleans was one of the few towns with an extensive river front, past which they had to drift unobtrusively and with special care at its difficult bridges. Orleans was hardly out of sight before they reached Beaugency with its interminable bridges of countless arches and its strange square tower. The river was blue and gold and green. The rocks above Nevers were succeeded by the gravel banks of the middle reaches, and now the gravel gave way to sand, golden sand amid the shimmering blue of the river whose water was a clear green overside. All the contrasted greens delighted Hornblower's eyes, the green of the never-ending willows, of the vineyards and the cornfields and the meadows.

They passed Blois, its steeply-humped bridge crowned by the pyramid whose inscription proclaimed the bridge to be the first public work of the infant Louis XV, and Chaumont and Amboise, their lovely châteaux towering above the river, and Tours – an extensive water front to sidle past here, too – and Langeais. The wild desolation of the island-studded river was punctuated everywhere by towers and châteaux and cathedrals on the distant banks. Below Langeais the big placid Vienne entered the river on their left, and appeared to convey some of its own qualities to the united stream, which was now a little slower and more regular in its course, its shallows becoming less and less frequent. After Saumur and the innumerable islands of Les Ponts de Cé, the even bigger Maine came in on their right, and finally deprived the wild river of all the characteristics which had endeared it to them. Here it was far deeper and far slower, and for the first time they found the attempt to make the river available for commercial traffic successful here – they had passed numerous traces of wasted work on Bonaparte's part higher up.

But below the confluence of the Maine the groynes and dykes had withstood the winter floods and the continual erosion, had piled up long beaches of golden sand on either bank, and had left in the centre a deep channel navigable to barges – they passed several working their way up to Angers from Nantes. Mostly they were being towed by teams of mules, but one or two were taking advantage of a westerly wind to make the ascent under vast gaff-mainsails. Hornblower stared hungrily at them, for they were the first sails he had seen for months, but he put aside all thought of stealing one. A glance at their clumsy lines assured him that it would be more dangerous to put to sea, even for a short distance, in one of those than in the cockleshell boat they had already.

That westerly wind that brought the barges up brought something else with it, too. Brown, diligently tugging at the sculls as he forced the boat into it, suddenly wrinkled his nose.

'Begging your pardon, sir,' he said, 'I can smell the sea.'

They sniffed at the breeze, all three of them.

'By God, you're right, Brown,' said Bush.

Hornblower said nothing, but he had smelt the salt as well, and it had brought with it such a wave of mixed feelings as to leave him without words. And that night after they had camped – there were just as many desolate islands to choose from, despite the changes in the river – Hornblower noticed that the level of the water had risen perceptibly above where it had stood when they beached the boat. It was not flood water like the time when after a day of heavy rain their boat had nearly floated during the night; on this evening above Nantes there had been no rain, no sign of it, for three days. Hornblower watched the water creep up at a rate almost perceptible, watched it reach a maximum, dally there for a space, and then begin to sink. It was the tide. Down at Paimboeuf at the mouth there was a rise and fall of ten or twelve feet, at Nantes one of four or six; up here he was witnessing the last dying effort of the banked up sea to hold the river back in its course.

*

There was a strange emotion in the thought. They had reached tidewater at last, the habitat on which he had spent more than half his life; they had travelled from sea to sea, from the Mediterranean to what was at least technically the Atlantic; this same tide he was witnessing here washed also the shores of England, where were Barbara, and Maria, and his unknown child, and the Lords Commissioners of the Admiralty. But more than that. It meant that their pleasant picnic on the Loire was over. In tidal water they could not hope to move about with half the freedom they had known inland; strange faces and new arrivals would be scanned with suspicion, and probably the next forty-eight hours or so would determine whether he was to reach England to face a court martial or be recaptured to face a firing squad. Hornblower knew that moment the old sensation of excitement, which he called fear to himself – the quickened heart beat, the dampening palms, the tingling in the calves of his legs. He had to brace himself to master these symptoms before returning to the others to tell them of his observations.

'High water half an hour back, sir?' repeated Bush in reply.

'Yes.'

'M'm,' said Bush.

Brown said nothing, as accorded with his position in life, but his face bore momentarily the same expression of deep cogitation. They were both assimilating the fact, in the manner of seamen. Hornblower knew that from now on, with perhaps a glance at the sun but not necessarily with a glance at the river, they would be able to tell offhand the state of the tide, producing the information without a thought by the aid of a subconscious calculating ability developed during a lifetime at sea. He could do the same himself – the only difference between them was that he was interested in the phenomenon while they were indifferent to it or unaware of it.

13

For their entrance into Nantes Hornblower decided that they must wear their uniforms as officials of the customs service. It called for long and anxious thought to reach this decision, a desperately keen balancing of chances. If they arrived in civilian clothes they would almost certainly be questioned, and in that case it would be almost impossible to explain their lack of papers and passports, whereas in uniform they might easily not be questioned at all, and if they were a haughty demeanour might still save them. But to pose as a colonel of douaniers would call for histrionic ability on the part of Hornblower, and he mistrusted himself – not his ability, but his nerve. With remorseless self-analysis he told himself that he had played a part for years, posing as a man of rigid imperturbability when he was nothing of the kind, and he asked himself why he could not pose for a few minutes as a man of swaggering and overbearing haughtiness, even under the additional handicap of having to speak French. In the end it was in despite of his doubts that he reached his decision, and put on the neat uniform and pinned the glittering Legion of Honour on his breast.

As always, it was the first moment of departure which tried him most – getting into the sternsheets of the boat and taking the tiller while Brown got out the sculls. The tension under which he laboured was such that he knew that, if he allowed it, the hand that rested on the tiller would tremble, and the voice which gave the orders to Brown would quaver. So he carried himself with the unbending rigidity which men were accustomed to see in him, and he spoke with the insensitive harshness he always used in action.

Under the impulse of Brown's sculls the river glided away behind them, and the city of Nantes came steadily nearer. Houses grew thicker and thicker on the banks, and then the river began to break up into several arms; to Hornblower the main channel between the islands was made obvious by the indications of traces of commercial activity along the banks – traces of the past, largely, for Nantes was a dying town, dying of the slow strangulation of the British blockade. The lounging idlers along the quays, the deserted warehouses, all indicated the dire effects of war upon French commerce.

They passed under a couple of bridges, with the tide running strongly, and left the huge mass of the ducal château to starboard; Hornblower forced himself to sit with careless ease in the boat, as though neither courting nor avoiding observation; the Legion of Honour clinked as it swung upon his breast. A side glance at Bush suddenly gave him enormous comfort and reassurance, for Bush was sitting with a masklike immobility of countenance which told Hornblower that he was nervous too. Bush could go into action and face an enemy's broadside with an honest indifference to danger, but this present situation was trying his nerves severely, sitting watched by a thousand French eyes, and having to rely upon mere inactivity to save himself from death or imprisonment. The sight was like a tonic to Hornblower.

His cares dropped from him, and he knew the joy and thrill of reckless bravery.

Beyond the next bridge the maritime port began. Here first were the fishing boats – Hornblower looked keenly at them, for he had in mind to steal one of them. His experience under Pellew in the blockading squadron years ago was serving him in good stead now, for he knew the ways of those fishing boats. They were accustomed to ply their trade among the islands of the Breton coast, catching the pilchards which the French persisted in calling 'sardines', and bringing their catch up the estuary to sell in the market at Nantes. He and Bush and Brown between them could handle one of those boats with ease, and they were seaworthy enough to take them safely out to the blockading squadron, or to England if necessary. He was practically certain that he would decide upon such a plan, so that as they rowed by he sharply ordered Brown to pull more slowly, and he turned all his attention upon them.

Below the fishing boats two American ships were lying against the quay, the Stars and Stripes fluttering jauntily in the gentle wind. His attention was caught by a dreary clanking of chains – the ships were being emptied of their cargoes by gangs of prisoners, each man staggering bent double under a bag of grain. That was interesting. Hornblower looked again. The chain gangs were under the charge of soldiers – Hornblower could see the shakos and the flash of the musket barrels – which gave him an insight into who the poor devils might be. They were military criminals, deserters, men caught sleeping at their posts, men who had disobeyed an order, all the unfortunates of the armies Bonaparte maintained in every corner of Europe. Their sentences condemned them to 'the galleys' and as the French Navy no longer used galleys in which they could be forced to tug at the oars, they were now employed in all the hard labour of the ports; twice as lieutenant in Pellew's *Indefatigable* Hornblower had seen picked up small parties of desperate men who had escaped from Nantes in much the same fashion as he himself proposed now to do.

And then against the quay below the American ships they saw something else, something which caused them to stiffen in their seats. The tricolour here was hoisted above a tattered blue ensign, flaunting a petty triumph.

'*Witch of Endor*, ten-gun cutter,' said Bush hoarsely. 'A French frigate caught her on a lee shore off Noirmoutier last year. By God, isn't it what you'd expect of the French? It's eleven months ago and they're still wearing French colours over British.'

She was a lovely little ship; even from where they were they could see the perfection of her lines – speed and seaworthiness were written all over her.

'The Frogs don't seem to have over-sparred her the way you'd expect 'em to,' commented Bush.

She was ready for sea, and their expert eyes could estimate the area of the furled mainsail and jib. The high graceful mast nodded to them, almost imperceptibly, as the cutter rocked minutely beside the quay. It was as if a prisoner were appealing to them for aid, and the flapping colours, tricolour over blue ensign, told a tragic story. In a sudden rush of impulse Hornblower put the helm over.

'Lay us alongside the quay,' he said to Brown.

A few strokes took them there; the tide had turned some time ago, and they headed against the flood. Brown caught a ring and made the painter fast, and first Hornblower, nimbly, and then Bush, with difficulty, mounted the stone steps to the top of the quay.

'Suivez-nous,' said Hornblower to Brown, remembering at the last moment to speak French.

Hornblower forced himself to hold up his head and walk with a swagger; the pistols in his side pockets bumped reassuringly against his hips, and his sword tapped against his thigh. Bush walked beside him, his wooden leg thumping with measured stride on the stone quay. A passing group of soldiers saluted the smart uniform, and Hornblower returned the salute nonchalantly, amazed at his new coolness. His heart was beating fast, but ecstatically he knew he was not afraid. It was worth running this risk to experience this feeling of mad bravery.

They stopped and looked at the *Witch of Endor* against the quay. Her decks were not of the dazzling whiteness upon which an English first lieutenant would have insisted, and there was a slovenliness about her standing rigging which was heartbreaking to contemplate. A couple of men were moving lackadaisically about the deck under the supervision of a third.

'Anchor watch,' muttered Bush. 'Two hands and a master's mate.'

He spoke without moving his lips, like a naughty boy in school, lest some onlooker should read his words and realize that he was not speaking French.

'Everyone else on shore, the lubbers,' went on Bush.

Hornblower stood on the quay, the tiny breeze

blowing round his ears, soldiers and sailors and civilians walking by, the bustle of the unloading of the American ships noisy in the distance. Bush's thoughts were following on the heels of his own. Bush was aware of the temptation Hornblower was feeling, to steal the *Witch of Endor* and to sail her to England – Bush would never have thought of it himself, but years of service under his captain made him receptive of ideas, however fantastic.

Fantastic was the right word. Those big cutters carried a crew of sixty men, and the gear and tackle were planned accordingly. Three men – one a cripple – could not even hope to be able to hoist the big mainsail, although it was just possible that the three of them might handle her under sail in the open sea in fair weather. It was that possibility which had given rise to the train of thought, but on the other hand there was all the tricky estuary of the Loire between them and the sea; and the French, Hornblower knew, had removed the buoys and navigation marks for fear of an English raid. Unpiloted they could never hope to find their way through thirty-five miles of shoals without going aground, and besides, there were batteries at Paimboeuf and Saint Nazaire to prohibit unauthorized entrance arid exit. The thing was impossible – it was sheer sentimentality to think of it, he told himself, suddenly self-critical again for a moment.

He turned away and strolled up towards the American ships, and watched with interest the wretched chain gangs staggering along the gang planks with their loads of grain. The sight of their misery sickened him; so did the bullying sergeants who strutted about in charge of them. Here, if anywhere, he told himself, was to be found the nucleus of that rising against Bonaparte which everyone was expecting. All that was needed was a desperate leader – that would be something worth reporting to the Government when he reached home. Farther down the river yet another ship was coming up to the port, her topsails black against the setting sun, as, with the flood behind her, she held her course close hauled to the faint southerly breeze. She was flying the Stars and Stripes – American again. Hornblower experienced the same feeling of exasperated impotence which he had known in the old days of his service under Pellew. What was the use of blockading a coast, and enduring all the hardships and perils of that service, if neutral vessels could sail in and out with impunity? Their cargoes of wheat were officially noncontraband, but wheat was of as vital importance to Bonaparte as ever was hemp, or pitch, or any other item on the contraband list – the more wheat he could import, the more men he could draft into his armies. Hornblower found himself drifting into the eternal debate as to whether America, when eventually she became weary of the indignities of neutrality, would turn her arms against England or France – she had actually been at war with France for a short time already, and it was much to her interest to help pull down the imperial despotism, but it was doubtful whether she would be able to resist the temptation to twist the British lion's tail.

The new arrival, smartly enough handled, was edging in now to the quay. A backed topsail took the way off her, and the warps creaked round the bollards. Hornblower watched idly, Bush and Brown beside him.

As the ship was made fast, a gang plank was thrown to the quay, and a little stout man made ready to walk down it from the ship. He was in civilian clothes, and he had a rosy round face with a ridiculous little black moustache with upturned ends. From his manner of shaking hands with the captain, and from the very broken English which he was speaking, Hornblower guessed him to be the pilot.

The pilot! In that moment a surge of ideas boiled up in Hornblower's mind. It would be dark in less than an hour, with the moon in its first quarter – already he could see it, just visible in the sky high over the setting sun. A clear night, the tide about to ebb, a gentle breeze, southerly with a touch of east. A pilot available on the one hand, a crew on the other. Then he hesitated. The whole scheme was rash to the point of madness – beyond that point. It must be ill-digested, unsound. His mind raced madly through the scheme again, but even as it did so he was carried away by the wave of recklessness. There was an intoxication about throwing caution to the winds which he had forgotten since his boyhood. In the tense seconds which were all he had, while the pilot was descending the gang plank and approaching them along the quay, he had formed his resolution. He nudged his two companions, and then stepped forward and intercepted the fat little pilot as he walked briskly past them.

'Monsieur,' he said. 'I have some questions to ask you. Will you kindly accompany me to my ship for a moment?'

The pilot noted the uniform, the star of the Legion of Honour, the assured manner.

'Why, certainly,' he said. His conscience was clear; he was guilty of no more than venal infringements of the Continental system. He turned and trotted alongside Hornblower. 'You are a newcomer to this port, Colonel, I fancy?'

'I was transferred here yesterday from Amsterdam,' answered Hornblower shortly.

Brown was striding along at the pilot's other elbow; Bush was bringing up the rear, gallantly trying to keep pace with them, his wooden leg thumping the pavement. They came up to the *Witch of Endor*, and made their way up her gang plank to her deck; the officer there looked at them with a little surprise. But he knew the pilot, and he knew the customs uniform.

'I want to examine one of your charts, if you please,' said Hornblower. 'Will you show us the way to the cabin?'

The mate had not a suspicion in the world. He signed to his men to go on with their work and led the way down the brief companion to the after cabin. The mate entered, and politely Hornblower thrust the pilot in next, before him. It was a tiny cabin, but there was sufficient room to be safe when they were at the farther end. He stood by the door and brought out his two pistols.

'If you make a sound,' he said, and excitement rippled his lips into a snarl, 'I will kill you.'

They simply stood and stared at him, but at last the pilot opened his mouth to speak – speech was irrepressible with him.

'Silence!' snapped Hornblower.

He moved far enough into the room to allow Brown and Bush to enter after him.

'Tie 'em up,' he ordered.

Belts and handkerchiefs and scarves did the work efficiently enough; soon the two men were gagged and helpless, their hands tied behind them.

'Under the table with 'em,' said Hornblower. 'Now, be ready for the two hands when I bring 'em down.'

He ran up on deck.

'Here, you two,' he snapped. 'I've some question to ask you. Come down with me.'

They put down their work and followed him meekly, to the cabin where Hornblower's pistols frightened them into silence. Brown ran on deck for a generous supply of line with which to bind them and to make the lashings of the other two more secure yet. Then he and Bush – neither of them had spoken as yet since the adventure began – looked to him for further orders.

'Watch 'em,' said Hornblower. 'I'll be back in five minutes with a crew. There'll be one more man at least to make fast.'

He went up to the quay again, and along to where the gangs of galley slaves were assembling, weary after their day's work of unloading. The ten chained men under the sergeant whom he addressed looked at him with lacklustre eyes, only wondering faintly what fresh misery this spruce colonel was bringing them.

'Sergeant,' he said. 'Bring your party down to my ship. There is work for them there.'

'Yes, Colonel,' said the sergeant.

He rasped an order at the weary men, and they followed Hornblower down the quay. Their bare feet made no sound, but the chain which ran from waist to waist clashed rhythmically with their stride.

'Bring them down on to the deck,' said Hornblower. 'Now come down into the cabin for your orders.'

It was all so easy, thanks to that uniform and star. Hornblower had to try hard not to laugh at the sergeant's bewilderment as they disarmed him and tied him up. It took no more than a significant gesture with Hornblower's pistol to make the sergeant indicate in which pocket was the key of the prisoner's chain.

'I'll have these men laid out under the table, if you please, Mr Bush,' said Hornblower. 'All except the pilot. I want him on deck.'

The sergeant and the mate and the two hands were laid out, none too gently, and Hornblower went out on deck while the others dragged the pilot after him; it was nearly quite dark now, with only the moon shining. The galley slaves were squatting listlessly on the hatch-coaming. Hornblower addressed them quietly. Despite his difficulty with the language, his boiling excitement conveyed itself to them.

'I can set you men free,' he said. 'There will be an end of beatings and slavery if you will do what I order. I am an English officer, and I am going to sail this ship to England. Does anyone not want to come?'

There was a little sigh from the group; it was as if they could not believe they were hearing aright – probably they could not.

'In England,' went on Hornblower, 'you will be rewarded. There will be a new life awaiting you.'

Now at last they were beginning to understand that they had not been brought on board the cutter for further toil, that there really was a chance of freedom.

'Yes, sir,' said a voice.

'I am going to unfasten your chain,' said Hornblower. 'Remember this. There is to be no noise. Sit still until you are told what to do.'

He fumbled for the padlock in the dim light, unlocked it and snapped it open – it was pathetic, the automatic gesture with which the first man lifted his arms. He was accustomed to being locked and unlocked daily, like an animal. Hornblower set free each man in turn, and the chain clanked on the deck; he stood back with his hands on the butts of his pistols ready in case of trouble, but there was no sign of any. The men stood dazed – the transition from slavery to freedom had taken no more than three minutes.

Hornblower felt the movement of the cutter under his feet as the wind swung her; she was bumping gently against the fends-off hung between her and the quay. A glance over the side confirmed his conclusions – the tide had not yet begun to ebb. There were still some minutes to wait, and he turned to Brown, standing restless aft of the mainmast with the pilot sitting miserably at his feet.

'Brown,' he said quietly, 'run down to our boat and bring me my parcel of clothes. Run along now – what are you waiting for?'

Brown went unhappily. It seemed dreadful to him that his captain should waste precious minutes over recovering his clothes, and should even trouble to think of them. But Hornblower was not as mad as he might appear. They could not start until the tide turned, and Brown might as well be employed fetching clothes as standing fidgeting. For once in his life Hornblower had no intention of posing before his subordinates. His head was clear despite his excitement.

'Thank you,' he said, as Brown returned, panting with the canvas bag. 'Get me my uniform coat out.'

He stripped off his colonel's tunic and put on the coat which Brown held for him, experiencing a pleasant thrill as his fingers fastened the buttons with their crown and anchor. The coat was sadly crumpled, and the gold lace bent and broken, but still it was a uniform, even though the last time he had worn it was months ago when they had been capsized in the Loire. With this coat on his back he could no longer be accused of being a spy, and should their attempt result in failure and recapture it would shelter both himself and his subordinates. Failure and recapture were likely possibilities, as his logical brain told him, but secret murder now was not. The stealing of the cutter would attract sufficient public attention to make that impossible. Already he had bettered his position – he could not be shot as a spy nor be quietly strangled in prison. If he were recaptured now he could only be tried on the old charge of violation of the laws of war, and Hornblower felt that his recent exploits might win him sufficient public sympathy to make it impolitic for Bonaparte to press even that charge.

It was time for action now. He took a belaying pin from the rail, and walked up slowly to the seated pilot, weighing the instrument meditatively in his hand.

'Monsieur,' he said, 'I want you to pilot this ship out to sea.'

The pilot goggled up at him in the faint moonlight.

'I cannot,' he gabbled. 'My professional honour – my duty –'

Hornblower cut him short with a menacing gesture of the belaying pin.

'We are going to start now,' he said. 'You can give instructions or not, as you choose. But I tell you this, monsieur. The moment this ship touches ground, I will beat your head into a paste with this.'

Hornblower eyed the white face of the pilot – his moustache was lopsided and ridiculous now after his rough treatment. The man's eyes were on the belaying pin with which Hornblower was tapping the palm of his hand, and Hornblower felt a little thrill of triumph. The threat of a pistol bullet through the head would not have been sufficient for this imaginative southerner. But the man could picture so clearly the crash of the belaying pin upon his skull, and the savage blows which would beat him to death, that the argument Hornblower had selected was the most effective one.

'Yes, monsieur,' said the pilot, weakly.

'Right,' said Hornblower. 'Brown, lash him to the rail, there. Then we can start. Mr Bush, will you take the tiller, if you please?'

The necessary preparations were brief; the convicts were led to the halliards and the ropes put in their hands, ready to haul on the word of command. Hornblower and Brown had so often before had experience in pushing raw crews into their places, thanks to the all-embracing activities of the British press-gangs, and it was good to see that Brown's French, eked out by the force of his example, was sufficient for the occasion.

'Cut the warps, sir?' volunteered Brown.

'No. Cast them off,' snapped Hornblower.

Cut warps left hanging to the bollards would be a sure proof of a hurried and probably illegal departure; to cast them off meant possibly delaying inquiry and pursuit by a few more minutes, and every minute of delay might be precious in the uncertain future. The first of the ebb was tightening the ropes now, simplifying the business of getting away from the quay. To handle the tiny fore-and-aft rigged ship was an operation calling for little either of the judgement or of the brute strength which a big square rigger would demand, and the present circumstances – the wind off the quay and the ebbing tide – made the only precaution necessary that of casting off the stern warp before the bow, as Brown understood as clearly as Hornblower. It happened in the natural course of events, for Hornblower had to fumble in the dim light to disentangle the clove hitches with which some French sailor had made fast, and Brown had completed his share long before him. The push of the tide was swinging the cutter away from the quay. Hornblower, in the uncertain light, had to time his moment for setting sail, making allowance for the unreliability of his crew, the eddy along the quayside, the tide and the wind.

'Hoist away,' said Hornblower, and then, to the men, 'Tirez'.

Mainsail and jib rose, to the accompaniment of the creaking of the blocks. The sails flapped, bellied, flapped again. Then they filled, and Bush at the tiller – the cutter steered with a tiller, not a wheel – felt a steady pressure. The cutter was gathering way; she was changing from a dead thing to a live. She heeled the tiniest fraction to the breeze with a subdued creaking of her cordage, and simultaneously Hornblower heard a little musical chuckle from the bows as her forefoot bubbled through the water. He picked up the belaying pin again, and in three strides was at the pilot's side, balancing the instrument in his hand.

'To the right, monsieur,' gabbled the individual. 'Keep well to the right.'

'Port your helm, Mr Bush. We're taking the starboard channel,' said Hornblower, and then, translating the further hurried instructions of the pilot. 'Meet her! Keep her at that!'

The cutter glided on down the river in the faint moonlight. From the bank of the river she must make a pretty picture – no one would guess that she was not setting forth on some quite legitimate expedition.

The pilot was saying something else now; Hornblower bent his ear to listen. It had regard to the advisability of having a man at work with the lead taking soundings, and Hornblower would not consider it for a moment. There were only Brown and himself who could do that, and they both might be wanted at any moment in case it should be necessary for the cutter to go about – moreover, there would be bound to be a muddle about fathoms and metres.

'No,' said Hornblower. 'You will have to do your work without that. And my promise still holds good.'

He tapped his palm with the belaying pin, and laughed. That laugh surprised him, it was so bloodcurdling in its implications. Anyone hearing it would be quite sure that Hornblower was determined upon clubbing the pilot to death if they went aground. Hornblower asked himself if he were acting and was puzzled to discover that he could not answer the question. He could not picture himself killing a helpless man – and yet he could not be sure. This fierce, relentless determination that consumed him was something new to him, just as it always was. He was aware of the fact that once he had set his hand to a scheme he never allowed any consideration to stop his carrying it through, but he always looked upon himself as fatalistic or resigned. It was always startling to detect in himself qualities which he admired in other men. But it was sufficient, and satisfactory, for the moment, to know that the pilot was quite sure that he would be killed in an unpleasant fashion if the cutter should touch ground.

Within half a mile it was necessary to cross to the other side – it was amusing to note how this vast estuary repeated on a grand scale the characteristics of the upper river, where the clear channel serpentined from shore to shore between the sandbanks. At the pilot's warning Hornblower got his motley crew together in case it might be necessary to go about, but the precaution was needless. Closehauled, and with the tide running fast behind her, the cutter glided across, Hornblower and Brown at the sheets, and Bush at the tiller demonstrating once more what an accomplished seaman he was. They steadied her with the wind again over her quarter, Hornblower anxiously testing the direction of the wind and looking up at the ghostly sails.

'Monsieur,' pleaded the pilot. 'Monsieur, these cords are tight.'

Hornblower laughed again, horribly.

'They will serve to keep you awake, then,' he said.

His instinct had dictated the reply; his reason confirmed it. It would be best to show no hint of weakness towards this man who had it in his power to wreck everything – the more firmly the pilot was convinced of his captor's utter pitilessness the less chance there was of his playing them false. Better that he should endure the pain of tight ligatures than that three men should risk imprisonment and death. And suddenly Hornblower remembered the four other men – the sergeant and the mate and the two hands – who lay gagged and bound in the cabin. They must be highly uncomfortable, and probably fairly near to suffocation. It could not be helped. No one could be spared for a moment from the deck to go below and attend them. There they must lie until there was no hope of rescue for them.

He found himself feeling sorry for them, and put the feeling aside. Naval history teemed with stories of recaptured prizes, in which the prisoners had succeeded in overpowering weak prize crews. He was going to run no risk of that. It was interesting to note how his mouth set itself hard at the thought without his own volition; and it was equally interesting to observe how his reluctance to go home and face the music reacted contrariwise upon his resolution to see this affair through. He did not want to fail, and the thought that he might be glad of failure because of the postponement of the settlement of his affairs only made him more set in his determination not to fail.

'I will loosen the cords,' he said to the pilot, 'when we are off Noirmoutier. Not before.'

14

They were off Noirmoutier at dawn, with the last dying puff of wind. The grey light found them becalmed and enwreathed in a light haze which drifted in patches over the calm surface of the sea, awaiting the rising of the sun to dissipate it. Hornblower looked round him as the details became more clear. The galley slaves were all asleep on the foredeck, huddled together for warmth like pigs in a sty, with Brown squatting on the hatch beside them, his chin on his hand. Bush still stood at the tiller, betraying no fatigue after his sleepless night; he held the tiller against his hip with his wooden leg braced against a ring bolt. Against the rail the pilot drooped in his bonds; his face which yesterday had been plump and pink was this morning drawn and grey with pain and fatigue.

With a little shudder of disgust Hornblower cut him loose.

'I keep my promise, you see,' he said, but the pilot only dropped to the deck, his face distorted with pain, and a minute later he was groaning with the agony of returning circulation.

The big mainsail boom came inboard with a clatter as the sail flapped.

'I can't hold the course, sir,' said Bush.

'Very well,' said Hornblower.

He might have expected this. The gentle night wind

which had wafted them down the estuary was just the sort to die away with the dawn, leaving them becalmed. But had it held for another half hour, had they made another couple of miles of progress, they would be far safer. There lay Noirmoutier to port, and the mainland astern; through the shredding mist he could make out the gaunt outlines of the semaphore station on the mainland – sixteen years ago he had been second in command of the landing party which Pellew had sent ashore to destroy it. The islands were all heavily garrisoned now, with big guns mounted, as a consequence of the incessant English raids. He scanned the distance which separated them from Noirmoutier, measuring it with his eye – they were out of big gun range, he fancied, but the tide might easily drift them in closer. He even suspected, from what he remembered of the set of the tides, that there was danger of their being drifted into the Bay of Bourgneuf.

'Brown,' he called, sharply. 'Wake those men up. Set them to work with the sweeps.'

On either side of every gun was a thole for a sweep, six on each side of the ship; Brown shoved his bleary-eyed crew into their positions and showed them how to get out the big oars, with the long rope joining the looms.

'One, two, three, pull!' shouted Brown.

The men put their weight on the oars; the blades bubbled ineffectively through the still water.

'One, two, three, pull! One, two, three, pull!'

Brown was all animation, gesticulating, running from man to man beating time with his whole body. Gradually the cutter gathered way, and as she began to move the oar blades began to bite upon the water with more effect.

'One, two, three, pull!'

It did not matter that Brown was counting time in English, for there was no mistaking his meaning, nor the meaning of the convulsive movements of his big body.

'Pull!'

The galley slaves sought for foothold on the deck as they tugged; Brown's enthusiasm was infectious, so that one or two of them even raised their voices in a cracked cheer as they leaned back. Now the cutter was perceptibly moving; Bush swung the tiller over, felt the rudder bite, and steadied her on her course again. She rose and fell over the tiny swell with a clattering of blocks.

Hornblower looked away from the straining men over the oily sea. If he had been lucky he might have found one of the ships of the blockading squadron close inshore – often they would come right in among the islands to beard Bonaparte. But today there was no sail in sight. He studied the grim outlines of the island for signs of life. Even as he looked the gallows-like arms of the semaphore station on the mainland sprang up to attention. They made no further movement, and Hornblower guessed that they were merely announcing the operators' readiness to receive a message from the station further inshore invisible to him – he could guess the purport of the message. Then the arms started signalling, moving jerkily against the blue sky, transmitting a brief reply to the interior. Another period of quiescence, and then Hornblower saw the signal arms swing round towards him – previously they had been nearly in profile. Automatically he turned towards Noirmoutier, and he saw the tiny speck of the flag at the masthead there dip in acknowledgement. Noirmoutier was ready to receive orders from the land. Round and round spun the arms of the semaphore; up and down went the flag in acknowledgement of each sentence.

Near the foot of the mast appeared a long jet of white smoke, rounding off instantly into a ball, and one after the other four fountains of water leaped from the glassy surface of the sea as a shot skipped over it, the dull report following after. The nearest fountain was a full half mile away, so that they were comfortably out of range.

'Make those men pull!' roared Hornblower to Brown.

He could guess what would be the next move. Under her sweeps the cutter was making less than a mile in the hour, and all day long they would be in danger, unless a breeze came, and his straining eye could see no hint of a breeze on the calm surface of the sea, nor in the vivid blue of the morning sky. At any moment boats crowded with men would be putting off towards them – boats whose oars would move them far faster than the cutter's sweeps. There would be fifty men in each, perhaps a gun mounted in the bows as well. Three men with the doubtful aid of a dozen galley slaves could not hope to oppose them.

'Yes I can, by God,' said Hornblower to himself.

As he sprang into action he could see the boats heading out from the tip of the island, tiny dots upon the surface of the sea. The garrison must have turned out and bundled into the boats immediately on receiving the order from the land.

'Pull!' shouted Brown.

The sweeps groaned on the tholes, and the cutter lurched under the impulse.

Hornblower had cleared away the aftermost six-pounder on the port side. There was shot in the locker under the rail, but no powder.

'Keep the men at work, Brown,' he said, 'and watch the pilot.'

'Aye aye, sir,' said Brown.

He stretched out a vast hand and took hold of the pilot's collar, while Hornblower dived into the cabin. One of the four prisoners there had writhed and wriggled his way to the foot of the little companion – Hornblower trod on him in his haste. With a curse he dragged him out of the way; as he expected there was a hatchway down into the lazarette. Hornblower jerked it open and plunged through; it was nearly dark, for the only light was what filtered through the cabin skylight and down the hatchway, and he stumbled and blundered upon the piled-up stores inside. He steadied himself; whatever the need for haste there was no profit in panic. He waited for his eyes to grow accustomed to the darkness, while overhead he could hear Brown still bellowing and the sweeps still groaning on the tholes. Then in the bulkhead before him he saw what he sought, a low doorway with a glass panel, which must indicate the magazine – the gunner would work in there by the light of a lantern shining through.

He heaved the piled-up stores out of his way, sweating in his haste and the heat, and wrenched open the door. Feeling about him in the tiny space, crouching nearly double, his hands fell upon four big hogsheads of gunpowder. He fancied he could feel the grittiness of gunpowder under his feet; any movement on his part might start a spark and blow the cutter to fragments – it was just like the French to be careless with explosives. He sighed with relief when his fingers encountered the paper – containers of ready charges. He had hoped to find them, but there had always been the chance that there were no cartridges available, and he had not been enamoured of the prospect of using a powder-ladle. He loaded himself with cartridges and backed out of the tiny magazine to the cabin, and sprang up on deck again, to the clear sunshine.

The boats were appreciably nearer, for they were no longer black specks but boats, creeping beetle-like over the surface towards them, three of them, already spaced out in their race to effect a recapture. Hornblower put down his cartridges upon the deck. His heart was pounding with his exertions and with excitement, and each successive effort that he made to steady himself seemed to grow less successful. It was one thing to think and plan and direct, to say 'Do this' or 'Go there', and it was quite another to have success dependent upon the cunning of his own fingers and the straightness of his own eye.

His sensations were rather similar to those he experienced when he had drunk a glass of wine too many – he knew clearly enough what he had to do, but his limbs were not quite as ready as usual to obey the orders of his brain. He fumbled more than once as he rigged the train-tackle of the gun.

That fumbling cured him; he rose from the task shaking his unsteadiness from him like Christian losing his burden of sin. He was cool now, set completely on the task in hand.

'Here, you,' he said to the pilot.

The pilot demurred for a moment, full of fine phrases regarding the impossibility of training a gun upon his fellow countrymen, but a sight of the alteration in Hornblower's expression reduced him to instant humble submission. Hornblower was unaware of the relentless ferocity of his glance, being only conscious of a momentary irritation at anyone crossing his will. But the pilot had thought that any further delay would lead to Hornblower's killing him, pitilessly – and the pilot may have been right. Between them they laid hold of the train-tackle and ran the gun back. Hornblower took out the tampion and went round to the breech; he twirled the elevating screw until his eye told him that the gun was at the maximum elevation at which it could be run out. He cocked the lock, and then, crouching over the gun so that the shadow of his body cut off the sunlight, jerked the lanyard. The spark was satisfactory.

He ripped open a cartridge, poured the powder into the muzzle of the gun, folded the paper into a wad, and rammed the charge home with the flexible rammer. A glance towards the boats showed that they were still probably out of range, so that he was not pressed for time. He devoted a few seconds to turning over the shot in the locker, selecting two or three of the roundest, and then strolled across the deck to the starboard side locker and made a selection from there. For long range work with a six-pounder he did not want shot that bounced about during its passage up the gun and was liable to fly off God-knew-where when it emerged. He rammed his eventual selection well down upon the wad – at this elevation there was no need for a second wad – and, ripping open a second cartridge, he primed the breach.

'Allons!' he snapped at the pilot, and then ran the gun up. Two men were the barest minimum crew for a six-pounder, but Hornblower's long slight body was capable of exerting extraordinary strength at the behest of his mind.

With a handspike he trained the gun round aft as far as possible. Even so, the gun did not point towards the leading boat, which lay far abaft the beam; the cutter would have to yaw to fire at her. Hornblower straightened himself up in the sunlight. Brown was chanting hoarsely at the galley slaves almost in his ear, and the aftermost sweep had been working right at his elbow, and he had not noticed either, so intent had he been on his task. For the cutter to yaw meant losing a certain amount of distance; he had to balance that certain loss against the chances of hitting a boat with a six-pounder ball at two thousand yards. It would not pay at present; it would be better to wait a little, for the range to shorten, but it was an interesting problem, even though it could have no exact solution in consequence of the presence of an unknown, which was the possibility of the coming of a wind.

Of that there was still no sign, long and anxiously though Hornblower stared over the glassy sea. As he looked round he caught the eye of Bush at the tiller directed anxiously at him – Bush was awaiting the order to yaw. Hornblower smiled at him and shook his head, resuming his study of the horizon, the distant islands, the unbroken expanse to seaward where lay freedom. A seagull was wheeling overhead, dazzling white against the blue, and crying plaintively. The cutter was nodding a little in the faint swell.

'Beggin' your pardon, sir,' said Brown in his ear. 'Beggin' your pardon, sir – Pull! – These men can't go on much longer, sir. Look at that one over there on the starboard side, sir – Pull!'

There could be no doubt of it; the men were swaying with fatigue as they reached forward with the long sweeps. Dangling from Brown's hand was a length of knotted cord; clearly he had already been using the most obvious argument to persuade them to work.

'Give 'em a bit of a rest, sir, and summat to eat an' drink, an' they'll go on all right, sir. Pull, you bastards! They haven't had no breakfast, sir, nor no supper yesterday.'

'Very good,' said Hornblower. 'You can rest 'em and get 'em fed. Mr Bush! Let her come slowly round.'

He bent over the gun, oblivious at once to the clatter of the released sweeps as the galley slaves ceased work, just as he was oblivious that he himself had not eaten or drunk or slept since yesterday. At the touch of the tiller and with her residual way the cutter turned slowly. The black mass of a boat appeared in the V of the dispart sight, and he waved his hand to Bush. The boat had disappeared again, and came back into his field of vision as Bush checked the turn with the tiller, but not quite in alignment with the gun. Hornblower eased the gun round with the handspike until the aim was true, drew himself up, and stepped out of the way of the recoil, lanyard in hand. Of necessity, he was far more doubtful of the range than of the direction, and it was vital to observe the fall of the shot. He took note of the motion of the cutter on the swell, waited for the climax of the roll, and jerked the lanyard. The gun roared out and recoiled past him; he sprang sideways to get clear of the smoke. The four seconds of the flight of the shot seemed to stretch out indefinitely, and then at last he saw the jet of water leap into brief existence, fully two hundred yards short and a hundred yards to the right. That was poor shooting.

He sponged out the gun and reloaded it, called the pilot to him with an abrupt gesture, and ran the gun out again. It was necessary, he realized, to get acquainted with the weapon if he wanted to do any fancy shooting with it, so that he made no alteration in elevation, endeavoured to lay the gun exactly as before, and jerked the lanyard at as nearly the same instant of the roll as possible. This time it appeared that the elevation was correct, for the shot pitched well up to the boat, but it was out to the right again, fifty yards off at least. It seemed likely that the gun, therefore, had a tendency to throw to the right. He trained the gun round a trifle to the left, and, still without altering the elevation, fired again. Too far to the left, and two hundred yards short again.

Hornblower told himself that a variation of two hundred yards in the fall of shot from a six-pounder at full elevation was only to be expected, and he knew it to be true, but that was cold comfort to him. The powder varied from charge to charge, the shot were never truly round, quite apart from the variations in atmospheric conditions and in the temperature of the gun. He set his teeth, aimed and fired again. Short, and a trifle to the left. It was maddening.

'Breakfast, sir,' said Brown at his elbow.

Hornblower turned abruptly, and there was Brown with a tray, bearing a basin of biscuit, a bottle of wine, a jug of water, a pewter mug; the sight made Hornblower realize that he was intensely hungry and thirsty.

'What about you?' asked Hornblower.

'We're all right, sir,' said Brown.

The galley slaves were squatting on the deck wolfing bread and drinking water; so was Bush, over by the tiller. Hornblower discovered that his tongue and the roof of his mouth were dry as leather – his hands shook as he mixed water with wine and gulped it down. Beside the cabin skylight lay the four men who had been left in bonds in the cabin. Their hands were free now, although their feet were still bound. The sergeant and one of the seamen were noticeably pale.

'I took the liberty of bringing 'em up, sir,' said Brown. 'Those two was pretty nigh dead, 'cause o' their gags, sir. But they'll be all right soon, I fancy, sir.'

It had been thoughtless cruelty to leave them bound, thought Hornblower. But going back in his mind through the events of the night he could not think of any time until now when any attention could have been spared for them. In war there was always plenty of cruelty.

'These beggars,' said Brown, indicating the galley slaves, 'wanted to throw the sojer overboard when they saw 'im, sir.'

He grinned widely, as though that were very amusing. The remark opened a long vista of thought, regarding the miseries of the life of a galley slave and the brutalities of their guards.

'Yes,' said Hornblower, gulping down a morsel of biscuit and drinking again. 'You had better set 'em all to work at the sweeps.'

'Aye aye, sir. I had the same idea, beggin' your pardon, sir. We can have two watches with all these men.'

'Arrange it as you like,' said Hornblower, turning back to the gun.

The nearest boat was appreciably nearer now; Hornblower judged it advisable to make a small reduction in the elevation, and this time the shot pitched close to the boat, almost among the oars on one side, apparently.

'Beautiful, sir!' said Bush beside the tiller.

Hornblower's skin was prickling with sweat and powder smoke. He took off his gold laced coat, suddenly conscious of the heavy weight of the pistols in the side pockets; he proffered them to Bush, but the latter shook his head and grinned, pointing to the bell-mouthed blunderbuss on the deck beside him. That would be a far more efficacious weapon if there was trouble with their motley crew. For an exasperated moment Hornblower wondered what to do with the pistols, and finally laid them handy in the scuppers before sponging out and reloading the gun. The next shot was a close one, too – apparently the small reduction of range had had a profound effect on the accuracy of the gun. Hornblower saw the shot pitch close to the bows of the boat; it would be a matter of pure chance at that range if he scored an actual hit, for no gun could be expected to be accurate to fifty yards.

'Sweeps are ready, sir,' said Brown.

'Very good. Mr Bush, kindly lay a course so that I can keep that boat under fire.'

Brown was a pillar of strength. He had had rigged only the three foremost sweeps on each side, setting six men to work on them. The others were herded together forward, ready to relieve the men at work when they were tired – six sweeps would only just give the big cutter steerage way, but continuous slow progress was preferable to an alternation of movement and passivity. What arguments he had used to persuade the four Frenchmen who were not galley slaves to work at the sweeps Hornblower judged it best not to inquire – it was sufficient that they were there, their feet hobbled, straining away at the sweeps while Brown gave them the time, his knotted rope's end dangling from his fist.

The cutter began to creep through the blue water again, the rigging rattling at each tug on the sweeps. To make the chase as long as possible she should have turned her stern to her pursuers, instead of keeping them on her quarter. But Hornblower had decided that the chance of scoring a hit with the gun was worth the loss in distance – a decision of whose boldness he was painfully aware and which he had to justify. He bent over the gun and aimed carefully, and this time the shot flew wide again. Watching the splash from the rail Hornblower felt a surge of exasperation. For a moment he was tempted to hand the gun over to Bush, for him to try his hand, but he put the temptation aside. In the face of stark reality, without allowing false modesty to enter into the debate, he could rely on himself to lay a gun better than Bush could.

'Tirez!' he snapped at the pilot, and between them they ran the gun up again.

The pursuing boats, creeping black over the blue sea, had shown no sign so far of being dismayed by the bombardment to which they were being subjected. Their oars kept steadily at work, and they maintained resolutely a course which would cut the *Witch of Endor*'s a mile or so further on. They were big boats, all three of them, carrying at least a hundred and fifty men between them – only one of them need range alongside to do the business. Hornblower fired again and then again, doggedly, fighting down the bitter disappointment at each successive miss. The range was little over a thousand yards now, he judged – what he would call in an official report 'long cannon shot'. He hated those black boats creeping onward, immune, threatening his life and liberty, just as he hated this cranky gun which would not shoot the same two rounds running. The sweat was making his shirt stick to him, and the powder-grains were irritating his skin.

At the next shot there was no splash; Hornblower could see no sign of its fall anywhere. Then he saw the leading boat swing half round, and her oars stop moving.

'You've hit her, sir,' called Bush.

Next moment the boat straightened on her course again, her oars hard at work. That was disappointing – it had hardly been likely that a ship's long boat could survive a direct hit from a six-pounder ball without injury to her fighting ability, but it was possible, all the same. Hornblower felt for the first time a sense of impending failure. If the hit he had scored with such difficulty was of no avail, what was the sense in continuing the struggle? Then, doggedly, he bent over the gun again, staring along the sights to allow for the small amount of right hand bias which the gun exhibited. Even as he looked he saw the leading boat cease rowing again. She wavered and then swung round, signalling wildly to the other boats. Hornblower trained the gun round upon her and fired again and missed, but he could see that she was perceptibly lower in the water. The other boats drew up alongside her, evidently to transfer her crew.

'Port a point, Mr Bush!' yelled Hornblower – already the group of boats was out of the field of fire of the gun, and yet was far too tempting a mark to ignore. The French pilot groaned as he helped to run the gun up, but Hornblower had no time for his patriotic protests. He sighted carefully, and fired. Again there was no sign of a splash – the ball had taken effect, but presumably upon the boat which had already been hit, for immediately afterwards the other two drew away from their waterlogged fellow to resume the pursuit.

Brown was changing over the men at the sweeps – Hornblower remembered now that he had heard him cheering hoarsely when he had scored his hit – and Hornblower found a second in which to admire his masterful handling of the men, prisoners of war and escaping slaves alike. There was time for admiration, but no time for envy. The pursuers were changing their tactics – one boat was heading straight at them, while the other, diverging a little, was still heading to intercept them. The reason was soon obvious, for from the bows of the former boat came a puff of smoke, and a cannon-ball raised a splash from the surface of the water on the cutter's quarter and skipped past the stern.

Hornblower shrugged his shoulders at that – a three-pounder boat gun, fired from a platform far more unsteady even than the *Witch of Endor*, could hardly do them any harm at that range, and every shot meant delay in the pursuit. He trained his gun round upon the intercepting boat, fired, and missed. He was already taking aim again before the sound of the second shot from the boat gun reached his ears, and he did not trouble to find out where the ball went. His own shot fell close to its target, for the range was shortening and he was growing more experienced with the gun and more imbued with the rhythm of the long Atlantic swell which rocked the *Witch of Endor*. Three times he dropped a shot so close to the boat that the men at the oars must have been wetted by the splashes – each shot deserved to be a hit, he knew, but the incalculable residuum of variables in powder and ball and gun made it a matter of chance just where the ball fell in a circle of fifty yards, radius, however well aimed. Ten guns properly controlled, and fired together in a broadside, would do the business, but there was no chance of firing ten guns together.

There was a crash from forward, a fountain of splinters from the base of a stanchion, and a shot scarred the deck diagonally close beside the fore hatchway.

'No you don't,' roared Brown, leaping forward with his rope's end. 'Keep pulling, you bastard!'

He jerked the scared galley slave who had dropped his sweep – the shot must have missed him by no more than a yard – back into position.

'Pull!' he shouted, standing, magnificent in his superb physique, right in the midst of them, the weary ones lying on the deck, the others sweating at the sweeps, the knotted rope swinging from his hand. He was like a lion tamer in a cage. Hornblower could see there was no need for him and his pistols, and he bent again, this time with a real twinge of envy, over his gun.

The boat which was firing at them had not closed in at all – if anything she had fallen a trifle back – but the other one was far nearer by now. Hornblower could see the individual men in her, the dark heads and the brown shoulders. Her oars were still for the moment, and there was some movement in her, as if they were rearranging the men at the oars. Now she was in motion again, and moving far faster, and heading straight at them. The officer in charge, having worked up as close as this, had double-banked his oars so as to cover the last, most dangerous zone with a rush, pouring out the carefully conserved energy of his men prodigally in his haste to come alongside.

Hornblower estimated the rapidly diminishing range, twirled the elevating screw, and fired. The shot hit the water ten yards from her bows and must have ricochetted clean over her. He sponged and loaded and rammed – a miss-fire now, he told himself, would be fatal, and he forced himself to go through the routine with all the exactness he had employed before. The sights of the gun were looking straight at the bows of the boat, it was point blank range. He jerked the lanyard and sprang instantly to reload without wasting time by seeing where the shot went. It must have passed close over the heads of the men at the oars, for when he looked along the sights again there she was, still heading straight at him. A tiny reduction in elevation, and he stepped aside and jerked the lanyard. He was dragging at the train tackles before he could look again. The bows of the boat had opened like a fan. In the air above her there was a black dot – a water breaker, presumably, sent flying like a football by the impact of the shot, which had hit clean and square upon her stem at water level. Her bows were lifted a little out of the water, the loose stakes spread wide, and then they came down again and the water surged in, and she was gunwale deep in a flash, her bottom smashed, presumably, as well as her bows, by the passage of the shot.

Brown was cheering again, and Bush was capering as well as he could with a wooden leg while steering, and the little French pilot at his side pulling in his breath with a sharp hissing noise. There were black dots on the surface of the blue water where men struggled for their lives – it must be bitter cold and they would die quickly, those who could not find support on the shattered hull, but nothing could be done to help them. Already they had more prisoners than they could conveniently handle, and any delay would bring the other boat alongside them.

'Keep the men at work!' said Hornblower, harshly, to Brown, and unnecessarily. Then he bent to reload the gun once more.

'What course, sir?' asked Bush, from the tiller. He wanted to know if he should steer so as to allow fire to be opened on the third boat, which had ceased firing now and was pulling hastily towards the wreck.

'Keep her as she is,' snapped Hornblower. He knew

perfectly well that the boat would not annoy them further; having seen two of her fellows sunk and being of necessity vastly overcrowded she would turn back sooner than maintain the contest. And so it proved. After the boat had picked up the survivors they saw her swing round and head towards Noirmoutier, followed by a derisive cheer from Brown.

Hornblower could look round him now. He walked aft to the taffrail beside Bush – it was curious how much more natural it felt to be there than at the gun – and scanned the horizon. During the fight the cutter had made very decided progress under her sweeps. The mainland was lost in the faint haze; Noirmoutier was already far behind. But there was still no sign of a breeze. They were still in danger – if darkness should find them where boats could reach them from the islands a night attack would tell a very different story. They needed every yard they could gain, and the men must go on slaving at the sweeps all through the day, all through the night too, if necessary.

He was conscious now that he ached in every joint after the frantic exertions of serving the gun the whole morning, and he had had a whole night without sleep – so had Bush, so had Brown. He felt that he stank of sweat and smoke, and his skin tingled with powder grains. He wanted rest, yet automatically he walked over to make the gun secure again, to put the unused cartridges out of harm's way, and to repocket the pistols which he noticed reproaching his carelessness from the scuppers.

15

At midnight, and not before, a tiny breeze came whispering over the misty surface of the water, at first merely swinging over the big mainsail and setting the rigging chattering, but then breathing more strongly until the sails could catch it and hold it, filling out in the darkness until Hornblower could give the word for the exhausted men at the sweeps to abandon their labour and the cutter could glide on with almost imperceptible motion, so slowly that there was hardly a bubble at her bows, yet even at that faster than the sweeps had moved her. Out of the east came that breath of wind, steady even though feeble; Hornblower could feel hardly any pull as he handled the mainsheet, and yet the cutter's big area of canvas was able to carry her graceful hull forward over the invisible surface as though in a dream.

It was like a dream indeed – weariness and lack of sleep combined to make it so for Hornblower, who moved about his tasks in a misty unreality which matched the misty darkness of the sea. The galley slaves and prisoners could lie and sleep – there was no fear of trouble from them at present, when they had spent ten hours out of the last twenty pulling at the sweeps with hands which by nightfall were running with blood, but there was no sleep for him nor for Bush and Brown. His voice sounded strange and distant in his own ears, like that of a stranger speaking from another room, as he issued his orders; the very hands with which he held the ropes seemed not to belong to him. It was as if there was a cleavage between the brain with which he was trying to think and the body which condescended to obey him.

Somewhere to the northwest lay the fleet which maintained its unsleeping watch over Brest; he had laid the cutter on a northwesterly course with the wind comfortably on her quarter, and if he could not find the Channel fleet he would round Ushant and sail the cutter to England. He knew all this – it made it more like a dream than ever that he could not believe it although he knew it. The memory of Marie de Graçay's upper boudoir, or of his battle for life in the flood-water of the Loire, was far more real to him than this solid little ship whose deck he trod and whose mainsheet he was handling. Setting a course for Bush to steer was like playing a make-believe game with a child. He told himself desperately that this was not a new phenomenon, that often enough before he had noticed that although he could dispense with one night's sleep without missing it greatly, on the second in succession his imagination began to play tricks with him, but it did not help to clear his mind.

He came back to Bush at the tiller, when the faint binnacle light made the lieutenant's face just visible in the darkness; Hornblower was even prepared to enter into conversation in exchange for a grasp at reality.

'Tired, Mr Bush?' he asked.

'No, sir. Of course not. But how is it with you, sir?'

Bush had served with his captain through too many fights to have an exaggerated idea of his strength.

'Well enough, thank you.'

'If this breeze holds, sir,' said Bush, realizing that this was one of the rare occasions when he was expected to make small talk with his captain, 'we'll be up to the fleet in the morning.'

'I hope so,' said Hornblower.

'By God, sir,' said Bush, 'what will they say of this in England?'

Bush's expression was rapt. He was dreaming of fame, of promotion, for his captain as much as for himself.

'In England?' said Hornblower vaguely.

He had been too busy to dream any dreams himself, to think about what the British public, sentimental as always, would think of an escaping British captain retaking almost single-handed a captured ship of war and returning in her in triumph. And he had seized the *Witch of Endor* in the first place merely because the opportunity had presented itself, and because it was the most damaging blow he could deal the enemy; since the seizure he had been at first too busy, and latterly too tired, to appreciate the dramatic quality of his action. His distrust of himself, and his perennial pessimism regarding his career, would not allow him to think of himself as dramatically successful. The unimaginative Bush could appreciate the potentialities better than he could.

'Yes, sir,' said Bush, eagerly – even with tiller and compass and wind claiming so much of his attention he could be loquacious at this point – 'It'll look fine in the *Gazette*, this recapture of the *Witch*. Even the *Morning Chronicle*, sir –'

The *Morning Chronicle* was a thorn in the side of the government, ever ready to decry a victory or make capital of a defeat. Hornblower remembered how during the bitter early days of his captivity at Rosas he had worried about what the *Morning Chronicle* would say regarding his surrender of the *Sutherland*.

He felt sick now, suddenly. His mind was active enough now. Most of its vagueness must have been due, he told himself, because he had been refusing in cowardly fashion to contemplate the future. Until this night everything had been uncertain – he might have been recaptured at any moment, but now, as sure as anything could be at sea, he would see England again. He would have to stand his trial for the loss of the *Sutherland*, and face a court martial, after eighteen years of service. The court might find him guilty of not having done his utmost in the presence of the enemy, and for that there was only one penalty, death – that Article of War did not end, as others did, with the mitigating words 'or such less penalty –'. Byng had been shot fifty years before under that Article of War.

Absolved on that account, the wisdom of his actions in command of the *Sutherland* might still be called into question. He might be found guilty of errors of judgement in hazarding his ship in a battle against quadruple odds, and be punished by anything from dismissal from the service, which would make him an outcast and a beggar, down to a simple reprimand which would merely wreck his career. A court martial was always a hazardous ordeal from which few emerged unscathed – Cochrane, Sydney Smith, half a dozen brilliant captains had suffered damage at the hands of a court martial, and the friendless Captain Hornblower might be the next.

And a court martial was only one of the ordeals that awaited him. The child must be three months old now; until this moment he had never been able to think clearly about the child – boy or girl, healthy or feeble. He was torn with anxiety for Maria – and yet, gulping at the pill of reality, he forced himself to admit that he did not want to go back to Maria. He did not want to. It had been in mad jealousy of the moment, when he heard of Lady Barbara's marriage to Admiral Leighton, that the child had been conceived. Maria in England, Marie in France – his conscience was in a turmoil about both of them, and underlying the turmoil was an unregenerate hunger for Lady Barbara which had remained quiescent during his preoccupation but which he knew would grow into an unrelenting ache, an internal cancer, the moment his other troubles ceased, if ever they did.

Bush was still babbling away happily beside him at the tiller. Hornblower heard the words, and attached no meaning to them.

'Ha – h'm,' he said. 'Quite so.'

He could find no satisfaction in the simple pleasures Bush had been in ecstasy about – the breath of the sea, the feeling of a ship's deck underfoot – not now, not with all these bitter thoughts thronging his mind. The harshness of his tone checked Bush in the full career of his artless and unwonted chatter, and the lieutenant pulled himself up abruptly. Hornblower thought it was absurd that Bush should still cherish any affection for him after the cutting cruelty with which he sometimes used him. Bush was like a dog, thought Hornblower bitterly – too cynical for the moment to credit Bush with any perspicacity at all – like a dog, coming fawning to the hand that beat him. Hornblower despised himself as he walked forward again to the mainsheet, to a long, long, period of a solitary black hell of his own.

There was just the faintest beginning of daylight, the barest pearly softening of the sombreness of night, a greyness instead of a blackness in the haze, when Brown came aft to Hornblower.

'Beggin' your pardon, sir, but I fancy I see the loom of something out there just now. On the port bow, sir – there, d'you see it, sir?'

Hornblower strained his eyes through the darkness. Perhaps there was a more solid nucleus to the black mist out there, a tiny something. It came and went as his eyes grew tired.

'What d'you make of it, Brown?'

'I thought it was a ship, sir, when I first saw it, but in this haze, sir –'

There was a faint chance she might be a French ship of war – it was about as likely as to find the king unguarded when leading from a suit of four to an ace. Much the most likely chance was that she was an English ship of war, and the next most likely that she was a merchantman. The safest course was to creep down upon her from the windward, because the cutter, lying nearer the wind than any square-rigged ship could do, could escape if necessary the way she came, trusting to the mist and darkness and surprise to avoid being disabled before she got out of range.

'Mr Bush, I fancy there's a sail to leeward. Put the cutter before the wind and run down to her, if you please. Be ready to go about if I give the word. Jib-sheet, Brown.'

Hornblower's head was clear again now, in the face of a possible emergency. He regretted the quickening of his pulse – uncertainly always had that effect. The cutter steadied upon her new course, creeping before the wind over the misty water, mainsail boom far out to port. Hornblower experienced a moment's doubt in case Bush was sailing her by the lee, but he would not allow himself to call a warning – he knew he could trust a sailor of Bush's ability not to risk a gibe in an emergency of this sort. He strained his eyes through the darkness; the mist was patchy, coming and going as he looked, but that was a ship without any doubt. She was under topsails alone – that made it almost certain that she was an English ship of war, one of the fleet which maintained unceasing watch over Brest. Another patch of mist obscured her again, and by the time they had run through it she was appreciably nearer, and dawn was at hand – her sails were faint grey in the growing light. Now they were close upon her.

Suddenly the stillness was rent by a hail, high-pitched, penetrating, its purity of quality almost unspoilt by the speaking trumpet – the voice which uttered it was trained in clarity in Atlantic gales.

'Cutter ahoy! What cutter's that?'

At the sound of the English speech Hornblower relaxed. There was no need now to go about, to claw to windward, to seek shelter in the mist. But on the other hand all the unpleasantness of the future which he had been visualizing was certain now. He swallowed hard, words failing him for the moment.

'What cutter's that?' repeated the hail, impatiently.

Unpleasant the future might be; he would fly his colours to the last, and if his career were ending, he would end it with a joke.

'His Britannic Majesty's armed cutter *Witch of Endor*, Captain Horatio Hornblower. What ship's that?'

'*Triumph*, Captain Sir Thomas Hardy – *what* did you say that cutter was?'

Hornblower grinned to himself. The officer of the watch in the strange sail had begun his reply automatically; it was only after he had stated the names of his ship and captain that it had suddenly dawned upon him that the cutter's statement was quite incredible. The *Witch of Endor* had been a prize to the French for nearly a year, and Captain Horatio Hornblower had been dead six months.

Hornblower repeated what he had said before; both Bush and Brown were chuckling audibly at a joke which appealed to them forcibly indeed.

'Come under my lee, and no tricks, or I'll sink you,' hailed the voice.

From the cutter they could hear the guns being run out in the *Triumph;* Hornblower could picture the bustle on board, hands being turned up, the captain being called – Sir Thomas Hardy must be Nelson's late flag captain at Trafalgar, two years Hornblower's senior in the captains' list. Hornblower had known him as a lieutenant, although since then their paths had hardly crossed. Bush eased the cutter under the stern of the two-decker, and brought her to the wind under her lee. Dawn was coming up fast now, and they could see the details of the ship, as she lay hove to, rolling in the swell, and a long shuddering sigh burst from Hornblower's breast. The sturdy beauty of the ship, the two yellow streaks along her sides, checkered with black gunports, the pendant at the main, the hands on the deck, the red coats of the marines, the boatswain's voice roaring at dilatory seamen – all the familiar sights and sounds of the Navy in which he had grown up moved him inexpressibly at this moment, the end of his long captivity and flight.

The *Triumph* had launched a boat, which came dancing rapidly over to them, and a young midshipman swung himself dexterously on board, dirk at his hip, arrogant suspicion on his face, four seamen at his back with pistols and cutlasses.

'What's all this?' demanded the midshipman. His glance swept the cutter's deck, observing the sleepy prisoners rubbing their eyes, the wooden-legged civilian at the tiller, the bare-headed man in a King's coat awaiting him.

'You call me "sir",' barked Hornblower, as he had done to midshipmen ever since he became a lieutenant.

The midshipman eyed the gold laced coat – undoubtedly it was trimmed in the fashion of the coat of a captain of more than three years' seniority, and the man who wore it carried himself as though he expected deference.

'Yes, sir,' said the midshipman, a little abashed.

'That is Lieutenant Bush at the tiller. You will remain here with these men under his orders, while I go to interview your captain.'

'Aye aye, sir,' said the midshipman, stiffening to attention.

The boat bore Hornblower to the *Triumph*'s side; the coxswain made the four-finger gesture which indicated the arrival of a captain, but marines and side-boys were not in attendance as Hornblower went up the side – the Navy could not risk wasting her cherished compliments on possible impostors. But Hardy was there on deck, his huge bulk towering over everyone round him; Hornblower saw the expression of his beefy face alter as he saw him.

'Good God, it's Hornblower all right,' said Hardy, striding forward, with his hand outstretched. 'Welcome back, sir. How do you come here, sir? How did you retake the *Witch*? How –'

What Hardy wanted to say was 'How have you risen from the grave?' but such a question seemed to savour of impoliteness. Hornblower shook hands, and trod gratefully the quarterdeck of a ship of the line once more. His heart was too full for speech, or his brain was too numb with fatigue, and he could make no reply to Hardy's questioning.

'Come below to my cabin,' said Hardy, kindly – phlegmatic though he was, he still could just appreciate the other's difficulty.

There was more ease in the cabin, sitting on the cushioned locker under the portrait of Nelson that hung on the bulkhead, and with the timbers groaning faintly all round, and the blue sea visible through the great stern window. Hornblower told a little of what happened to him – not much, and not in detail; only half a dozen brief sentences, for Hardy was not a man with much use for words. He listened with attention, pulling at his whiskers, and nodding at each point.

'There was a whole *Gazette*,' he remarked, 'about the attack in Rosas Bay. They brought Leighton's body back for burial in St Paul's.'

The cabin swam round Hornblower; Hardy's homely face and magnificent whiskers vanished in a mist.

'He was killed, then?' Hornblower asked.

'He died of his wounds at Gibraltar.'

So Barbara was a widow – had been one for six months now.

'Have you heard anything of my wife?' asked Hornblower. The question was a natural one to Hardy, little use though he himself had for women; and he could see no connexion between it and the preceding conversation.

'I remember reading that she was awarded a Civil List pension by the government when the news of – of your death arrived.'

'No other news? There was a child coming.'

'None that I know of. I have been four months in this ship.'

Hornblower's head sunk on his breast. The news of Leighton's death added to the confusion of his mind. He did not know whether to be pleased or sorry about it. Barbara would be as unattainable to him as ever, and perhaps there would be all the jealous misery to endure of her remarriage.

'Now,' said Hardy. 'Breakfast?'

'There's Bush and my coxswain in the cutter,' said Hornblower. 'I must see that all is well with them first.'

16

A midshipman came into the cabin as they ate breakfast.

'The fleet's in sight from the masthead, sir,' he reported to Hardy.

'Very good.' As the midshipman went out again Hardy turned back to Hornblower. 'I must report your arrival to His Lordship.'

'Is he still in command?' asked Hornblower, startled. It was a surprise to him that the government had left Admiral Lord Gambier in command of the Channel Fleet for three years, despite the disastrous waste of opportunity at the Basque Roads.

'He hauls down his flag next month,' said Hardy, gloomily. Most officers turned gloomy when discussing 'Dismal Jimmy'. 'They whitewashed him at the court martial, and had to leave him his full three years.'

A shade of embarrassment appeared in Hardy's expression; he had let slip the mention of a court martial to a man who soon would endure the same ordeal.

'I suppose they had to,' said Hornblower, his train of thought following that of his fellow captain as he wondered if there would be any whitewash employed at his trial.

Hardy broke the embarrassed silence which followed.

'Would you care to come on deck with me?' he asked.

Over the horizon to leeward was appearing a long line of ships, closehauled. They were in rigid, regular line, and as Hornblower watched they went about in succession in perfect order, as if they were chained together. The Channel Fleet was at drill – eighteen years of drill at sea had given them their unquestioned superiority over any other fleet in the world.

'*Victory*'s in the van,' said Hardy, handing his glass to Hornblower. 'Signal midshipman! "*Triumph* to flag. Have on board –".'

Hornblower looked through the glass while Hardy dictated his message. The three-decker with her admiral's flag at the main was leading the long line of ships, the broad stripes on her side glistening in the sunlight. She had been Jervis's flagship at St Vincent, Hood's in the Mediterranean, Nelson's at Trafalgar. Now she was Dismal Jimmy's – a tragedy if ever there was one. Signal-hoists were soaring up to her yardarms; Hardy was busy dictating replies.

'The Admiral is signalling for you to go on board, sir,' he said at last, turning back to Hornblower. 'I trust you will do me the honour of making use of my barge?'

The *Triumph*'s barge was painted primrose yellow picked out with black, and so were the oarblades; her crew wore primrose-coloured jumpers with black neckcloths. As Hornblower took his seat, his hand still tingling with Hardy's handclasp, he reminded himself gloomily that he had never been able to afford to dress his barge's crew in a fancy rig-out; he always felt sore on the point. Hardy must be a wealthy man with his Trafalgar prize money and his pension as Colonel of Marines. He contrasted their situations – Hardy, a baronet, moneyed, famous, and he himself poor, undistinguished, and awaiting trial.

They piped the side for him in the *Victory*, as Admiralty regulations laid down – the marine guard at the present, the side-boys in white gloves to hand him up, the pipes of the boatswain's mates all a-twittering; and there was a captain on the quarterdeck ready to shake hands with him – odd, that was to Hornblower, seeing that soon he would be on trial for his life.

'I'm Calendar, Captain of the Fleet,' he said. 'His Lordship is below, waiting for you.'

He led the way below, extraordinarily affable.

'I was first of the *Amazon*,' he volunteered, 'when you were in *Indefatigable*. Do you remember me?'

'Yes,' said Hornblower. He had not risked a snub by saying so first.

'I remember you plainly,' said Calendar. 'I remember hearing what Pellew had to say about you.'

Whatever Pellew said about him would be favourable – he had owed his promotion to Pellow's enthusiastic recommendation – and it was pleasant of Calendar to remind him of it at this crisis of his career.

Lord Gambier's cabin was not nearly as ornate as Captain Hardy's had been – the most conspicuous item of furniture therein was the big brass-bound Bible lying on the table. Gambier himself, heavy-jowled, gloomy, was sitting by the stern window dictating to a clerk who withdrew on the arrival of the two captains.

'You can make your report verbally, sir, for the present,' said the Admiral.

Hornblower drew a deep breath and made the plunge. He sketched out the strategic situation at the moment when he took the *Sutherland* into action against the French squadron off Rosas. Only a sentence or two had to be devoted to the battle itself – these men had fought in battles themselves and could fill in the gaps. He described the whole crippled mass of ships drifting helpless up Rosas Bay to where the guns of the fortress awaited them, and the gunboats creeping out under oars.

'One hundred and seventeen killed,' said Hornblower. 'One hundred and forty-five wounded, of whom forty-four died before I was removed from Rosas.'

'My God!' said Calendar. It was not the deaths in hospital which called forth the exclamation – that was a usual proportion – but the total casualty list. Far more than half the crew of the *Sutherland* had been put out of action before surrendering.

'Thompson in the *Leander* lost ninety-two out of three hundred, my lord,' he said. Thompson had surrendered the *Leander* to a French ship of the line off Crete after a defence which had excited the admiration of all England.

'I was aware of it,' answered Gambier. 'Please go on, Captain.'

Hornblower told of how he witnessed the destruction of the French squadron, of how Caillard arrived to take him to Paris, of his escape, first from his escort and then from drowning. He made only a slight mention of Count de Graçay and of his voyage down the Loire – that was not an admiral's business – but he descended to fuller details when he told of his recapture of the *Witch of Endor*. Details here were of importance, because in the course of the manifold activities of the British Navy it might easily happen that a knowledge of harbour arrangements at Nantes and of the navigational difficulties of the lower Loire might be useful.

'Good God Almighty, man,' said Calendar, 'how can you be so cold-blooded about it? Weren't you –'

'Captain Calendar,' interrupted Gambier, 'I have requested you before not to allude to the Deity in that blasphemous fashion. Any repetition will incur my serious displeasure. Kindly continue, Captain Hornblower.'

There was only the brush with the boats from Noirmoutier to be described now. Hornblower continued, formally, but this time Gambier himself interrupted him.

'You say you opened fire with a six-pounder,' he said. 'The prisoners were at the sweeps, and the ship had to be steered. Who laid the gun?'

'I did, my lord. The French pilot helped me.'

'M'm. And you frightened 'em off?'

Hornblower confessed that he had succeeded in sinking two out of the three boats sent against him. Calendar whistled his surprise and admiration, but the hard lines in Gambier's face only set harder still.

'Yes?' he said. 'And then?'

'We went on under sweeps until midnight, my lord, and then we picked up a breeze. We sighted *Triumph* at dawn.'

There was silence in the cabin, only broken by the noises on deck, until Gambier stirred in his chair.

'I trust, Captain,' he said, 'that you have given thanks to the Almighty for these miraculous preservations of yours. In all these adventures I can see the finger of God. I shall direct my chaplain at prayers this evening to make a special mention of your gratitude and thankfulness.'

'Yes, my lord.'

'Now you will make your report in writing. You can

have it ready by dinner time – I trust you will give me the pleasure of your company at dinner? I will then be able to enclose it in the packet I am about to despatch to Their Lordships.'

'Yes, my lord.'

Gambier was still thinking deeply.

'*Witch of Endor* can carry the despatches,' he said. Like every admiral the world over, his most irritating and continuous problem was how to collect and disseminate information without weakening his main body by detachments; it must have been an immense relief to him to have the cutter drop from the clouds as it were, to carry these despatches. He went on thinking.

'I will promote this lieutenant of yours, Bush, into her as Commander,' he announced.

Hornblower gave a little gasp. Promotion to Commander meant almost certain post rank within the year, and it was this power of promotion which constituted the most prized source of patronage an Admiral in command possessed. Bush deserved the step, but it was surprising that Gambier should give it to him – Admirals generally had some favourite lieutenant, or some nephew or some old friend's son awaiting the first vacancy. Hornblower could imagine Bush's delight at the news that he was at last on his way to becoming an admiral himself if he lived long enough.

But that was not all, by no means all. Promotion of a captain's first lieutenant was a high compliment to the captain himself. It set the seal of official approval on the captain's proceedings. This decision of Gambler's was a public – not merely a private – announcement that Hornblower had acted correctly.

'Thank you, my lord, thank you,' said Hornblower.

'She is your prize, of course,' went on Gambier. 'Government will have to buy her on her arrival.'

Hornblower had not thought of that. It meant at least a thousand pounds in his pocket.

'That coxswain of yours will be in clover,' chuckled Calendar. 'He'll take all the lower deck's share.'

That was true, too. Brown would have a quarter of the value of the *Witch of Endor* for himself. He could buy a cottage or land and set up in business on his own account if he wished to.

'*Witch of Endor* will wait until your report is ready,' announced Gambier. 'I will send my secretary in to you. Captain Calendar will provide you with a cabin and the necessities you lack. I hope you will continue to be my guest until I sail for Portsmouth next week. It would be best, I think.'

The last words were a delicate allusion to that aspect of the matter which had occupied most of Hornblower's thoughts on his arrival, and which had not as yet been touched upon – the fact that he must undergo court martial for the loss of the *Sutherland*, and was of necessity under arrest until that time. By old established custom he must be under the supervision of an officer of equal rank while under arrest; there could be no question of sending him home in the *Witch of Endor*.

'Yes, my lord,' said Hornblower.

Despite all Gambler's courtesy and indulgence towards him, despite Calendar's open admiration, he still felt a constriction of the throat and a dryness of the mouth at the thought of that court martial; they were symptoms which persisted even when he tried to settle down and compose his report with the aid of the competent young clergyman who made his appearance in the cabin to which Calendar conducted him.

'Arma virumque cano,' quoted the Admiral's secretary after the first halting sentences – Hornblower's report naturally began with the battle of Rosas. 'You begin in medias res, sir, as every good epic should.'

'This is an official report,' snapped Hornblower. 'It continues the last report I made to Admiral Leighton.'

His tiny cabin only allowed him to walk three paces each way, and crouching nearly double at that – some unfortunate lieutenant had been turned out to make room for him. In a flagship, even in a big three-decker like the *Victory*, the demand for cabins always greatly exceeded the supply, what with the Admiral, and the Captain of the Fleet, and the flag lieutenant, and the secretary, and the chaplain, and the rest of the staff. He sat down on the breech of the twelve-pounder beside the cot.

'Continue, if you please,' he ordered. '"Having regard to these conditions, I therefore proceeded –"'

It was finished in the end – it was the third time that morning that Hornblower had recounted his adventures, and they had lost all their savour for him now. He was dreadfully tired – his head drooped forward at his breast as he squatted on the gun, and then he woke with a snort. He was actually falling asleep while he sat.

'You are tired, sir,' said the secretary.

'Yes.'

He forced himself to wake up again. The secretary was looking at him with eyes shining with admiration, positive hero-worship. It made him feel uncomfortable.

'If you will just sign this, sir, I will attend to the seal and the superscription.'

The secretary slipped out of the chair and Hornblower took the pen and dashed off his signature to the document on whose evidence he was soon to be tried for his life.

'Thank you, sir,' said the secretary, gathering the papers together.

Hornblower had no more attention to spare for him. He threw himself face downward on to the cot, careless of appearances. He went rushing giddily down a tremendous slope into blackness – he was snoring before the secretary had reached the door, and he never felt the touch of the blanket with which the secretary returned, five minutes later, tiptoeing up to the cot to spread it over him.

17

Something enormously painful was recalling Hornblower to life. He did not want to return. It was agony to wake up, it was torture to feel unconsciousness slipping away from him. He clung to it, tried to recapture it, unavailingly. Remorselessly it eluded him. Somebody was gently shaking his shoulder, and he came back to complete consciousness with a start, and wriggled over to see the Admiral's secretary bending over him.

'The Admiral will dine within the hour, sir,' he said. 'Captain Calendar thought you might prefer to have a little time in which to prepare.'

'Yes,' grunted Hornblower. He fingered instinctively the long stubble on his unshaven chin. 'Yes.'

The secretary was standing very stiff and still, and Hornblower looked up at him curiously. There was an odd, set expression on the secretary's face, and he held a newspaper imperfectly concealed behind his back.

'What's the matter?' demanded Hornblower.

'It is bad news for you, sir,' said the secretary.

'What news?'

Hornblower's spirits fell down into the depths of despair. Perhaps Gambier had changed his mind. Perhaps he was going to be kept under strict arrest, tried, condemned, and shot. Perhaps –

'I remembered having seen this paragraph in the *Morning Chronicle* of three months ago, sir,' said the secretary. 'I showed it to his Lordship, and to Captain Calendar. They decided it ought to be shown to you as early as possible. His Lordship says –'

'What is the paragraph?' demanded Hornblower, holding out his hand for the paper.

'It is bad news, sir,' repeated the secretary, hesitatingly.

'Let me see it, damn you.'

The secretary handed over the newspaper, one finger indicating the paragraph.

'The Lord giveth, the Lord taketh away,' he said. 'Blessed be the name of the Lord.'

It was a very short paragraph.

We regret to announce the death in childbed, on the seventh of this month of Mrs Maria Hornblower, widow of the late Captain Horatio Hornblower, Bonaparte's martyred victim. The tragedy occurred in Mrs Hornblower's lodgings at Southsea, and we are given to understand that the child, a fine boy, is healthy.

Hornblower read it twice, and he began on it a third time. Maria was dead, Maria the tender, the loving.

'You can find consolation in prayer, sir –' said the secretary, but Hornblower paid no attention to what the secretary said.

He had lost Maria. She had died in childbed, and having regard to the circumstances in which the child had been engendered, he had as good as killed her. Maria was dead. There would be no one, no one at all, to welcome him now on his return to England. Maria would have stood by him during the court martial, and whatever the verdict, she would never have believed him to be at fault. Hornblower remembered the tears wetting her coarse red cheeks when she had last put her arms round him to say goodbye. He had been a little bored by the formality of an affectionate goodbye, then. He was free now – the realization came creeping over him like cold water in a warm bath. But it was not fair to Maria. He would not have bought his freedom at such a price. She had earned by her own devotion his attention, his kindness, and he would have given them to her uncomplainingly for the rest of his life. He was desperately sorry that she was dead.

'His Lordship instructed me, sir,' said the secretary, 'to inform you of his sympathy in your bereavement. He told me to say that he would not take it amiss if you decided not to join him and his guests at dinner but sought instead the consolation of religion in your cabin.'

'Yes,' said Hornblower.

'Any help which I can give, sir –'

'None,' said Hornblower.

He continued to sit on the edge of the cot, his head bowed, and the secretary shuffled his feet.

'Get out of here,' said Hornblower, without looking up.

He sat there for some time, but there was no order in his thoughts; his mind was muddled. There was a continuous undercurrent of sadness, a hurt feeling indistinguishable from physical pain, but fatigue and excitement and lack of sleep deprived him of any ability to think clearly. Finally, with a desperate effort he pulled himself together. He felt as if he was stifling in the stuffy cabin; he hated his stubbly beard and the feelings of dried sweat.

'Pass the word for my servant,' he ordered the sentry at his door.

It was good to shave off the filthy beard, to wash his body in cold water, to put on clean linen. He went up on deck, the clean sea air rushing into his lungs as he breathed. It was good, too, to have a deck to pace, up and down, up and down, between the slides of the quarterdeck carronades and the line of ringbolts in the deck, with all the familiar sounds of shipboard life as a kind of lullaby to his tired mind. Up and down he walked, up and down, as he had walked so many hours before, in the *Indefatigable*, and the *Lydia*, and the *Sutherland*. They left him alone; the officers of the watch collected on the other side of the ship and only stared at him unobtrusively, politely concealing their curiosity about this man who had just heard of the death of his wife, who had escaped from a French prison, who was waiting his trial for surrendering his ship – the first captain to strike his colours in a British ship of the line since Captain Ferris in the *Hannibal* at Algeciras. Up and down he walked, the goodly fatigue closing in upon him again until his mind was stupefied with it, until he found that he could hardly drag one foot past the other. Then he went below to the certainty of sleep and oblivion. But even in his sleep tumultuous dreams came to harass him – dreams of Maria, against which he struggled, sweating, knowing that Maria's body was now only a liquid mass of corruption; nightmares of death and imprisonment; and, ever-recurring, dreams of Barbara smiling to him on the farther side of the horrors that encompassed him.

From one point of view the death of his wife was of benefit to Hornblower during those days of waiting. It provided him with a good excuse for being silent and unapproachable. Without being thought impolite he could find a strip of deck and walk by himself in the sunshine. Gambier could walk with the captain of the fleet or the flag captain, little groups of lieutenants and warrant officers could walk together, chatting lightly, but they all kept out of his way; and it was not taken amiss that he should sit silent at the Admiral's dinner table and hold himself aloof at the Admiral's prayer meetings.

Had it not been so he would have been forced to mingle in the busy social life of the flagship, talking to officers who would studiously avoid all reference to the fact that shortly they would be sitting as judges on him at his court martial. He did not have to join in the eternal technical discussions which went on round him, stoically pretending that the responsibility of having surrendered a British ship of the line sat lightly on his shoulders. Despite all the kindness with which he was treated, he felt a pariah. Calendar could voice open admiration for him, Gambier could treat him with distinction, the young lieutenants could regard him with wide-eyed hero-worship, but they had never hauled down their colours. More than once during his long wait Hornblower found himself wishing that a cannon ball had killed him on the quarterdeck of the *Sutherland*. There was no one in the world who cared for him now – the little son in England, in the arms of some unknown foster-mother, might grow up ashamed of the name he bore.

Suspecting, morbidly, that the others would treat him like an outcast if they could, he anticipated them and made an outcast of himself, bitterly proud. He went through all that period of black reaction by himself, without companionship, during those last days of Gambier's tenure of command, until Hood came out in the *Britannia* to take over the command, and, amid the thunder of salutes, the *Victory* sailed for Portsmouth. There were headwinds to delay her passage; she had to beat up the Channel for seven long days before at last she glided into Spithead and the cable roared out through the hawse-hole.

Hornblower sat in his cabin – he felt no interest in the green hills of the Isle of Wight nor in the busy prospect of Portsmouth. The tap which came at his cabin door heralded, he supposed, the arrival of the orders regarding his court martial.

'Come in!' he said, but it was Bush who entered, stumping along on his wooden leg, his face wreathed in smiles, his arms burdened with packages and parcels.

At the sight of that homely face Hornblower's depression evaporated like mist. He found himself grinning as delightedly as Bush, he wrung his hand over and over again, sat him down in the only chair, offered to send for drinks for him, all trace of self-consciousness and reserve disappearing in the violence of his reaction.

'Oh, I'm well enough, sir, thank you,' said Bush, in reply to Hornblower's questions. 'And this is the first chance I've had of thanking you for my promotion.'

'Don't thank me,' said Hornblower, a trace of bitterness creeping back into his voice. 'You must thank his Lordship.'

'I know who I owe it to, all the same,' said Bush, sturdily. 'They're going to post me as captain this week. They won't give me a ship – not with this leg of mine

– but there's the dockyard job at Sheerness waiting for me. I should never be captain if it weren't for you, sir.'

'Rubbish,' said Hornblower. The pathetic gratitude in Bush's voice and expression made him feel uncomfortable.

'And how is it with you, sir?' asked Bush, regarding him with anxious blue eyes.

Hornblower shrugged his shoulders.

'Fit and well,' he said.

'I was sorry to hear about Mrs Hornblower, sir,' said Bush.

That was all he needed to say on that subject. They knew each other too well to have to enlarge on it.

'I took the liberty, sir,' said Bush, hastily, 'of bringing you out your letters – there was a good deal waiting for you.'

'Yes?' said Hornblower.

'This big package is a sword, I'm sure, sir,' said Bush. He was cunning enough to think of ways of capturing Hornblower's interest.

'Let's open it, then,' said Hornblower, indulgently.

A sword it was, sure enough, with a gold-mounted scabbard and a gold hilt, and when Hornblower drew it the blue steel blade bore an inscription in gold inlay. It was the sword 'of one hundred guineas' value' which had been presented to him by the Patriotic Fund for his defeat of the *Natividad* in the *Lydia*, and which he had left in pawn with Duddingstone the ship's chandler at Plymouth, as a pledge for payment for captain's stores when he was commissioning the *Sutherland*.

'A sight too much writing on this for me,' Duddingstone had complained at the time.

'Let's see what Duddingstone has to say,' said Hornblower, tearing open the note enclosed in the package.

Sir,

It was with great emotion that I read today of your escape from the Corsican's clutches and I cannot find words to express my relief that the reports of your untimely death were unfounded, nor my admiration of your exploits during your last commission. I cannot reconcile it with my conscience to retain the sword of an officer so distinguished, and have therefore taken the liberty of forwarding the enclosed to you, hoping that in consequence you will wear it when next you enforce Britannia's dominion of the seas.

Your obedient and humble servant to command.

J. DUDDINGSTONE

'God bless my soul!' said Hornblower.

He let Bush read the note; Bush was a captain and his equal now, as well as his friend, and there was no disciplinary objection to allowing him to know to what shifts he had been put when commissioning the *Sutherland*. Hornblower laughed a little self-consciously when Bush looked up at him after reading the note.

'Our friend Duddingstone,' said Hornblower, 'must have been very moved to allow a pledge for forty guineas to slip out of his fingers.' He spoke cynically to keep the pride out of his voice, but he was genuinely moved. His eyes would have grown moist if he had allowed them.

'I'm not surprised, sir,' said Bush, fumbling among

the newspapers beside him. 'Look at this, sir, and at this. Here's the *Morning Chronicle*, and *The Times*. I saved them to show you, hoping you'd be interested.'

Hornblower glanced at the columns indicated; somehow the gist of them seemed to leap out at him without his having to read them. The British press had let itself go thoroughly. As even Bush had foreseen, the fancy of the British public had been caught by the news that a captain whom they had imagined to be foully done to death by the Corsican tyrant had succeeded in escaping, and not merely in escaping, but in carrying off a British ship of war which had been for months a prize to the Corsican. There were columns in praise of Hornblower's daring and ability. A passage in *The Times* caught Hornblower's attention and he read it more carefully. 'Captain Hornblower still has to stand his trial for the loss of the *Sutherland*, but, as we pointed out in our examination of the news of the battle of Rosas Bay, his conduct was so well advised and his behaviour so exemplary on that occasion, whether he was acting under the orders of the late Admiral Leighton or not, that although the case is still *sub judice*, we have no hesitation in predicting his speedy reappointment.'

'Here's what the *Anti-Gallican* has to say, sir,' said Bush.

What the *Anti-Gallican* had to say was very like what the other newspapers had said; it was beginning to dawn upon Hornblower that he was famous. He laughed uncomfortably again. All this was a most curious experience and he was not at all sure that he liked it. Cold-bloodedly he could see the reason for it. Lately there had been no naval officer prominent in the affections of the public – Cochrane had wrecked himself by his intemperate wrath after the Basque Roads, while six years had passed since Hardy had kissed the dying Nelson; Collingwood was dead and Leighton too, for that matter – and the public always demanded an idol. Like the Israelites in the desert, they were not satisfied with an invisible object for their devotion. Chance had made him the public's idol, and presumably Government were not sorry, seeing how much it would strengthen their position to have one of their own men suddenly popular. But somehow he did not like it; he was not used to fame, he distrusted it, and his ever-present personal modesty made him feel it was all a sham.

'I hope you're pleased, sir,' said Bush, looking wonderingly at the struggle on Hornblower's face.

'Yes. I suppose I am,' said Hornblower.

'The Navy bought the *Witch of Endor* yesterday at the Prize Court!' said Bush, searching wildly for news which might delight this odd captain of his. 'Four thousand pounds was the price, sir. And the division of the prize money where the prize has been taken by an incomplete crew is governed by an old regulation – I didn't know about it, sir, until they told me. It was made after that boat's crew from *Squirrel*, after she foundered, captured the Spanish plate ship in '97. Two thirds to you, sir – that's two thousand six hundred pounds. And a thousand to me and four hundred for Brown.'

'H'm,' said Hornblower.

Two thousand six hundred pounds was a substantial bit of money – a far more concrete reward than the acclamation of a capricious public.

'And there's all these letters and packets, sir,' went on Bush, anxious to exploit the propitious moment.

The first dozen letters were all from people unknown to him, writing to congratulate him on his success and escape. Two at least were from madmen, apparently – but on the other hand two were from peers; even Hornblower was a little impressed by the signatures and the coroneted notepaper. Bush was more impressed still when they were passed over to him to read.

'That's very good indeed, sir, isn't it?' he said. 'There are some more here.'

Hornblower's hand shot out and picked one letter out of the mass offered him the moment he saw the handwriting, and then when he had taken it he stood for a second holding it in his hand, hesitating before opening. The anxious Bush saw the hardening of his mouth and the waning of the colour in his cheeks; watched him while he read, but Hornblower had regained his self-control and his expression altered no farther.

London,
129 Bond Street.
3rd June 1811

Dear Captain Hornblower

It is hard for me to write this letter, so overwhelmed am I with pleasure and surprise at hearing at this moment from the Admiralty that you are free and well. I hasten to let you know that I have your son here in my care. When he was left orphaned after the lamented death of your wife I ventured to take charge of him and make myself responsible for his upbringing, while my brothers

Lords Wellesley and Wellington consented to act as his godfathers at his baptism, whereat he was consequently given the names Richard Arthur Horatio. Richard is a fine healthy boy with a wonderful resemblance to his father and he has already endeared himself greatly to me, to such an extent that I shall be conscious of a great loss when the time comes for you to take him away from me. Let me assure you that I shall look upon it as a pleasure to continue to have charge of Richard until that time, as I can easily guess that you will be much occupied with affairs on your arrival in England. You will be very welcome should you care to call here to see your son, who grows in intelligence every day. It will give pleasure not only to Richard, but to

Your firm friend,
Barbara Leighton

Hornblower nervously cleared his throat and reread the letter. There was too much crowded in it for him to have any emotion left. Richard Arthur Horatio Hornblower, with two Wellesleys as godfathers, and growing in intelligence every day. There would be a great future ahead of him, perhaps. Up to that moment Hornblower had hardly thought about the child – his paternal instincts had hardly been touched by any consideration of a child he had never seen; and they further were warped by memories of the little Horatio who had died of smallpox in his arms so many years ago. But now he felt a great wave of affection for the unknown little brat in London who had managed to endear himself to Barbara.

And Barbara had taken him in charge; possibly

because, widowed and childless, she had sought for a convenient orphan to adopt – and yet it might be because she still cherished memories of Captain Hornblower, whom at the time she had believed to be dead at Bonaparte's hands.

He could not bear to think about it any more. He thrust the letter into his pocket – all the others he had dropped on the deck – and with immobile face he met Bush's gaze again.

'There are all these other letters, sir,' said Bush, with masterly tact.

They were letters from great men and from madmen – one contained an ounce of snuff as a token of some eccentric squire's esteem and regard – but there was only one which caught Hornblower's attention. It was from some Chancery Lane lawyer – the name was unfamiliar – who wrote, it appeared, on hearing from Lady Barbara Leighton that the presumption of Captain Hornblower's death was unfounded. Previously he had been acting under the instructions of the Lords Commissioners of the Admiralty to settle Captain Hornblower's estate, and working in conjunction with the Prize Agent at Port Mahon. With the consent of the Lord Chancellor, upon the death intestate of Mrs Maria Hornblower, he had been acting as trustee to the heir, Richard Arthur Horatio Hornblower, and had invested for the latter in the Funds the proceeds of the sale of Captain Hornblower's prizes after the deduction of expenses. As Captain Hornblower would see from the enclosed account, there was the sum of three thousand two hundred and ninety-one pounds six and fourpence invested in the Consolidated Fund, which would naturally revert to him. The lawyer awaited his esteemed instructions.

The enclosed accounts, which Hornblower was about to thrust aside, had among the innumerable six and eightpences and three and fourpences one set of items which caught his eye – they dealt with the funeral expenses of the late Mrs Hornblower, and a grave in the cemetery of the church of St Thomas à Beckett, and a headstone, and fees for grave-watchers; it was a ghoulish list which made Hornblower's blood run a little colder. It was hateful. More than anything else it accentuated his loss of Maria – he would only have to go on deck to see the tower of the church where she lay.

He fought down the depression which threatened to overmaster him once more. It was at least a distraction to think about the news in that lawyer's letter, to contemplate the fact that he owned three thousand odd pounds in the Funds. He had forgotten all about those prizes he had made in the Mediterranean before he came under Leighton's command. Altogether that made his total fortune nearly six thousand pounds – not nearly as large as some captains had contrived to acquire, but handsome enough. Even on half-pay he would be able to live in comfort now, and educate Richard Arthur Horatio properly, and take his place in a modest way in society.

'The captain's list has changed a lot since we saw it last, sir,' said Bush, and he was echoing Hornblower's train of thought rather than breaking into it.

'Have you been studying it?' grinned Hornblower.

'Of course, sir.'

Upon the position of their names in that list depended

the date of their promotion to flag rank – year by year they would climb it as death or promotion eliminated their seniors, until one day, if they lived long enough, they would find themselves admirals, with admirals' pay and privileges.

'It's the top half of the list which has changed most, sir,' said Bush. 'Leighton was killed, and Ball died at Malta, and Troubridge was lost at sea – in Indian waters, sir – and there's seven or eight others who've gone. You're more than half-way up now.'

Hornblower had held his present rank eleven years, but with each coming year he would mount more slowly, in proportion to the decrease in number of his seniors, and it would be 1825 or so before he could fly his flag. Hornblower remembered the Count de Graçay's prediction that the war would end in 1814 – promotion would be slower in peace time. And Bush was ten years older than he, and only just beginning the climb. Probably he would never live to be an admiral, but then Bush was perfectly content with being a captain. Clearly his ambition had never soared higher than that; he was fortunate.

'We're both of us very lucky men, Bush,' said Hornblower.

'Yes, sir,' agreed Bush, and hesitated before going on. 'I'm giving evidence at the court martial, sir, but of course you know what my evidence'll be. They asked me about it at Whitehall, and they told me that what I was going to say agreed with everything they knew. You've nothing to fear from the court martial, sir.'

18

Hornblower told himself often during the next twenty-four hours that he had nothing to fear from the court martial, and yet it was nervous work waiting for it – to hear the repeated twitter of pipes and stamping of marines' boots overhead as the compliments were given to the captains and admirals who came on board to try him, to hear silence close down on the ship as the court assembled, and to hear the sullen boom of the court martial gun as the court opened, and the click of the cabin door latch as Calendar came to escort him before his judges.

Hornblower remembered little enough afterwards of the details of the trial – only a few impressions stood out clearly in his memory. He could always recall the flash and glitter of the gold lace on the coats of the semicircle of officers sitting round the table in the great cabin of the *Victory*, and the expression on Bush's anxious, honest face as he declared that no captain could have handled a ship with more skill and determination than Hornblower had handled *Sutherland* at Rosas Bay. It was a neat point which Hornblower's 'friend' – the officer the Admiralty had sent to conduct his defence – made when his question brought out the fact that just before the surrender Bush had been completely incapacitated by the loss of his foot, so that he bore no responsibility whatever for the surrender and had no interest in presenting as good a case as possible. There was an officer who read, seemingly for an eternity, long extracts from depositions and official reports, in a spiritless mumble – the greatness of the occasion apparently made him nervous and affected his articulation, much to the annoyance of the President of the Court. At one point the President actually took the paper from him, and himself read, in his nasal tenor, Admiral Martin's pronouncement that the *Sutherland*'s engagement had certainly made the eventual destruction of the French squadron more easy, and in his opinion was all that had made it possible. There was an awkward moment when a discrepancy was detected between the signal logs of the *Pluto* and *Caligula*, but it passed away in smiles when someone reminded the Court that signal midshipmen sometimes made mistakes.

During the adjournment there was an elegant civilian in buff and blue, with a neat silk cravat, who came into Hornblower with a good many questions. Frere, his name was, Hookham Frere – Hornblower had a vague acquaintance with the name. He was one of the wits who wrote in the *Anti-Gallican*, a friend of Canning's, who for a time had acted as ambassador to the patriot government of Spain. Hornblower was a little intrigued by the presence of someone deep in cabinet secrets, but he was too preoccupied, waiting for the trial to re-open, to pay much attention to him or to answer his questions in detail.

And it was worse when all the evidence had been given, and he was waiting with Calendar while the Court considered its decision. Hornblower knew real fear, then. It was hard to sit apparently unmoved, while the minutes dragged by, waiting for the summons to the great cabin, to hear what his fate would be. His heart was beating hard as he went in, and he knew himself to be pale. He jerked his head erect to meet his judges' eyes, but the judges in their panoply of blue and gold were veiled in a mist which obscured the whole cabin, so that nothing was visible to Hornblower's eyes save for one little space in the centre – the cleared area in the middle of the table before the President's seat, where lay his sword, the hundred-guinea sword presented by the Patriotic Fund. That was all Hornblower could see – the sword seemed to hang there in space, unsupported. And the hilt was towards him; he was not guilty.

'Captain Hornblower,' said the President of the Court – that nasal tenor of his had a pleasant tone – 'This Court is of the unanimous opinion that your gallant and unprecedented defence of His Majesty's ship *Sutherland*, against a force so superior, is deserving of every praise the country and this Court can give. Your conduct, together with that of the officers and men under your command, reflects not only the highest honour on you, but on the country at large. You are therefore most honourably acquitted.'

There was a little confirmatory buzz from the other members of the Court, and a general bustle in the cabin. Somebody was buckling the hundred-guinea sword to his waist; someone else was patting his shoulder. Hookham Frere was there, too, speaking insistently.

'Congratulations, sir. And now, are you ready to accompany me to London? I have had a post chaise horsed and waiting this last six hours.'

The mists were only clearing slowly; everything was still vague about him as he allowed himself to be led away, to be escorted on deck, to be handed down into

instance, that Hornblower was wholeheartedly on the government side, and that Hornblower had fought at Rosas Bay and had escaped from France solely to maintain a dozen politicians in office. It rather damped Hornblower's spirits. He sat silent, listening to the rattle of the wheels.

'HRH is none too helpful,' said Frere. 'He didn't turn us out when he assumed the Regency, but he bears us no love – the Regency Bill didn't please him. Remember that, when you see him tomorrow. He likes a bit of flattery, too. If you can make him believe that you owe your success to the inspiring examples both of HRH *and* of Mr Spencer Perceval you will be taking the right line. What's this? Horndean?'

The postillion drew the horses to a halt outside the inn, and ostlers came running with a fresh pair.

'Sixty miles from London,' commented Mr Frere. 'We've just time.'

The inn servants had been eagerly questioning the postillion, and a knot of loungers – smocked agricultural workers and a travelling tinker – joined them, looking eagerly at Hornblower in his blue and gold. Someone else came hastening out of the inn; his red face and silk cravat and leather leggings seemed to indicate him as the local squire.

'Acquitted, sir?' he asked.

'Naturally, sir,' replied Frere at once. 'Most honourably acquitted.'

'Hooray for Hornblower!' yelled the tinker, throwing his hat into the air. The squire waved his arms and stamped with joy, and the farm hands echoed the cheer.

'Down with Boney!' said Frere. 'Drive on.'

'It is surprising how much interest has been aroused in your case,' said Frere a minute later. 'Although naturally one would expect it to be greatest along the Portsmouth Road.'

'Yes,' said Hornblower.

'I can remember,' said Frere, 'when the mob were howling for Wellington to be hanged, drawn, and quartered – that was after the news of Cintra. I thought we were gone then. It was his court of inquiry which saved us as it happened, just as yours is going to do now. Do you remember Cintra?'

'I was commanding a frigate in the Pacific at the time,' said Hornblower, curtly.

He was vaguely irritated – and he was surprised at himself at finding that he neither liked being cheered by tinkers nor flattered by politicians.

'All the same,' said Frere, 'it's just as well that Leighton was hit at Rosas. Not that I wished him harm, but it drew the teeth of that gang. It would have been them or us otherwise, I fancy. His friends counted twenty votes on a division. You know his widow, I've heard?'

'I have that honour.'

'A charming woman for those who are partial to that type. And most influential as a link between the Wellesley party and her late husband's.'

'Yes,' said Hornblower.

All the pleasure was evaporating from his success. The radiant afternoon sunshine seemed to have lost its brightness.

'Petersfield is just over the hill,' said Frere. 'I expect there'll be a crowd there.'

Frere was right. There were twenty or thirty people

waiting at the Red Lion, and more came hurrying up, all agog to hear the result of the court martial. There was wild cheering at the news, and Mr Frere took the opportunity to slip in a good word for the government.

'It's the newspapers,' grumbled Frere, as they drove on with fresh horses. 'I wish we could take a lead out of Boney's book and only allow 'em to publish what we think they ought to know. Emancipation – Reform – naval policy – the mob wants a finger in every pie nowadays.'

Even the marvellous beauty of the Devil's Punch Bowl was lost on Hornblower as they drove past it. All the savour was gone from life. He was wishing he was still an unnoticed naval captain battling with Atlantic storms. Every stride the horses were taking was carrying him nearer to Barbara, and yet he was conscious of a sick, vague desire that he was returning to Maria, dull and uninteresting and undisturbing. The crowd that cheered him at Guildford – market day was just over – stank of sweat and beer. He was glad that with the approach of evening Frere ceased talking and left him to his thoughts, depressing though they were.

It was growing dark when they changed horses again at Esher.

'It is satisfactory to think that no footpad or highwayman will rob us,' laughed Frere. 'We have only to mention the name of the hero of the hour to escape scot free.'

No footpad or highwayman interfered with them at all, as it happened. Unmolested they crossed the river at Putney and drove on past the more frequent houses and along the dark streets.

'Number Ten Downing Street, postie,' said Frere.

What Hornblower remembered most vividly of the interview that followed was Frere's first sotto voce whisper to Perceval – 'He's safe' – which he overheard. The interview lasted no more than ten minutes, formal on the one side, reserved on the other. The Prime Minister was not in talkative mood apparently – his main wish seemed to be to inspect this man who might perhaps do him an ill turn with the Prince Regent or with the public. Hornblower formed no very favourable impression either of his ability or of his personal charm.

'Pall Mall and the War Office next,' said Frere. 'God, how we have to work!'

London smelt of horses – it always did, Hornblower remembered, to men fresh from the sea. The lights of Whitehall seemed astonishingly bright. At the War Office there was a young Lord to see him, someone whom Hornblower liked at first sight. Palmerston was his name, the Under Secretary of State. He asked a great many intelligent questions regarding the state of opinion in France, the success of the last harvest, the manner of Hornblower's escape. He nodded approvingly when Hornblower hesitated to answer when asked the name of the man who had given him shelter.

'Quite right,' he said. 'You're afraid some damned fool'll blab it out and get him shot. Some damned fool probably would. I'll ask you for it if ever we need it badly, and you will be able to rely on us then. And what happened to these galley slaves?'

'The first lieutenant in the *Triumph* pressed them for the service, my lord.'

'So they've been hands in a King's ship for the last three weeks? I'd rather be a galley slave myself.'

Hornblower was of the same opinion. He was glad to find someone in high position with no illusions regarding the hardships of the service.

'I'll have them traced and brought home if I can persuade your superiors at the Admiralty to give 'em up. I can find a better use for 'em.'

A footman brought in a note which Palmerston opened.

'His Royal Highness commands your presence,' he announced 'Thank you, Captain. I hope I shall again have the pleasure of meeting you shortly. This discussion of ours has been most profitable. And the Luddites have been smashing machinery in the north, and Sam Whitbread has been raising Cain in the House, so that your arrival is most opportune. Good evening, Captain.'

It was those last words which spoilt the whole effect. Lord Palmerston planning a new campaign against Bonaparte won Hornblower's respect, but Lord Palmerston echoing Frere's estimate of the political results of Hornblower's return lost it again.

'What does His Royal Highness want of me?' he asked of Frere, as they went down the stairs together.

'That's to be a surprise for you,' replied Frere archly. 'You may even have to wait until tomorrow's levee to find out. It isn't often Prinny's sober enough for business at this time in the evening. Probably he's not. You may find tact necessary in your interview with him.'

It was only this morning, thought Hornblower, his head whirling, that he had been sitting listening to the evidence at his court martial. So much had already happened today. He was surfeited with new experiences. He was sick and depressed. And Lady Barbara and his little son were in Bond Street, not a quarter of a mile away.

'What time is it?' he asked.

'Ten o'clock. Young Pam keeps late hours at the War Office. He's a glutton for a work.'

'Oh,' said Hornblower.

God only knew at what hour he would escape from the palace. He would certainly have to wait until tomorrow before he called at Bond Street. At the door a coach was waiting, coachmen and footmen in the royal red liveries.

'Sent by the Lord Chamberlain,' explained Frere. 'Kind of him.'

He handed Hornblower in through the door and climbed after him.

'Ever met His Royal Highness?' he went on.

'No.'

'But you've been to Court?'

'I have attended two levees. I was presented to King George in '98.'

'Ah! Prinny's not like his father. And you know Clarence, I suppose?'

'Yes.'

The carriage had stopped at a doorway brightly lit with lanterns; the door was opened, and a little group of footmen were awaiting to hand them out. There was a glittering entrance hall, where somebody in uniform and powder and with a white staff ran his eyes keenly over Hornblower.

'Hat under your arm,' he whispered. 'This way, please.'

'Captain Hornblower. Mr Hookham Frere,' somebody announced.

It was an immense room, dazzling with the light of

its candles; a wide expanse of polished floor, and at the far end a group of people bright with gold lace and jewels. Somebody came over to them, dressed in naval uniform – it was the Duke of Clarence, pop-eyed and pineapple-headed.

'Ah, Hornblower,' he said, hand held out, 'welcome home.'

Hornblower bowed over the hand.

'Come and be presented. This is Captain Hornblower, sir.'

'Evenin', Captain.'

Corpulent, handsome, and dissipated, weak and sly, was the sequence of impressions Hornblower received as he made his bow. The thinning curls were obviously dyed; the moist eyes and the ruddy pendulous cheeks seemed to hint that His Royal Highness had dined well, which was more than Hornblower had.

'Everyone's been talkin' about you, Captain, ever since your cutter – what's its name, now? – came in to Portsmouth.'

'Indeed, sir?' Hornblower was standing stiffly at attention.

'Yes. And, damme, so they ought to. So they ought to, damme, Captain. Best piece of work I ever heard of – good as I could have done myself. Here, Conyngham, make the presentations.'

Hornblower bowed to Lady This and Lady That, to Lord Somebody and to Sir John Somebody-else. Bold eyes and bare arms, exquisite clothes and blue Garter-ribbons, were all the impressions Hornblower received. He was conscious that the uniform made for him by the *Victory*'s tailor was a bad fit.

'Now let's get the business done with,' said the Prince. 'Call those fellows in.'

Someone was spreading a carpet on the floor, someone else was bearing in a cushion on which something winked and sparkled. There was a little procession of three solemn men in red cloaks. Someone dropped on one knee to present the Prince with a sword.

'Kneel, sir,' said Lord Conyngham to Hornblower.

He felt the accolade and heard the formal words which dubbed him knight. But when he rose, a little dazed, the ceremony was by no means over. There was a ribbon to be hung over his shoulder, a star to be pinned on his breast, a red cloak to be draped about him, a vow to be repeated and signatures written. He was being invested as a Knight of the Most Honourable Order of the Bath, as someone loudly proclaimed. He was Sir Horatio Hornblower, with a ribbon and star to wear for the rest of his life. At last they took the cloak from his shoulders again and the officials of the order withdrew.

'Let me be the first to congratulate you, Sir Horatio,' said the Duke of Clarence, coming forward, his kindly imbecile face wreathed in smiles.

'Thank you, sir,' said Hornblower. The broad star thumped his chest as he bowed again.

'My best wishes, Colonel,' said the Prince Regent.

Hornblower was conscious of all the eyes turned on him at that speech; it was that which warned him that the Prince was not making a slip regarding his rank.

'Sir?' he said, inquiringly, as seemed to be expected of him.

'His Royal Highness,' explained the Duke, 'has been pleased to appoint you one of his Colonels of Marines.'

A Colonel of Marines received pay to the amount of twelve hundred pounds a year, and did no duty for it. It was an appointment given as a reward to successful captains, to be held until they reach flag rank. Six thousand pounds he had already, Hornblower remembered. Now he had twelve hundred a year in addition to his captain's half pay at least. He had attained financial security at last, for the first time in his life. He had a title, a ribbon and star. He had everything he had ever dreamed of having, in fact.

'The poor man's dazed,' laughed the Regent loudly, delighted.

'I am overwhelmed, sir,' said Hornblower, trying to concentrate again on the business in hand. 'I hardly know how to thank your Royal Highness.'

'Thank me by joining us at hazard. Your arrival interrupted a damned interesting game. Ring that bell, Sir John and let's have some wine. Sit here beside Lady Jane, Captain. Surely you want to play? Yes, I know about you, Hookham. You want to slip away and tell John Walter that I've done my duty. You might suggest at the same time that he writes one of his damned leaders and has my Civil List raised – I work hard enough for it, God knows. But I don't see why you should take the Captain away. Oh, very well then, damn it. You can go if you want to.'

'I didn't imagine,' said Frere, when they were safely in the coach again, 'that you'd care to play hazard. *I* wouldn't, not with Prinny, if he were using his own dice. Well, how does it feel to be Sir Horatio?'

'Very well,' said Hornblower.

He was digesting the Regent's allusion to John Walter.

This was the editor of *The Times*, he knew. It was beginning to dawn upon him that his investiture as Knight of the Bath and appointment as Colonel of Marines were useful pieces of news. Presumably their announcement would have some influence politically, too – that was the reason for haste. They would convince doubting people that the government's naval officers were achieving great things – it was almost as much a political move to make him a knight as was Bonaparte's scheme to shoot him for violating the laws of war. The thought took a great deal of the pleasure out of it.

'I took the liberty,' said Frere, 'of engaging a room for you at the Golden Cross. You'll find them expecting you; I had your baggage sent round. Shall I stop the coach there? Or do you want to visit Fladong's first?'

Hornblower wanted to be alone; the idea of visiting the naval coffee house tonight – for the first time in five years – had no appeal for him, especially as he felt suddenly self-conscious in his ribbon and star. Even at the hotel it was bad enough, with host and boots and chambermaid all unctuously deferential with their 'Yes, Sir Horatio' and 'No, Sir Horatio', making a procession out of lighting him up to his room, and fluttering round him to see that he had all he wanted, when all he wanted now was to be left in peace.

There was little enough peace for him, all the same, when he climbed into bed. Resolutely as he put out of his mind all recollection of the wild doings of the day, he could not stop himself thinking about the fact that tomorrow he would be seeing his son and Lady Barbara. He spent a restless night.

19

'Sir Horatio Hornblower,' announced the butler, holding open the door for him.

Lady Barbara was there; it was a surprise to see her in black – Hornblower had been visualizing her as dressed in the blue gown she had worn when last he had seen her, the grey-blue which matched her eyes. She was in mourning now, of course, for Leighton had been dead less than a year still. But the black dress suited her well – her skin was creamy white against it. Hornblower remembered with a strange pang the golden tang of her cheeks in those old days on board the *Lydia*.

'Welcome,' she said, her hands outstretched to him. They were smooth and cool and delicious – he remembered their touch of old. 'The nurse will bring Richard directly. Meanwhile, my heartiest congratulations on your success.'

'Thank you,' said Hornblower. 'I was extremely lucky, ma'am.'

'The lucky man,' said Lady Barbara, 'is usually the man who knows how much to leave to chance.'

While he digested this statement he stood awkwardly looking at her. Until this moment he had forgotten how Olympian she was, what self-assurance – kindly self-assurance – she had, which raised her to inaccessible heights and made him feel like a loutish schoolboy. His knighthood must appear ridiculously unimportant to her, the daughter of an earl, the sister of a marquis and of a viscount who was well on his way towards a dukedom. He was suddenly acutely conscious of his elbows and hands.

His awkwardness only ended with the opening of the door and the entrance of the nurse, plump and rosy in her ribboned cap, the baby held to her shoulder. She dropped a curtsey.

'Hullo, son,' said Hornblower, gently.

He did not seem to have much hair yet, under his little cap, but there were two startling brown eyes looking out at his father; nose and chin and forehead might be as indeterminate as one would expect in a baby, but there was no ignoring those eyes.

'Hullo, baby,' said Hornblower, gently, again.

He was unconscious of the caress in his voice. He was speaking to Richard as years before he had spoken to little Horatio and little Maria. He held up his hands to the child.

'Come to your father,' he said.

Richard made no objections. It was a little shock to Hornblower to feel how tiny and light he was – Hornblower, years ago, had grown used to older children – but the feeling passed immediately.

'There, baby, there,' said Hornblower.

Richard wriggled in his arms, stretching out his hands to the shining gold fringe of his epaulette.

'Pretty?' asked Hornblower.

'Da!' said Richard, touching the threads of bullion.

'That's a man!' said Hornblower.

His old skill with babies had not deserted him.

Richard gurgled happily in his arms, smiled seraphically as he played with him, kicked his chest with tiny kicks through his dress. That good old trick of bowing the head and pretending to butt Richard in the stomach had its never-failing success. Richard gurgled and waved his arms in ecstasy.

'What a joke!' said Hornblower. 'Oh, what a joke!'

Suddenly remembering, he looked round at Lady Barbara. She had eyes only for the baby, her serenity strangely exalted, her smile tender. He thought then that she was moved by her love for the child. Richard noticed her too.

'Goo!' he said, with a jab of an arm in her direction.

She came nearer, and Richard reached over his father's shoulder to touch her face.

'He's a fine baby,' said Hornblower.

'O' course he's a fine babby,' said the wet-nurse, reaching for him. She took it for granted that godlike fathers in glittering uniforms would only condescend to notice their children for ten seconds consecutively, and would need to be instantly relieved of them at the end of that time.

'He's a saucy one,' said the wet-nurse, the baby back in her arms. He wriggled there, those big brown eyes of his looking from Hornblower to Barbara.

'Say "bye bye",' said the nurse. She held up his wrist and waved his fat fist at them. 'Bye bye.'

'Do you think he's like you?' asked Barbara, as the door closed behind the nurse and baby.

'Well –' said Hornblower, with a doubtful grin.

He had been happy during those few seconds with the baby, happier than he had been for a long long time.

The morning up to now had been one of black despondency for him. He had told himself that he had everything heart could desire, and some inner man within him had replied that he wanted none of it. In the morning light his ribbon and star had appeared gaudy gew-gaws. He never could contrive to feel proud of himself; there was something vaguely ridiculous about the name 'Sir Horatio Hornblower', just as he always felt there was something vaguely ridiculous about himself.

He had tried to comfort himself with the thought of all the money he had. There was a life of ease and security before him; he would never again have to pawn his gold-hilted sword, nor feel self-conscious in good society about the pinchbeck buckles on his shoes. And yet the prospect was frightening now that it was certain. There was something of confinement about it, something reminiscent of these weary weeks in the Château de Graçay – how well he remembered how he fretted there. Unease and insecurity, which had appeared such vast evils when he suffered under them, had something attractive about them now, hard though that was to believe.

He had envied brother captains who had columns about themselves in the newspapers. Surfeit in that way was attained instantaneously, he had discovered. Bush and Brown would love him neither more nor less on account of what *The Times* had to say about him; he would scorn the love of those who loved him more – and he had good reason to fear that there would be rivals who would love him less. He had received the adulation of crowds yesterday; that did not heighten his good opinion of crowds, and he was filled with a bitter contempt for the upper circle that rules those crowds. Within him the fighting man and the humanitarian both seethed with discontent.

Happiness was a Dead Sea fruit that turned to ashes in the mouth, decided Hornblower, generalizing recklessly from his own particular experience. Prospect, and not possession, was what gave pleasure, and his cross-grainedness would deprive him, now that he had made that discovery, even of the pleasure in prospect. He misdoubted everything so much. Freedom that could only be bought by Maria's death was not a freedom worth having; honours granted by those that had the granting of them were no honours at all; and no security was really worth the loss of insecurity. What life gave with one hand she took back with the other. The political career of which he had once dreamed was open to him now, especially with the alliance of the Wellesley faction, but he could see with morbid clarity how often he would hate it; and he had been happy for thirty seconds with his son, and now, more morbidly still, he asked himself cynically if that happiness could endure for thirty years.

His eyes met Barbara's again, and he knew she was his for the asking. To those who did not know and understand, who thought there was romance in his life when really it was the most prosaic of lives, that would be a romantic climax. She was smiling at him, and then he saw her lips tremble as she smiled. He remembered how Marie had said he was a man whom women loved easily, and he felt uncomfortable at being reminded of her.

Also available in the Hornblower series by C.S. Forester

A Ship of the Line

Admiral Hornblower

Hornblower and the Atropos

Hornblower and the Crisis

Hornblower and the Hotspur

Hornblower in the West Indies

Lieutenant Hornblower

Lord Hornblower

Mr Midshipman Hornblower

The Commodore

The Earthly Paradise

The Happy Return

The Ship